THE HUNGER MOON

ALSO BY
SUZANNE MATSON

Durable Goods (poems)
Sea Level (poems)

THE HUNGER MOON

SUZANNE MATSON

W. W. NORTON & COMPANY
NEW YORK LONDON

The text of this book is composed in Perpetua with the display set in Eaglefeather.
Desktop composition by Chelsea Dippel
Manufacturing by The Haddon Craftsmen, Inc.
Book design by Charlotte Staub

Library of Congress Cataloging-in-Publication Data

Matson, Suzanne, date.
The hunger moon / Suzanne Matson.
p. cm.
ISBN 0-393-04099-2
I. Title.
PS3563.A8378H86 1997
813'.54—dc21 96-45286 CIP

W. W. Norton & Company, Inc., 500 Fifth Avenue, New York, N.Y. 10110
http://www.wwnorton.com

W. W. Norton & Company Ltd., 10 Coptic Street, London WC1A 1PU
3 4 5 6 7 8 9 0

FOR JOE, NICK, AND HENRY

THE HUNGER MOON

RENATA WAS HAPPIEST DRIVING, knowing she was *en route*. She loved poring over road maps to find towns with names like Knockemstiff, Pep, Peerless, and Bean Blossom. She loved stopping for meals at diners with EAT outlined in neon against the evening sky, and finding motels at night that had a little angled parking space right in front of each blue or green or orange front door. She appreciated the way the roadside markers changed colors and typography with the states, so that she always knew she was getting someplace new.

It was different now, traveling with a baby, but in a way it was even better—just the two of them, the car a little world in which they were perfectly alone. Charlie was so good. Sometimes, when they had driven for more than an hour and she couldn't hear his soft snores, she reached one arm in back of her to pat his head where he lay in his rear-facing infant seat. Even that wasn't enough; she needed to trail her fingers gently down the front of his face until she reached his mouth, parted slightly in sleep. Only then, when he'd latch on to her fingertip and start sucking, was she reassured. "Just checking, pal," she'd tell him.

Charlie liked the road as much as she did. For the two months that they had been drifting eastward across the country, Charlie had grown to sleep and wake according to the car's engine, enabling Renata to regulate his daytime schedule perfectly. It was when they stopped in some town for a few days so Renata could catch her breath that Charlie seemed disoriented, and forgot how to nap. Those days Renata sometimes took elaborate sightseeing drives to make him feel at home.

At night in their motel rooms she made the baby a nest of pillows and blankets on one side of their queen-size bed; she didn't think she should indulge in the pleasure of holding him close to her all night. The few nights she had given in and cradled him next to her, he had nursed on and off continually, like a puppy. Somehow that seemed too decadent; she had read that it was better for the baby to have regular feeding times. Regularity in his life would let him know that he could count on things, and this was important to her.

Soon he would be able to roll off the side of the bed, and so she would need to get one of those portable cribs. Renata had so far bought as little baby gear as possible. She liked the feeling of their lightness: her one large duffel with both their clothes, the car seat, the folding stroller. She stopped two or three times a week at a Laundromat to do their laundry while Charlie dozed in the stroller. He liked the hum of the washing machines almost as much as he liked riding in the car, and when she scooped their clothes out of the dryer, she would lay the baby in the midst of them to kick and chuckle in the warm pile.

People were friendly in the middle of the country; they often wanted to know where Renata was headed with such a young baby, and wasn't she afraid to drive alone? In Nevada she had bought herself a thin wedding band for sixty-five dollars at a pawnshop. Town by town she honed her story until she had a version that she liked: her husband was in the military and she was moving to a town nearer his base. Their furniture was being transported separately. She had driven rather than flown so that she could stop on the way and spend time with the baby's grandparents. The location of the base and the grandparents changed according to what part of the country Renata was in, but it was always distant enough so that locals wouldn't ask her questions she couldn't answer.

Having a baby made people considerate and respectful toward her. Men who before would have come on to her now simply held doors wide for the stroller or helped to raise it up over a curb. Women who would have watched her like a hawk because of their men now smiled and asked how old the baby was. She was welcomed into an invisible country of mothers that behaved the same wherever she went. She was given nice big booths by restaurant hostesses to accommodate the car seat; waitresses dandled the baby while she paid the check; and one young mother she met in a Nebraska laundromat even gave Charlie a darling little overall fresh from the dryer that she said her own baby boy was just out of.

As long as they kept moving, Renata felt that nothing bad could ever touch them, so she drove from Eugene to Boise, down to Reno then Flagstaff, up to Salt Lake City and Billings, on to Casper and Rapid City, then through North Platte via Valentine, and so on. She didn't like interstates because they were too straight and too fast. Renata looked for long cuts, wrong turns, detours, and backtracks. She wasn't in a hurry. She had enough money in her account for now, and with her bank card she could get at it just about anywhere. The future would take care of itself, Renata felt sure, just as soon as she got them to Massachusetts. But they had plenty of time until then, and she thought there might never be days like this again, a perfect union of Charlie and Renata, with no one to interfere and nothing to take her attention away from him. Driving, her foot keeping the accelerator a conservative fifty-five, Renata had time to plan things as she stared at the horizon, and time even to go over the important episodes of her life, rehearsing the ways she would make sure Charlie would have a better start than she had.

She thought she made a pretty good mother, enough to make up for the fact that her baby would never know his natural father.

Charlie's father did not know he had a child. They had gone together for a year while Renata was waitressing in Venice, California. In the early months of her pregnancy she broke it off and went to live in Oregon with her sister until the baby was born.

Charlie's father, Bryan, was not a bad guy; he was funny, and handsome, and romantic. But he was living a prolonged adolescence on the beach in Venice—bartending just enough to pay the rent in an old house he shared with four other guys. He usually ate for free at Renata's beachfront café when her manager wasn't around, and he drank for free at his own restaurant on his nights off. If they did anything else, Renata often found herself picking up the check, or one of his friends paid. His lack of responsibility made her impatient, but that wasn't why she had left without telling him they were having a baby.

Bryan was marked for tragedy. He was literally marked, with a puckered scar running down his back from when his mother had tried to kill them both by jumping from the roof of their house when he was a baby. She hadn't succeeded then, although she had done enough damage to herself to require long hospital stays and painkiller prescriptions that she stockpiled until she had enough pills to finish the job. Bryan had been eighteen months old at the time of the big leap, as he liked to call it. One of the guardian angels in charge of infants must have swooped down just in time to cradle him gently above the ground while his mother's bones shattered under him. Actually, they had found him wailing inside her unconscious arms, which embraced him so tightly that he had to be pried from her by two strong men. A row of shrubbery alongside the house had broken their fall. Bryan's only injury had been the open gash on his back, which required eighteen stitches, one for every month of his life. No one ever told him what it was on the way down that had cut him open; but the uncles and aunts he grew up with, rotating among their families in six-month shifts, always reminded him how lucky he was to have survived with only the single wound.

Renata saw it differently. She believed Bryan's survival to be a reprieve, and a harbinger of some final fall that lay in store for him. This was not mere superstition, brought on by the awe she felt every time she imagined the darkness surrounding Bryan's mother before she jumped, but information coming from Bryan himself. She had at first been attracted to his easygoing humor, his perpetual air of having just come from the beach, the fine premature creases around his eyes from being tanned year-round since he was a child. It was only after they had become lovers that she discovered that grief was his only true companion, the one he was already married to.

The first night she heard it, she woke in a cold dread, wondering what evil had entered the room to be with them, what sobbing ghost. As her mind cleared and her eyes adjusted to the darkness, she realized that the moaning was coming from the man she was in bed with, whose anguished face bore no resemblance to her laid-back boyfriend. Gradually she became used to Bryan's dreams, of which he claimed he remembered nothing the next morning, but she could never get used to the loneliness of making love with him. When he was inside her she would open her eyes to see him looking through her. His bereft stare was enough to bring tears to her own eyes. At that point the joking Bryan would return to her, solicitous and kind. She never told him that she was crying on his behalf, knowing that she could never hold him securely enough to convince him he was not falling.

Renata had left because the bottomless nature of Bryan's sadness scared her, and once you gave a child a father, you couldn't unmake the link. She knew how it was with bad parents. You kept them, for better or for worse; and whether they did right by you or not, they were yours to haul around for life. With Bryan forming the third point of their triangle, there would be an unstable corner, like a table that wobbled, always worrying the back of her mind when she put something weighty on it. She would rather raise her daughter by herself—for Renata had been certain that she would have a girl. She had pictured a smaller Renata, the same dark hair as her own, which she would comb and braid for her daughter as her mother had done when she was a girl.

Now that she had Charlie, she wondered why having a baby used to mean to her that she would be creating a small replica of herself. Charlie was so much his own person. If pressed, she could see in him some of Bryan's mouth, and maybe a little of the comically sloping brows of his father above his wide blue eyes. But having a boy now, she couldn't imagine anything different. Already she felt they were comrades, pals, in a way that suggested a jolly soldiering forward. Raising a boy meant that she would have to respect some essential difference between them: it would have been too easy to assume that a daughter would be feeling all her feelings.

There were times she thought she might have made a mistake in running away from Bryan. Perhaps he could have risen to the occasion; being a father might possibly have allowed him to go inside himself and shut off the infant's memory loop of gutters and shingles and tree branches rushing by. This might, in fact, have been his chance to grab hold of some real person, instead of just the ghost of a person, but at the time she discovered herself pregnant, Renata didn't think she could risk it, and it was too late to second-guess herself now.

She had lived with the secret of her pregnancy for three months; being as slender as she was, her jeans and sweatshirts continued to fit just fine. One day, though, when they were lying on the beach, Bryan rubbed his hand over her stomach above her bikini bottom and teased her about having had too big a lunch. That was when Renata began making plans.

She had never set out to become pregnant and certainly had not intentionally missed a couple of days of her pill cycle. They had driven to Santa Barbara to spend the weekend with one of Bryan's friends when she discovered that she had not packed her birth control pills. She shrugged it off, thinking to herself that two days probably would not make much of a difference since she had been taking the pills faithfully for years. As soon as she missed her period, she knew. She also realized, much to her surprise, that she had no doubts about having the baby. It was as if she had been waiting all these years for life to deliver some compelling role for her, some decisive turn of events that she could embrace with her whole self. Though she would not have pictured herself a mother at this stage—if anything, would have laughed at the thought—once the test came out positive, and she realized with a shock that the baby was already with her, made from her, and tied to her, she loved it with a startling passion.

Bryan had been surprised when she announced that she wanted to break up, but he took it well. Too well. He sat there watching her talk with a funny half-smile, and he didn't even press for explanations beyond the weak ones she offered about needing more freedom and time to herself. Renata took this as a confirmation that she had made the right decision: why provide a child with a father who would give up on people so easily? She still remembered feeling his eyes on her back as she moved to the door of his bedroom, her small knapsack bulging with the few articles she had to pack—a toothbrush, a pair of flip-flops, a short fake-silk kimono that she used to throw on when she had to use the shared bathroom down the hall. If he had spoken then, there's no telling how things might have worked out, because at the moment when her hand turned the doorknob, she felt a grief inside so large that she would have welcomed the chance to share it, to turn around and pour some of it into his arms.

But he had said nothing. Without turning to look, she pictured him sitting on his sandy mattress on the floor watching her go, and at that moment she could honestly say that she hated him. She stayed in Venice another month, and then, just when she would have needed to buy a new set of waitressing skirts, she packed everything in her car and drove north, leaving only her sister's post office box number in Oregon with the manager of the restaurant.

The first motel she stopped at on the way to Eugene was called the Piney Bower, and had a horseshoe-shaped yard with picnic tables right in back of the mint-green motel building. She pulled in after driving eight hours, queasy from the fast-food hamburgers she had eaten. In the office of the Piney Bower she used the name Mrs. John Rivera to sign the register, even though her pregnancy didn't show much yet, and if really married, she never would have referred to herself in such an old-fashioned way. "John" was nobody, the beginning of the phantom husband she would invent for strangers.

Taking a cup of Sanka from the Piney Bower hospitality bar with her to her room, she undressed and stood under the cool shower. One thing about traveling, even from one county to the next, was that the smell of the water kept shifting with you, reminding you that beneath the freeway exits with their identical Denny's and Howard Johnsons, water ran so deep it could not be made to resemble anything but its original self. Sulfur or sweet, or tangy like rain, water revealed its true nature right away, unlike people.

She loved passing through places with her secret, knowing that as she dipped her feet into the icy snow-melt waters of Lake Shasta or climbed out of her car to take a breath of astringent air in the Siskiyous she only looked as if she were traveling alone. She talked to the baby regularly, asking if it needed a refreshment break, or if it liked the Magic Fingers bed massager she had turned on for a quarter. She was almost to Medford, Oregon, a cowboy town where boys still wanted boots and saddles for their eighth birthdays, when she first thought the baby answered back. Just as she was moving up in line to order a soft vanilla cone at the Dairy Queen, she felt something like a ripple, as if brushed by the tiniest minnow in a still lake. Surprised, she looked over her shoulder, and saw only teenagers hanging out in the parking lot in the weak March sun, their oversized sweatshirts knotted at their waists. Then she looked down at her stomach, and, as if in confirmation, the minnow moved again. After that, Renata was careful about what she tuned in on the radio; she made sure that the music was not harsh, or the voice talking not overheated with opinion. She sang all the pretty songs she knew to the baby, and when lying in bed at night, massaged her barely rounded stomach in even, comforting circles.

Her sister, a legal secretary eight years older than Renata, had been glad enough to see her, as she herself was recently divorced and had two preschool children whom she was able to take out of day care while Renata was living with them. Renata lived at Marcia's house for six months, taking care of Jess and Tommy and helping with the housework and cooking. The two sisters got to know each other better than they ever had growing up, since the age difference had pretty much guaranteed that they were never interested in the same things at the same time. Now, however, they had Renata's prepared-childbirth breathing to practice together, and a layette to assemble, and Marcia's failed marriage to dissect as they sat up nights on the patio with chilled white wine for Marcia and seltzer water for Renata. When they brought Charlie home from the hospital, and Marcia pulled the bassinet her children had used close beside Renata's bed, bringing meals to her on trays for the first couple of days, Renata felt like she was living in the first home she had ever known.

"Why leave now?" Marcia had asked, shaking her head with disbelief, a month after Charlie was born, when Renata had begun collecting road maps from AAA and circling classified ads for a newer car. It was true that Renata's urge to drive somewhere distant seemed ill-timed. She had a newborn, and her sister's family was in Eugene. She couldn't adequately explain why she needed to be in motion just then, without an address, instead of getting a job down the road at the Sizzler and renting an apartment near Marcia. It wasn't possible to say out loud that her sister's life depressed her. Despite the fact that Marcia had been a smiling, lace-and-sequin–covered bride, certain that she was marrying for love and forever, she was now a short-tempered, overtired, divorced mother. Renata saw how the current of her sister's anger filled the house and passed through her children's small bodies, and how it made them whiny and uncertain. Just as Renata had needed to insulate herself from what she thought of as Bryan's damaged psyche, she now feared contact with her sister's bitterness. Since her pregnancy, Renata had been cushioned by a sense of peace that was new to her, and she wanted to preserve it away from the corrosive atmosphere of Marcia's disappointment. Unlike Marcia, Renata was choosing to raise her child alone; no one had failed them, and no one would.

As soon as the baby was safely born and pronounced robust, and Renata found herself miraculously shrinking back to her former shape, her soreness leaving her like the memory of some unrepeatable athletic feat, she began to feel restless. She kept thinking of the highway motels she had stayed at on their way to Oregon, with their racks of glossy invitations to sights and attractions, and the surprise of opening each desk or nightstand drawer to discover printed stationery you could mail to someone or just take with you. Eugene itself began to feel intolerably close and small, just three miles from her childhood home in Springfield. She resolved to leave; and though Marcia wouldn't understand, Renata couldn't help that. She left.

When Renata turned down the thin acrylic blankets and stiffly starched motel sheets every night, she felt like she was peeling back the skin of a new life. And every morning, as she heaped their damp towels in a considerate pile for the maid and refolded their slender store of clothes into the duffel, Renata felt her heart lift with the knowledge that once again she and Charlie had left no trace. She liked counting the number of states that Charlie had passed through in his first months of infancy, feeling that as the sum ticked up, she was giving him some kind of insurance policy against the future, much as other parents of newborns invest in mutual funds.

She knew that money was the least important gift she could give to her son, and when she tried to imagine what the ideal one would be, all she could see was the sky in front of her, laden with cumulus clouds one minute, flat and shiny as the blue hood of her car the next.

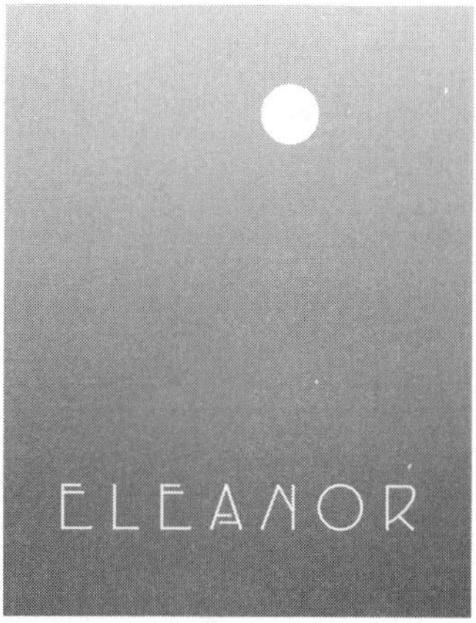

NOVEMBER IN BOSTON CAN BE INDECISIVE. Winter posits an arrival with a sudden nor'easter squall or a short, fervent cold snap, and then lapses into stretches of benign autumn warmth, luring people back out of their houses for walks along the Charles, or last strolls without a coat on Newbury Street. Department stores begin to hang garlands although it is not yet Thanksgiving, and hardware stores make prominent displays of snow shovels outside their front doors. Television weathermen grow more animated, knowing the power of suspense they have over their viewers who stay awake a few extra minutes into the eleven o'clock broadcast to see if the weather is about to take a definitive turn for the worse.

This particular November, the good weather brazenly hung on, giving folks a false sense of security. The woolens were unpacked but not yet called for, crowding everyone's closets and making dressing in the morning a vague, uncertain exercise. College students, already past their mid-semester examinations, pressed the season as far as they could, wearing shorts with their sweatshirts, although the summer tans they brought back to campus had long since faded and their bare legs now looked goose-pimply and pale.

The new year in Boston is measured by the academic clock, and the sense of initiative the city feels every Labor Day, when moving trucks and station wagons are unloading student goods on every street, begins to abate by November, when it becomes clear to all that the hopeful expectancy of September was just a trick of equinoctial light.

Eleanor was trying to overcome just such a period of high expectations followed by flagging energy. In September she had sold the home she had lived in for fifty years. She had coped with the grating cheeriness of her realtor, battled the wills of her increasingly bossy children, and overseen the sorting, selling, packing, and moving of all her personal effects. During the closing Eleanor met the young couple with a toddler and a baby who were buying her Belmont home; they were nervous and excited the way she remembered herself and Robert at the signing over of the deed. When they bought the house, Eleanor had been pregnant with Helen. The births of Janice and Peter soon followed, so that her first seven years in the house were spent erecting gates across the stairs and putting all the breakable things in the attic. Not that they had much, breakable or otherwise. Eleanor had not yet begun law school, and Robert was just starting his residency at Mass. General. Buying the house had represented a tremendous leap of faith for them, and things had gone well. By the time the last child was out of the house, Robert was chief attending surgeon at MGH and Eleanor was a judge in family court.

When she finally sold the house, Eleanor had been retired seven years and widowed ten. She had had one fall down the cellar stairs, one hip replacement surgery, and could no longer do her own pruning of the dogwood trees and rhododendrons. She was beginning to fear driving, although she still used her eight-year-old sedan, limiting herself to routes she knew well and trips made before dark and between rush hours. On a day last summer when all her children were in Boston at the same time, they converged at her house for a cookout and what Eleanor later suspected had been a coordinated assault.

"Mother, when will you admit that this house is too big for

you?" Helen had pressed. She lived the farthest away, in Houston, with her engineer husband and two high-school age children. Eleanor always detected a shade of guilt in her oldest daughter's voice when they talked about her living alone. But now Janice and Peter added their voices to the argument, and she knew that to her grown children the fact that she stayed in the house irritated them, worried them, and lived in their minds as a problem to be solved.

Peter was an academic and shared a house in Durham, New Hampshire, with a painter. Eleanor suspected that her son was gay, but what pained her was not that his brief marriage had failed, or that he had been living with a man for the last ten years, but that he could not tell her this simple truth about himself.

Janice was unmarried and lived in Cambridge, where she was getting her third graduate degree, this one in public policy at the Kennedy School. She was an inveterate student, having studied French literature at Mount Holyoke, gotten a master's in education at Harvard, followed by an MBA at Simmons. She had dabbled with a job in college administration, but was now attracted to working in government. Eleanor privately thought Janice would never settle on a career, preferring instead to spend her trust fund on degree after degree until retirement age. Janice seemed deeply afraid of beginning her life, something that Eleanor could not understand.

Eleanor would not have allowed her children to talk her into selling if she had not been ready. The truth was, a house as large as hers required ballast, and Eleanor's hollowed out bones were no match for its Victorian hulk. She was tired of telling the landscapers to put a proper edge to the flower beds, and of nagging the housecleaner to dust the light fixtures and sweep behind the stove. The house longed for entropy: its shingles flew off during storms, its pipes corroded, its steps sagged, its boiler cracked. It wanted to sink into a blowzy old age with her, and she had enough work to do in getting herself up and groomed every morning, and out into the world for her few errands. She agreed to sell, and chose a sleek modern apartment in Brookline with no nooks and crannies, no architectural complications of any sort. Her new apartment was utterly without history, her own or any other, as the building was so new. She moved into it with relief, and an immense lightening of spirit.

IT WAS A DAY IN NOVEMBER, unseasonably warm, and Eleanor was rummaging for the scissors when the phone rang. She frowned, pushed her short-distance glasses up on her nose, and left the kitchen drawer open while she went to answer.

"Hello?"

"Please hold while we connect you to receive this important call. . . . "

For a brief second, Eleanor didn't understand. Who was calling her? It was a man's tinny voice, excited and sincere like a television commercial. That was it—a commercial advertisement was calling her. She slammed the phone down. Did they think the world was full of imbeciles? Did people actually wait in their own homes while a recording put them on hold? She took a deep breath and went back to the kitchen. The drawer was open, but it took her a few moments to remember why. Scissors.

Though she had been in the apartment for two months, the packing boxes were still stacked neatly around her apartment; in some cases they had been draped with scarves and doilies so that they resembled odd cubes of furniture. Items had started to collect on them—hats, mail, a flower arrangement Helen had wired her for her birthday. It was the clutter on top that finally spurred her to finish unpacking. She had circled this day on her kitchen calendar, a Monday at the beginning of a clear week that bore no neatly jotted medical appointments, no lunch with Janice, no library books due. It was the white expanse of a whole week that finally gave her the courage to slice one box decisively down the center of its strip of clear packing tape and see what was inside.

The memories of her Belmont house that were attached to the familiar objects were almost overpowering. Oddly, she had not thought much about the house on Rosewood Avenue since the day she had met with her broker to convert the check from its sale into various neat certificates and folders and slim bank books. She had thought she would miss the house more than she did, had imagined dreaming for months about its many rooms and hallways, but in fact she had not had one dream about the house. Any dream that she now woke up remembering was strangely placeless, or the place was free of walls and ceilings, like a great field or stretch of sand.

Inside the box were white tissue-wrapped bundles, Eleanor's handiwork. She wouldn't let any of her children help her pack, knowing they would place things haphazardly inside, mixing up rooms, using insufficient paper for padding, forgetting to label the outside. This box was marked LIVING ROOM: MEMENTOS AND OBJECTS. Such labeling had allowed her to unpack the necessary items when she first moved in, and set up a functional, if spartan, household. She had put away items from KITCHEN: FLATWARE, EVERYDAY DISHES, COFFEE AND BASIC COOKING, DISHTOWELS; BATHROOM: TOWELS AND TOILETRIES; and BEDROOM: SHEETS AND BEDDING. She had hung the clothes packed in suitcases, but not opened the cartons labeled CLOTHING: SUMMER; CLOTHING: RESORT; CLOTHING: ACCESSORIES; or any of the other seasons or categories. In fact, she had found that she did very well living in a few pairs of stretch pants, loafers, and half a dozen sweaters and cotton jerseys, with one heavier coat hanging alone in her hall closet. But it was November now, and she should probably at least get at CLOTHING: WINTER OUTERWEAR and, maybe, if she felt up to it, CLOTHING: PARTY. She would probably be going out to a concert or an eggnog party, as well as her daughter's annual Christmas Day dinner.

Gingerly, Eleanor unwrapped the first bundle. It was a clay figurine of a peasant woman she had bought in Mexico a few years ago. She placed it on her bookshelf and turned to the next bundle: a painting on linen from India. She placed it on the carpet to wait for hammer and nail for hanging. Gradually the wrinkled sheets of tissue paper formed a pile beside her and the souvenirs of her travels assumed their accustomed places on her shelves and tables. Eleanor sat back on her heels and surveyed the room. The apartment was starkly white, with a sliding glass door to the deck and wall-to-wall slate-gray carpeting. Her exotic dolls, ornamental paperweights, rice-paper fans, brass animal statuettes, and porcelain plates suddenly annoyed her. Their placement around the living room had been too automatic: the doll from Kenya by the lamp, the Japanese tea set arranged in a semicircle on the top shelf of the bookcase. And yet, for all their familiarity, the objects were alien clutter in this room. What had accumulated naturally in her house over the years now seemed a grotesque and ridiculous assortment. Eleanor began to rewrap the objects, packing the box as full and snug as it had been before. She found a roll of packing tape and sealed it shut.

The walls were bare, the bookshelves bare. This disturbed her children, but Eleanor had grown used to the spare lines and empty space. The hollow feeling pleased her. What was jarring was the gathering of junk on top of the boxes, and the bulky presence of the boxes themselves, neatly stacked as they were. She tested the weight of LIVING ROOM: MEMENTOS AND OBJECTS, and found she could lift it. Bending at the knees, she hefted the box and walked it into the spare room. Laboriously she collected all the boxes from the rooms where the movers had placed them and transferred them to the empty second bedroom. The boxes she couldn't lift she pushed along the carpet. Finally she collected all the catalogs and junk mail she had been building up and swept them into the trash. The flowers, past their prime, went too. When she was done, the apartment seemed uninhabited: sofa, armchair, bare bookcase, and walls. End tables with nothing on them.

She drifted absently from kitchen to sliding glass door, sipping a glass of water, trailing her fingers along the smooth surfaces that everywhere met her fingers. No distractions. No busy colors. She wondered why she hadn't thought of it earlier: the release that pure emptiness could bring, the relief of letting your eyes rest on nothing but white.

JUNE

SHE WAS GOING TO BE LATE, AS USUAL. Somehow the hour she had to kill before the appointment with Mrs. MacGregor had drifted away over a newspaper in the student center and now she was running to the Kenmore station. Not a great way to start a new job. June saw the C train coming, and breathed a sigh. A break.

Settling into the first available seat, she tucked her parka under her, resting her arms on her red nylon backpack. The woman next to her was knitting something garish out of cheap acrylic yarn. Her face, puffy, middle-aged, a blunt fringe of bangs and bright slash of lipstick, was a picture of happy industry. She reminded June of her mother—cheerful and scatterbrained, unconcerned about her appearance, with dozens of half-begun craft projects littering the house, filling every inch of empty space after the divorce.

June had been discouraged from getting to know her father's new wife, who lived with him in Chicago. Melanie the Elegant. With her Chanel suits and lacquered nails, she was definitely not the arts-and-crafts type. Melanie had long red hair, the only wife June had ever seen with hair all the way down her back. Her mother's hair was short and brown, and she had kept June's similarly mousy hair clipped short when she was a child. June's hair was now down to her waist; she gave it a henna rinse every three weeks.

After her father left, she had tried to give her mother makeovers from the pages of her *Seventeen* magazines, but Alice had resisted June's offered hairstyles and tips for applying make-up, the calorie-counter tables and low-fat recipes. By thirteen June had given up on trying to create a new mother, a sophisticated one like Melanie, and instead had gone to work on herself. Her mother, distracted with her weaving and stenciling classes, scarcely seemed to notice June's transformation. Her daughter had emerged from a slightly pudgy junior high school student into a swanlike teenager. June had decided that food was less necessary to her than wearing size three jeans. For breakfast she had an instant chocolate drink that was guaranteed to contain all the vitamins and nutrients she would need in a day. For lunch she bought a salad at the school cafeteria and drizzled the merest teaspoon of French dressing on it. Dinner could be skipped, or if she had been so starved that she ate a full portion or, worse, a double one, she could always make herself throw it up afterward. Her mother was too preoccupied to cook. Like single women living in the same house, they were in the habit of making themselves sandwiches or microwaving frozen food as the mood struck them.

June eventually increased her caloric intake when she read an article about eating disorders in *Glamour* magazine. She decided that hers was only a borderline disorder. After all, her eating habits in high school had not been too different from any of the other girls'. Sometimes she starved. Sometimes she gorged and purged. After reading the article, she convinced herself she didn't really have a problem. Whatever it was, she would cure herself. She decided that she would allow herself to grow a size, and began eating lunch and dinner. That was the kind of will June had. Actually, she grew two sizes, which meant that she still had to watch herself, because if she ever completely gave up control, there was no telling how big she might get.

SHE GOT OFF THE TRAIN AT WASHINGTON STREET, and walked up the street, toward the address the job-placement office had given her. Her stomach was growling, but she had learned to ignore its complaints. When she buzzed apartment 712, the security lock clicked open. She walked by the concierge, a guy about her age who looked up from his book to smile at her, and took the elevator to the seventh floor.

The door opened and an immaculately dressed old woman peered out at her over tortoise-shell half-glasses; she wore black stretch pants and a red sweater. Her white hair was pulled back into a chignon. June was immediately impressed with the woman's makeup. It was complete and flawless down to the carefully lined red lipstick.

"Come in. You must be June."

The apartment, white and modern, was completely bare except for the furniture. No pictures, no books on the shelf, no decorations of any kind.

Mrs. MacGregor was appraising her.

"As you see, June, I don't have a whole lot that needs cleaning. I'm not sure you'll find the job worth your while; with some grocery shopping, it will be just a few hours a week. I wouldn't have advertised, really, but my children think I need someone coming by. To check on me." Mrs. MacGregor smiled slightly.

"I don't mind short hours." June willed Mrs. MacGregor to hire her. She didn't have even ten dollars left in her checking account.

"Well, then. Would you like a cup of tea?"

While Mrs. MacGregor prepared their tea in the kitchen, June stared out the sliding glass door to the balcony. Three different bird feeders were stocked with seeds; at the moment, no birds were in sight. Overnight the weather had gone from warm to wintry. The sky was low and the color of eggshells. Mrs. MacGregor had two patio chairs and a little table on her deck; these were neatly bundled in plastic with twine.

"Let me help you," June said, springing up to relieve Mrs. MacGregor of the tray she was carrying. She noticed that the older woman walked with a bit of a limp. "What pretty tea things."

"Thank you. They're English, from my mother's side of the family. Now," she announced, settling herself into an armchair, "I must ask you to pour. I'm a bit unsteady these days. Cream and sugar, please, two lumps, very white. And help yourself to a cookie. None for me."

June poured them each a cup and self-consciously served Mrs. MacGregor.

"Please tell me about yourself, June. What do you study?"

"Psychology and dance. What I really want to do is be a dancer, but I know that you can't make a career out of that very easily, so my mom said I should have something to fall back on."

June paused; was the woman listening or not? She seemed to be staring off at the balcony, as if waiting for something. June took a tiny bite of the cookie, guessing it to be about seventy-five calories, mentally adding that to the day's total so far of twelve hundred thirty. Round off at thirteen hundred, she decided, giving herself five calories' grace.

"I see." Mrs. MacGregor fastened her gray eyes on her. "And where were you raised?"

"Worcester." June wrinkled her nose. "I like living in Boston a lot better. There's so much more to do. When I can afford it I go see all the dance companies that come to town. Alvin Ailey was here last week."

There was a short silence.

"What about you? Where are you from?" June asked. She didn't know if she was allowed to ask questions back; Mrs. MacGregor seemed to be conducting a kind of interview.

"Just outside of New York," the older woman said without elaborating.

"I've been to New York a couple of times," June said. It's a very exciting city. Overwhelming, though. I've always been a little bit scared when I've been there."

"Yes. It used to be very different." Mrs. MacGregor stood, folding her napkin. "Well, June. I don't have anything for you to clean today, but perhaps you can walk to the market for me. It looks as though we might be in for bad weather, and I should get some things stocked up. I've made a list, and you can take my grocery cart. Finish your tea first; no hurry."

Mrs. MacGregor gave June two twenty-dollar bills and a neat list made out in a spidery hand. She had specified brand names and sizes.

In the market, June realized that Mrs. MacGregor had also listed the items in the order in which you came to them if you walked up and down the aisles one after another, beginning with the first one by the door. She finished the shopping in less than half an hour and was back at the apartment, letting herself in with the key she had been given. Mrs. MacGregor was in the armchair, a book open on her lap.

"Thank you, June. I'll put those away. Just leave them on the counter. Did you have enough money?"

"Yes, plenty. You've got change here." June put the money with the receipt by the groceries. Mrs. MacGregor had already washed up the tea things. "Are you sure I can't put the groceries away for you?" she asked her.

"No, thank you. I need to have something to do. I know you haven't used up your two hours, but I think that's all I'll need for the first day. I've written out your check for the full amount. It's on the desk there. On Friday I'll have some cleaning for you."

Dismissed, June lay the apartment key on the desk. Mrs. MacGregor saw her to the door. June waited until she was in the elevator to look at her check: twenty dollars. Twice a week at Mrs. MacGregor's would barely keep her in groceries, but it would help. She would still need to find another job.

On the walk back to the train, June saw that it had begun to snow small, almost invisible flakes. By the time her stop came, the wind was driving the snow sideways, into her face, and the flakes had formed sharp, stinging edges. The streets were emptying of pedestrians, and cars were turning on their lights although it was only three o'clock.

June's basement studio apartment seemed dark and cluttered after Mrs. MacGregor's, even though she really didn't own that much. Her books were on pine planks supported by cinder blocks. Her futon was folded up along one wall of the apartment. Along the length of the other wall was a barre that June had installed herself, where she did her stretching exercises. Dance posters covered the walls, hiding the fine network of cracks and nail holes from previous tenants. She had a small closet that held her collection of sweaters and blue jeans, along with a few Indian print rayon skirts. Plastic milk crates stacked in the corner separated her socks, underwear, and T-shirts.

The small painted table she had bought at a yard sale was her combination desk and dining area, and she had inherited two mismatched chairs from the former tenants. June's kitchen consisted of a two-burner electric stovetop with a half-size refrigerator below a miniature sink. Part of her two feet of counter space was taken up by a toaster oven and various jars of bulk pasta, rice, beans, and tea. She usually made herself big batches of soup or spaghetti sauce and ate it for several days, stopping on her way home from class to pick up some fresh bread.

June had studying to do, but didn't feel like it. Instead of working, she decided to do some stretching. She popped a tape she had made into the stereo on her bookshelf, and slipped out of her jeans and shoes so that she was standing in just socks, underwear, and a long-sleeved T-shirt. When the jazz music began, she started with head rolls, then shoulder rolls, then rib circles. Working her way down the body, she finished her warm-up with ankle circles, then assumed first position and waited for the Chopin to begin her pliés. After moving through the ballet positions for pliés and relevés, the African drums started. June left the barre to do some improvisational moving, dancing into all the odd spaces of her cramped studio, working with the space, against it, defining it, becoming the space and the drums.

When the music stopped, she heard the phone.

"June! It's Dad." Her father always began this way, practically shouting her name, as if she were a brand-new discovery of his.

"Hi, Dad. This is a surprise." Somehow, words to her father that started out sarcastically in June's head always came out in actual conversation sounding mild and pleasant.

"Listen, I've got to be in Boston tomorrow on business. Let's have lunch together."

"I have classes all day."

"Do you have one at noon?"

"No, but I've got one that ends at eleven-thirty, and another one that begins at one."

"Perfect! I'll have a driver for the day. We'll pick you up and go somewhere close. You choose the place, but not any of that Indian shit again, June. Pick a place with normal food. I may not get to see you over the holidays, so this will be it, kiddo."

"Okay, Dad."

"That's my girl. Melanie sends her love."

June flinched. Melanie did no such thing, but her father thought that by saying that she could be fooled.

"Yeah. See you tomorrow, Dad."

June hung up the phone, her stomach tight. Her apartment had a new flatness to it in the aftermath of her father's voice. She saw her cheap furniture for what it was; she saw the glue traps for the roaches gathering dust in the corners. Her dance posters, with their pictures of unattainably perfect bodies, all of a sudden seemed a pitiable way to decorate a room.

June rummaged around her cupboard for something to eat. She craved something sweet, like one of Mrs. MacGregor's ginger cookies. There were bananas and oranges on the counter, but they wouldn't do. She compromised by toasting some bread and spreading jam on it. She was restless, and paced the tiny apartment as she ate the bread, annoyed by the ugliness of everything she saw.

As she toasted a second slice, she mentally added up the calories. This would be her dinner. She wanted to put in another tape, but her hands were sticky, and putting down her toast to wash them seemed too difficult.

She toasted two more pieces, leaving one on her table while she paced. She didn't bother to toast the bread after that; it irritated her to wait for the slices to pop up. She was out of jam but had some honey. The honey was difficult to spread. Now the knife was sticky, as well as her hands and the table. She tasted nothing, was not conscious of fullness. Her mind was blank. She felt no emotion except a desperate restlessness, and the voracious need to keep taking food inside her. Because she had long ago stopped adding calories to her total, she felt as if some mechanism had broken, resulting in an unexpected freedom—as if a parking meter had quit working so that she could not be cited.

When she had finished the loaf of bread, she opened the cupboard doors again to see if there was something she had overlooked. There was nothing but uncooked pasta, beans, rice, and spices. She considered going out for a sack of doughnuts, but that would mean stopping at a cash machine first. And she had nothing in the bank. June sat at the table, breathing shallowly, gradually feeling her pulse moderate. Slowly the room gained depth again, and colors returned. She washed her hands and put on a tape. She sponged off the table and straightened the kitchen. Everything was back to normal. She went into the bathroom and held her finger down her throat until she threw up. Again. Again.

RENATA

RENATA HAD TRAVERSED THREE QUARTERS of the country. She felt the airiness of distance, as if all the roads she had taken had dried into husks and blown away behind her—no way to find them ever again. She could close her eyes and feel as ghost presences the winding pitches and great level stretches of ground she had covered. Dust had collected in all the seams and crannies of the car. During this time, Charlie had outgrown some of his first sleepers, and Renata had left them carefully folded on motel beds, dotted across Iowa and Illinois.

She was somewhere outside of Bloomington, Indiana, when she decided to stop for a picnic. The temperature was nearly seventy degrees, like early summer, though it was November. She picked up a hamburger and soda for herself at a drive-through, and followed the signs to a state park, where she left the car and transferred a sleeping Charlie to his stroller. With the diaper bag over her shoulder and her lunch tucked into the stroller's carrier, Renata followed the trail that led into a woods. She walked for about ten minutes, stretching her legs and listening to the crow caws and squirrel chatter. Selecting a sunny open piece of ground cushioned with fallen red maple leaves, she spread a blanket and lay the baby down, moving the stroller so that it shaded his eyes. While he was still asleep, Renata ate her hamburger and watched him. Every part of him was perfect: his fine blond hair that stood up in back with a crazy cowlick, his delicately veined eyelids, his fat cheeks, his precisely shaped mouth, which now was pursed and sucking with a dream of nursing. Then, as if suddenly aware that the earth had ceased to move under him, Charlie's eyes flew open and he cried. He always woke that way, with bewilderment. Renata liked to be hovering right above his face when this happened, so the first thing he would see when his eyes cleared would be her smile, and her eyes looking into his.

"I'm right here, Charlie; right here, buddy," she crooned. Abruptly, the cries stopped and he looked at her with astonished delight. Then, as he always did, his face became a wreath of smiling, and his whole body started fidgeting with pleasure. Renata laughed at his excitement, which doubled the baby's pleasure. He began laughing his breathy little laugh, and waving his arms. She picked him up and lifted her shirt, undoing her bra cup to nurse him. As soon as he saw the breast he began to squirm and fuss.

"Hold on, tiger. Okay, okay, there you go." Charlie latched on and began sucking with greed. A little rivulet of milk leaked from the side of his mouth, his lids drooped, and his eyes rolled partway up into his head, so that just the whites showed. The baby's wild drive to nurse had shocked Renata at first; from birth he had grabbed on to her nipple with a lunge and almost a little growl.

His first hunger satisfied, Charlie slowed down to a more methodical pace, then opened his eyes again to stare up at her.

"Hello, little boy; hi, baby," she murmured.

He opened his mouth to smile and the nipple escaped him. He cooed and babbled a few syllables, then started to look around. The older he got, the more frequently he lost his place while nursing, distracted by sights.

"What do you see, huh?" She propped him in to a sitting position so he could take in the trees and grass. "Do you see the squirrel? See the fat little squirrel?" Charlie babbled and drooled, bringing his hands together in front of him to suck with great smacking noises.

Through the woods she suddenly heard the low sound of men talking. They were coming down the trail in her direction. Renata fumbled to close her bra and pull down her shirt with one hand, holding Charlie with the other. The silence and dappled sunlight darkened around them; she realized how isolated they were sitting there. The men's voices came nearer. As they rounded a bend she could see briefly through a gap in the trees that there were three of them. She had an irrational urge to hide, but there was no place to screen herself completely, especially with the stroller. With Charlie, she couldn't run, not fast enough to get away from someone.

Renata never used to be afraid. But the warm, trusting weight of Charlie, and her knowledge of his absolute helplessness, her absolute necessity to him, filled her at times with this sudden panic. She had felt it while driving over a mountain pass in Montana when a blinding rainstorm hit and she was forced to pull over to the muddy shoulder to wait for it to pass, the hazard lights on the car blinking in rhythm with her heart. Fear had electrified her one night in one of the little stucco motel rooms, when there was a sharp knock on the door at nine P.M.—the manager asking her if she would move her car to accommodate a truck that needed to park. Now her skin rose into bumps as she thought of how alone and exposed they were, with three strange men coming upon them. *You are being ridiculous,* she told herself. *They are taking a walk through a state park. They are here for the same reason you are, no other*. Adrenaline fired her pulse. How many other cars had been in the parking lot? Was hers the only one?

Charlie, who had been hypnotized by the light and shadows, decided to cry, to remind her that he was only halfway through his meal.

"Shh-shh," she whispered, jiggling him and then putting him against her shoulder, rubbing his back.

The men's voices suddenly dropped, or maybe it was a trick of the woods throwing their voices away from her, or maybe Charlie's whimpering drowned them out.

Upset because the breast wasn't forthcoming, Charlie leaned his head back and cried full force. She could hear nothing now but him.

"Charlie, sweetheart, wait just a minute," Renata pleaded, rocking him back and forth. He screamed, his eyes tight with rage, his face red, tears rolling down his cheeks. Renata had no choice but to push up her shirt again and undo the other cup.

As soon as she put him to the breast, his cries stopped, and he sucked passionately with closed eyes, the tears beading on his eyelashes, and small, reproachful whimpers issuing intermittently from low in his throat.

Renata adjusted the shirt so that it covered all of the breast, showing just the back of the baby's head, and waited. She held Charlie close to her.

The men strode into view, looking straight at her. They had quit talking among themselves. She thought they looked surprised, then uncertain. One of them said something and they all laughed. They were about twenty yards from her. They wore boots and jeans and black leather motorcycle jackets. Two had a beard and a ponytail, another a mustache and longish dirty hair over his collar. In that instant when one spoke to the others, Renata imagined that they shifted from their tentative individual glances at her to a unit of masculine confidence. She thought she saw it in their walk, and in the set of their mouths, half-smiling.

Renata stared at them and felt a fierceness so complete begin to build in her that it colored her vision and made her slightly lightheaded. Charlie was still nursing, his whimpers having turned into rhythmic swallowing. With this animal mother rage flooding her, she thought that if they approached her she could tear them apart, rip them to pieces if she needed to. They had better not come near her child.

Another said something and they laughed again, a low chuckle. A six-pack dangled from the fingers of the one with a mustache, who was stocky verging on fat.

Renata's eyes were locked on them.

They were coming up even with her picnic blanket. They were close enough so that she could see the sheen of oil on the skin of the shorter one with the ponytail. She could see the silver coiled snake that was his belt buckle, and the dirty cracked leather of their boots. She stared. *Better not*, her eyes warned. *Better not. I will kill you if you touch my child. I swear to God I will kill you with my bare hands.*

"How ya doin'," the fat one said.

"Nice day," said one of the others.

Renata nodded without speaking, tensed. She wasn't sure if they hesitated or not. Then they were past her, their conversation resumed, their backs disappearing into the woods.

That was all. Renata was limp with exhaustion; she felt like weeping. She looked down and saw Charlie staring up at her, wide-eyed. When her eyes met his, he released the nipple to smile.

"Hi, Charlie," she whispered. "Come on, sweetheart, time to go." As she strapped the baby into his stroller and folded up the blanket, she was made dizzy by the thought of how utterly her baby belonged to her.

AFTER THAT, RENATA STOPPED ONLY at municipal parks crowded with mothers and children, or rest stops that had at least half a dozen cars clustered in the parking lot. When she spread a blanket on the grass, she hugged the margins of large family groups; she made eye contact right away with the other parents and smiled and nodded. She began to wish to belong somewhere. If not in a family, then a neighborhood, a mother's circle, somewhere. There should be someone besides herself to know about Charlie's existence, and to miss him if he suddenly were not there.

Renata began to feel impatient to get to Boston. Her destination had been a whim originally. A guy named Rick whom she had waited tables with in Venice was from Boston, and he had told her about the cobblestone and brick sidewalks on Beacon Hill, and about the Public Garden, where they had ice skating in the winter and swan boats in the summer. He showed her a picture of his parents' brownstone, the roof rounded with snow like a house in a children's book, the shrubs frosted white in a doll-sized garden.

She was driving to that picture as much as anything else, because it represented nothing she had come from; in such a place you could begin your life, the one you were supposed to have.

Renata had no family to leave behind except Marcia and her kids. Her parents were dead, and their parents, the grandparents she never knew, were all dead. Although her father had had some half-brothers and -sisters in California from his mother's second marriage, he hadn't known them. Her mother's family, the O'Conners, were originally from New York City, but the children had dispersed all over the country. Her mother never spoke of her family, other than to say, "You're better off not knowin' 'em, sweet," when Renata had asked why she didn't have grandparents and uncles and aunts, like the other kids at school.

Not that much of her life growing up resembled that of the other kids. Even Marcia's arms around Renata in their bedroom when they were children could not have protected her from the sound of their parents yelling and screaming down the hall. No number of stories Marcia told, in which a princess named Renata escaped from a gloomy castle through a window no bigger than a keyhole, could have reassured. But even those sisterly comforts, slight though they were, proved fleeting. Soon after entering high school, Marcia left Renata to fend for herself. She fell in love her sophomore year, and moved in with her future husband just after graduation.

With Marcia gone, Renata was on her own when her mother died. Though her mother used to drink almost as heavily as her father, she was not a mean drunk, and stayed glassily affectionate to her daughters until she passed out. Renata was always "Rennie" to her mother, who made up a song about "Rennie, Rennie, bright as a penny; Rennie the lass from Kilkenny." Renata was in junior high when her mother's cancer slipped in between her ribs like a snake and sucked her from their lives in less than a month. Her father became sober for the first time in years, and actually tried, Renata noticed, to fill in some of the gap in their house, coming straight home after work to cook hamburgers or hot dogs or Kraft macaroni and cheese for them. But to Renata this silent, clear-eyed man was a stranger, and though she did not necessarily prefer the slurring, sarcastic man who cursed her and slammed things, she did know what to expect from him, as she did not from this new father.

They didn't have much to say to each other, although Renata longed to have a conversation between them, tell him how much she missed her mother, and ask him if he ever missed her, too. She wanted to know things about him: what his days were like; if he had chosen to be a printer or if that was just what had happened to him; whether he was sorry he had had a family so early; if he loved his daughters. But there was no way to pose these questions, and he, in his turn, seemed incurious about her life at school, though Renata at the time was earning straight A's, and being asked about her thoughts on going to college by the school guidance counselor. She thought it might be her fault that she and her father could not talk at suppertime, because, try as she would, she could not present a cheerful face to him. She guessed that her sadness must have looked like sullenness, since somewhere along the line her father seemed to have given up on her, staying late after work again to drink with his buddies, forgetting to leave any food in the refrigerator.

For a while Renata used her baby-sitting money to buy McDonald's, then she began writing her father notes to please leave grocery money on the hall table. He did this, and she started doing all the food-shopping for them, as well as cleaning the house when she felt like it. Though her father had returned to his drinking, his outbursts were rarer now, so while they lived together in the house during Renata's high school years, she could do pretty much as she pleased as long as she stayed out of his way. Both of them started spending nights away from home, she with her twenty-year-old boyfriend who already had an apartment, and her father who knows where. Renata had smoked marijuana first as an experiment at some junior high parties, then because she liked it. She started sleeping in and missing classes in her senior year, and barely graduated. After graduation, she got a job as a waitress at the International House of Pancakes, and saved for a car.

Her grown-up life began with the car. At the age of nineteen, she knew that anytime she needed to, she could pack clothes and leave: she had the keys to her used Toyota, she had waitressing experience and had discovered she wasn't afraid of hard work, and, more important, she had nothing at home in Springfield that she would be sorry to leave.

One day just short of her twentieth birthday, she did leave, but it was boredom, rather than unhappiness, which caused her to go. By then she had moved in with her boyfriend, and their lives had settled into a routine. After work they hung out at a local tavern. Renata sat on the barstool and smoked, feeding the jukebox; Mike played pool. She thought that they never fought because they were so well matched temperamentally, but on Valentine's Day, when he suggested they get married, Renata had the revelation that she had never cared enough about him to have an argument. It was his proposal which made up her mind to go to California. When Mike gave her the ring at the Red Rustler steak house, where he liked to go to celebrate all important occasions, she took it because she didn't know what else to say. In fact, she was touched at the amount of saving he must have done to produce a diamond so big.

She accepted the ring, and then, like a coward, dropped it in the mail to him on her way out of town. She wrote two letters, notes really, one to her father and one to Mike. To her father she said only that she was going to California for a while. She would send him an address and hoped he stayed well. To Mike she wrote that she thought she was too young to settle down, though if she were ready, it would be with him. This last part was not true, but she owed him at least that much sentiment. She insured the ring for $2,000 and sent him the receipt in a separate envelope in case he needed to make a claim.

Renata lived in San Francisco for a few years, but was drawn eventually to the sun in Southern California. She sent her father her address every time she moved, but heard from him only once, on her twenty-fifth birthday. Why the twenty-fifth, and not the twenty-third, or even the twenty-first, which would have made sense, she didn't know. Actually, it was on her sister's birthday that he sent the card, but since Renata's birthday had been only two weeks before, she forgave the mistake. Inside was a check for a hundred dollars, which Renata kept uncashed for a month while she pondered what to do with it. Finally she decided to get herself a very expensive haircut at one of the salons in Santa Monica, and, with whatever money was left, buy lunch overlooking the ocean.

She told the stylist to go very short, and the slim young man whose own hair was a brilliant platinum cropped close to his skull and whose close-fitting white jeans and white T-shirt gave him the appearance of an angel, nodded his head approvingly. First he tilted Renata's head from side to side, scrutinizing the lines of her profile. Then he robed her and led her to the marble shampoo sink, where he gathered her dark shoulder-length hair in his hand and gently sprayed it, cradling her head as he worked. She watched as he deftly combed her wet hair back from her forehead and experimented with several natural parts. He told her she had a serious face, and she agreed, thinking that it was almost too serious a face for Los Angeles. As her hair fell to the floor under the hairdresser's quick scissors, Renata grew more and more pleased. By the time he was through with her, her eyes were enormous, and her mouth and nose suddenly had a strong, classic shape. Even the hairdresser was surprised at the difference he had made in her looks.

"Don't ever hide underneath your hair again," he scolded her kindly, rubbing a dollop of scented mousse between his hands and working it through her hair with authority. Her hair, freed from the weight of six inches or so, was now wavy and caught the light with a subdued sheen. He had shaped it close around her head, with short, feathery bangs. From the salon she drove to a restaurant in Malibu where she had never eaten and ordered a margarita. Her table was outside on the deck under a large umbrella. She faced the wide, blue expanse of the Pacific. Since it was a Wednesday around two, she had the deck almost to herself except for one or two customers who looked like Malibu locals, probably record-industry moguls or something, with their casual running shorts, beach sandals, and frayed cotton shirts.

Renata had just ordered her meal and was beginning to drink her second margarita when two guys came out on the deck and took the table next to hers. One of them kept staring at her. She avoided his eyes and studied the ocean. Renata was taking pleasure in reminding herself that she was her father's guest for lunch, as if that fact were nothing very extraordinary, as if he had even chosen the restaurant and the view. Then the wind blew the baseball cap off the table of the guy who had been watching her, and into her lap. She caught it in surprise and he laughed.

"Good catch," he told her. "Now let me buy you a drink."

She allowed them to join her. The three of them drank pitchers of margaritas and she laughed at their jokes. Finally she stood up to go.

"You shouldn't drive," he told her, catching her arm and sitting her down again. "Listen, Rod's house is just up the beach. What do you say we leave your car here and go grill something on his deck for dinner?"

She stared doubtfully.

"Come on," he said. "I'm a nice guy. Look." He pointed to his eyes. "Use your intuition." She stared into his blue eyes, remembering that Ted Bundy was a nice guy; the Hillside Strangler was probably a nice guy. The sun was going down and she was floating on waves of alcohol and ocean breezes that carried wood-burning scents of charred meats and garlic. She ran her fingers through her hair and felt a quick thrill at the surprise of the new haircut. She felt fantastic. She felt reckless.

"Great hair," he told her, petting her like a cat. "Really great hair."

From that evening when she stayed over at Rod's Malibu house, wearing her dress to bed with Bryan on the futon in the living room, her bare legs twined around his jeaned ones, they were a couple. It was a week or two before they finally made love, though they slept together every night from the day they met. From the very beginning they loved just to curl up together, almost like children.

MARCIA CALLED HER TO SAY THEIR FATHER had been in a serious car accident and was not expected to live; would she fly home? The day Renata received this news she had been seeing Bryan about a month. She almost said no, hating to leave town at this moment of heady physical addiction. It was Bryan who told her to go. "You only have one father," he said. "You don't have a choice about this."

As soon as she was on the plane she realized the wisdom of his advice. She hardly remembered her mother's funeral, so dazed and tired had she been, but she could vividly recall the calm, restored look on her mother's face in the coffin. Neither the ravages of drinking and smoking nor the toll of the cancer had destroyed her looks. She was buried looking like the mother Renata wished she had always been: self-possessed, faintly amused, beautiful. Her father that day had dressed in his best black suit, the one he had been married in, and had combed his dark hair back until it gleamed. Seeing him bending slightly over her mother's body, which wore the green dress she always put on for special occasions, Renata believed he mourned her.

Marcia met her at the airport and drove them to the hospital where their father lay in a coma. Renata sat with him while Marcia went home to her kids. There was nothing to do but stare at his bruised and puffy face, and his shaved head where he had needed dozens of stitches. If he was going to die from this accident, Renata was sorry that it would be looking like this. He had been a vain man, with a lean frame and white skin that she had inherited. It didn't seem fair that the one thing in life he had been lucky with—

his looks—should be taken from him at the end.

She tried, and failed, to feel some grief during her vigil. As it was, she sat and read magazines for two days in the intensive-care ward while nurses came and went, adjusting the IV that dripped something into her father's veins. She stood outside to smoke, and ate in the hospital cafeteria off Styrofoam trays. She didn't call Bryan, because she could hardly remember Bryan's face. And although she was staying at the house she grew up in, she found she could remember practically nothing about her childhood even when she was staring at the familiar varnished bookcase that still housed all the *Reader's Digest Condensed Books* her mother had once collected. She was in a limbo of nonfeeling; she knew only the present tense, and it gleamed with the coldness of hospital chrome.

When their father died during the middle of the third night of her visit, Renata was ashamed for feeling relieved. He never regained consciousness, never had any last message or advice or apology for her. She stayed in Springfield just long enough to help Marcia arrange for the cremation and empty the house to prepare it for sale. Marcia kept a small cherry desk that her mother had used to pay bills, and a silver tray, their parents' nicest wedding gift. Renata chose a small gold locket of her mother's. There was no picture in the locket. She looked through her father's dresser for a keepsake, finally settling on a silver-plated cigarette case stamped with his initials: FJR, for Francis James Rivera. She liked to think that the locket and cigarette case were presents her parents had given each other. She hunted for some photographs from her childhood, but discovered that her parents had not taken many, and the ones they had were blurry and out of focus. She kept them anyway, along with a photograph of her parents' wedding, the colors of which had turned bilious. A dealer was summoned to give them a flat fee for the rest of the furniture and haul it away.

Surprisingly, Frank Rivera had left a will. Even more surprising, his job had provided him with life insurance, so although he had never earned much in his lifetime and had no savings, the sisters suddenly found themselves with the proceeds of a small ranch house worth about seventy thousand dollars to split, as well as thirty thousand each in life insurance. The lawyer in Marcia's office who was handling the probate for them said that in a few months they would have checks.

Renata didn't know why, upon returning to California, she never mentioned the money to Bryan. She certainly didn't think he'd try to get his hands on it, aside from his usual casual sponging of movies and meals. He seemed never to actually want for money; he always had enough cash somehow to produce a few lines of coke when he wanted to get them high before bed. But she decided to pretend, even to herself, that the inheritance did not exist, except for allowing herself the indulgence of monthly trips to get her hair cut at the Santa Monica salon, where they always greeted her with a glass of lemon-scented mineral water. The lawyer in Eugene helped her invest the bulk of the money, and then she stopped thinking about it.

It was the money, really, which gave her the courage to have the baby on her own. Though, looking at Charlie now, she told herself that no matter how poor she would have been without her father's death, she still would have had him. Surely she would have. Wasn't Charlie her fate, her future, this one particular boy?

But since the incident in the park, the sole responsibility of him was beginning to weigh on her. She slept fitfully, with dreams of Charlie accidentally locked alone inside the car, Charlie left behind at a roadside stop in a moment of amnesia, or Charlie stolen from her motel room while she slept. The dreams never ended with tragedy; Renata woke just before something horrible happened, her heart pounding from the effort to rescue him. Then she would raise herself up on her elbow, waiting for her baby to take shape out of the nothingness as her eyes adjusted to the dark. He would be there beside her in the bed, protected from the edge by a barricade of pillows, protected from drafts by a zippered sleeper, protected from the outside world by a single door chain.

RENATA SIGNED THE LEASE on an apartment in Brookline just before Thanksgiving, but was not able to move in until the first of December. Overwhelmed by Boston, she and Charlie drove to Cape Cod for the holiday, finding a room in Hyannis. The Cape and Hyannis were places she had heard of before, associating them with blueberry pie and white-sand beaches, but she was disappointed. She knew the weather would most likely be cold and possibly wet, but she hadn't expected the relentlessly grim rain of the Cape and the ugly asphalt sprawl of Hyannis. And she couldn't find the beaches. Every time she followed a road that was supposed to lead to the shore, she found either a tiny stretch of seaweed-strewn sand that soon became private on either side or a boat dock. She was homesick for California, where the weather would be cool but sunny now, and if you wanted ocean you just pointed yourself west until you came upon the vast, straight line of the Pacific.

On Thanksgiving, she propped Charlie up with pillows on their motel bed, his arms encircling a bright pumpkin almost as large as himself, and snapped pictures. Renata wanted him to have holidays. Her mother and father observed them erratically when she was growing up. On a good year, her mother would be up dressing the turkey by six A.M., and have pies ready to bake by ten. Her father would be jovial with his beer and chips in front of the football games on television. With luck they would make it through dinner before the drinking her parents had done that day either started them fighting or caused them to pass out in the living room.

On a bad year, the drinking would be so heavy the night before the holiday that either the arguing would have cast its bitter pall over everything and her mother would refuse to cook, or her parents would still be sleeping at noon, both of them so hung over that when they awoke her mother was not able to cook, or it would be too late. The raw turkey would sit for days in the refrigerator, its watery pink blood collecting at the bottom of the plastic wrapper, then they would throw it out. One year, when Marcia was twelve, she cooked the turkey herself, sitting Renata on a high stool in the kitchen to watch her. She read the cookbook to get the right oven temperature and set the timer to baste the turkey at regular intervals. When she was struggling with the weight of the pan as she tried to slide it back into the oven, some fat splashed over the side of the roaster. A few minutes later the burning fat set off the smoke alarm, waking their father, who ran to the kitchen in a foggy confusion, saw Marcia in a panic at the open oven door waving away billows of black smoke, and Renata in the middle of the kitchen, crying. Without asking any questions, he shoved Marcia aside and reached for the roaster without a pot holder. He burned his hand, cursed, and slapped Marcia hard across the cheek, yelling that she was burning the house down. Marcia and Renata ran to their bedroom, and clung and sobbed together under the covers of Marcia's bed. That Thanksgiving they ate nothing until nine P.M., when their mother finally put on a robe and ordered a pizza to be delivered.

Renata always had a week of feeling sick to her stomach when her friends at school talked excitedly about their families' holiday plans. She would make hers up, fabricating grandparents who came over with pies and cookies, uncles who teased her and gave her money, cousins she would play catch with in the backyard while her mother and aunts cooked. After Christmas vacation in the third grade, when her classmates came back to school with stories of gifts they had received, Renata told them that a fire had burned all their Christmas presents. At first kids were shocked and sorry for her. Then, after school, some of them rode their bikes past her house and came back to school the next day to say that Renata Rivera was a liar. If fire had burned her presents, why not her house, too, or at least part of it? Renata wished that a fire *had* burned the house to the ground, so everyone could see that she wasn't making things up. In fact, she longed for the house to burn. She knew it could easily happen, that fire started quickly if you held a cigarette lighter to paper. That was how her mother had burned the Christmas presents in the bathtub after her father had gone out by himself on Christmas Eve and not come back until the next day.

CHARLIE WOULD HAVE HOLIDAYS, beginning now. The place she picked to have Thanksgiving dinner was crowded with retirees, and the hubbub and warm, steamy atmosphere put him to sleep in his carrier the minute they were seated.

"Darling baby," the waitress said.

"Yes." Renata felt the waitress's implicit question hanging in the air. Why weren't they with their family on Thanksgiving? Where was the darling baby's father? Now that Charlie's hair was lightening to a straw-colored blond, and his eyes had remained their startling blue, he looked more like Bryan than ever. People never failed to tell her that the baby must look like his daddy. Just because it was true didn't mean that Renata wasn't annoyed by the suggestion that they weren't a complete unit themselves, Charlie and Renata, without reference to any third party.

She ordered a turkey dinner, the first she would be eating since her mother died. When she lived with her first boyfriend, she made a joke of Thanksgiving, saying she didn't do holidays, and though he was a little disappointed, he humored her, and they always made it a point to eat something weird on that day, like corn dogs or chow mein. The one Thanksgiving she had shared with Bryan, they went hiking in the mountains and slept in a tent, drinking champagne and eating Ritz crackers and Raisinets. But this was Charlie's first Thanksgiving, and in his honor she would eat turkey, dressing, cranberry sauce, pumpkin pie—all of it.

Charlie slept through the whole meal, allowing her to eat slowly and look around. She wasn't sorry to be single. The old couples looked like sleepy cows munching away, two by two. Some hardly talked to each other. They probably knew every thought the other had, had heard every possible conversational gambit the other could offer. Maybe they held virtual conversations in their heads, or virtual arguments, or replayed a Thanksgiving scene from years ago. One woman cut her husband's meat for him as he placidly looked on. Another couple had brought paperbacks, and read silently across the table from each other as they chewed. It was pathetic, really.

Back at the motel, Renata called her sister.

"Hey, Jess," she said when her five-year-old niece answered.

"Aunt Rennie, where are you?" Jess whined. "I want to play that game you taught me with the cards."

"Concentration," Renata said. "We will. Did you guys have a nice dinner?"

"I don't like turkey."

"Well, how about pie?"

"I don't like pie."

"Jess, are you having a bad day, honey? Why are you being such a down-in-the-mouth girl?"

"I'm not. Can I talk to Charlie?"

"Charlie's sleeping, baby."

"Charlie's nicer than Tommy, Aunt Rennie. Tommy hits. I wish Charlie was my baby brother and not Tommy."

"Don't say that, honey. Tommy won't hit if you show him that it's not nice. He's little, and he has to be taught things."

"When is Charlie coming back?"

"We'll visit again."

"Christmas?"

"No, not this year."

"How will I give Charlie his present? I'm making him something at school."

"That's nice, sweetie. Maybe your mommy will help you send it to him."

"It's not the same. I won't get to see him play with it."

"You will when we visit. Jess, can I talk to your mommy for a minute? You can get back on after. And you can help Tommy talk on the phone, too."

"Tommy doesn't know how to talk on the phone. Only I do."

"Jess—"

Renata heard the phone drop with a clatter. Minutes later, Marcia came on.

"Hello?" She sounded puzzled.

"Didn't Jess tell you I was on the line?"

"She said you called, past tense. She didn't say you were waiting."

"Well, for Christ's sake, Marcia. I'm going to call on Thanksgiving, talk to Jess, and hang up?"

"Happy Thanksgiving to you, too. I thought she hung up on *you*. You know how she is with the phone. And how am I supposed to call you back when I don't even know where the hell you are?"

"If you know how she is with the phone, why don't you supervise her when she answers?"

"Look, Renata, lighten up. Give me lectures when you have two kids and your two-year-old is busy stuffing mashed potatoes in the toilet. You run to the phone then to supervise your five year old." Marcia paused. "How's my Charlie baby, anyway?"

"I'm sorry." Renata stopped. "He's doing great, just great. He laughs all the time now, you should see him. He thinks everything's hilarious."

"How am I going to see him? First you go to California and miss most of Jess and Tommy's baby years, and then you take off to God knows where so we have to miss Charlie's. That's not healthy, Renata."

"Uh-oh. You must have gone to one of your group-therapy sessions tonight."

"You should try a few. They help."

"Yeah, well." Renata paused. "Mashed potatoes in the toilet, huh?"

"That's what you have to look forward to. Did you get a place yet?"

"Yep, signed a lease and everything. It's nice—real modern and clean, two bedrooms, a deck, underground garage. Then I went to a furniture rental place and picked out a bunch of stuff. They're going to deliver it on the thirtieth, so when I show up on the first it will be all set up. How's that for painless?"

"Mm-hmm."

"Don't sound so enthusiastic." Renata hated the undercurrent of disapproval that ran through Marcia's side of these conversations. Why couldn't she understand that not everyone went about things the same way? Let her go to her support groups. They didn't, however, seem to cheer her up.

"Look, don't expect me to applaud. I didn't want you to leave, and I don't want you to stay there. We miss you."

Renata fingered the cord, looked around at the generic motel furnishings. It was the first time it occurred to her that Marcia might have needed *her*. That Renata had let her down.

"What do you think of Boston?" Marcia asked.

"I don't know. It's quaint. All these tiny little streets jammed with cars. It takes some getting used to." She didn't say that she had driven straight to the neighborhoods of the storybook brownstones with their diminutive walks and been told that the rents were two thousand a month and up.

"Why did you sign a lease? Maybe you won't like it."

"We'll see."

"Did you start looking for work yet?"

"When I'm settled. I have a lead from Rick, that waiter I knew in California who came from here."

"Speaking of California. Renata, Bryan called me looking for you. He says he ran into Rick, who told him you were moving to Boston."

Instinctively, Renata glanced at Charlie. He was sleeping soundly beside her on the bed in their motel room. Renata leaned over and wiped a little bit of drool from his chin with her index finger.

"Bryan?"

"You know. The father of your child?"

"Marcia, you didn't tell him." She pulled the extra blanket up from the foot of the bed and tucked it around herself and Charlie.

"No, I didn't. But he was real insistent that he get ahold of you. Maybe Rick told him."

"Well, Rick didn't know."

"Are you sure?"

Renata wasn't sure. She had started to show the slightest bit by the time she quit working, but she didn't think anyone was scrutinizing her under her loose waitressing blouses. Rick had covered her station once when she had to go to the john and throw up, but she had told him that she was hung over.

"Of course I'm sure."

"I don't know what Bryan wanted, but I was able to tell him the truth—that I don't know your new address. Are you going to give it to me?"

"Yeah. I'll call you with it later. It's packed away right now and I can't remember the street number. I'll call you when my phone's working." Renata needed time to think.

"Well, he gave me his number. He said he just moved, and you wouldn't know it. He wants you to call him. You want it?"

"No."

"Renata—"

"Keep the number for me, Marcia. I don't want it right now."

After hanging up, Renata curled herself around Charlie, her knees and arms forming a circle around him. He stirred and whimpered slightly in his sleep, rooting to find a nipple. As Renata was pulling her shirt up for him, his mouth suctioned onto the back of her hand and began working.

"You missed, you kooky little boy," Renata said, gently disengaging him and repositioning him at the breast. Charlie nursed without waking up. Renata felt the tingling in her breasts as they swelled with blood and milk. As the milk flowed from her to him, Renata relaxed again. When she was nursing the baby there was nothing she wanted, nobody she needed. Before Charlie was born she had had to work hard to feel like this—two or three drinks, a joint, a line of coke. And always the high had an edge to it: she'd be a shade too jumpy, or too out of control, or too foggy, or too speeding. Then there was the coming off of the feeling, like a door opening to a draft, or like a toothache starting. This was an entirely different matter. When Charlie nursed, or when she got Charlie to laugh, she felt as if the feathers of a great white wing were lightly brushing them both. That was how she pictured it: first a darkness, like space, all empty and cold; then a white wing unfolding so large it covered all the darkness, bringing its own warmth and light; then Renata and her baby were nestled inside the wing—cushioned, safe, flying somewhere together.

They were all right by themselves, Charlie and Renata. If she involved Bryan in any way, no matter how small, he would bring his history into it. He would look at Charlie and see himself—for Charlie was daily becoming the image of his father—and they would all start falling again. Bryan would fall, and Renata and the baby would fall right with him, out of the soft rescue of the wing.

THEY SPENT ANOTHER WEEK ON THE CAPE, going to Provincetown, and taking the ferry from Hyannis to Nantucket. Renata didn't want to stop driving. This was the last week of their nomadic life and she was nervous about setting up house—it marked the end of their time outside normal rules. On the ferry coming back from Nantucket on the morning of December first, Renata stood at the rail with Charlie and stared at the green water. She loosened her pawnshop wedding band and tossed it into the foaming wake. When she turned around, an old man sitting on deck in a wool coat and muffler was staring curiously at her.

Renata took her time driving back to Boston. She kept to the speed limit, stayed in the middle lane. When they entered the city it was late afternoon, and dusk was already settling in, making the buildings look like a painting in a dark museum. She got off the expressway and drove out Beacon Street toward Brookline. Red ribbons festooned the gaslight-style lampposts. Many of the brownstones already had Christmas wreaths and lights in their windows.

Renata parked in the loading zone under the apartment awning, unbelted Charlie from his car seat, and ran into the manager's office to get her keys.

"Your furniture got here fine yesterday," the manager said. "They were in and out in an hour."

"Thanks a lot for letting them come in a day early."

"No problem. And you sure have been getting a lot of packages. I had Sam, the maintenance man, put them in your apartment this morning."

"I appreciate that."

"That's what we're here for. You let us know if you need to borrow a hammer or a stepladder or anything, and I'll send Sam by your unit to give you a hand. Welcome to the building. And you, too, little guy," he said, pinching Charlie's cheek. Renata hated it when strangers touched him. Charlie took it in stride though, grinning and drooling at everyone without favoritism.

The key card worked smoothly, admitting them to the garage. Renata drove to her assigned spot and unloaded her bags. There were two pieces of luggage now: the large duffel they began with and another tote that Renata had picked up for the extra clothing and blankets Charlie was accumulating. Now that they were settled, Renata would have to buy herself some cold-weather clothes and boots. She couldn't stand this shivering much longer. With the baby on her arm and the bags at her feet, she pushed the elevator button.

"We're here, Charlie," she said, nuzzling him. "Here in your first home." He smiled, digging his hard little shoes into her side.

When they got to her floor she managed to carry the baby and bags in one ungainly trip down the hall. When she reached her door, she plopped the bags to the ground and fished for the key. The manager had already inserted a printed card with her name into the holder on the door: R. RIVERA.

Inside, the furniture had been arranged according to the floor plan she had left with the rental company. Somehow the place looked just like the motels Renata had been staying at.

"Are you ready?" she asked Charlie, bouncing him slightly so that he knew he should feel excited. "Ready for Charlie's room?" He razzed and brought his hands together to suck. Renata turned on the light and saw the crib with the matching dresser, changing table, and rocker. She gave him a tour of his nursery, stopping so he could grab on to each piece of furniture.

Her packages, piled up in the hall, were from Sears. She had picked up a catalog as soon as she knew what her address would be and ordered things over the phone to be delivered: sheets for her bed and for the crib, towels, dishes, cooking pots, flatware, shower curtain, a touch-tone phone with an answering machine, comforter, baby monitor, baby seat. She set up Charlie's new bounce seat first so he could watch her open the boxes. Then she gathered all the new baby bedding together to wash.

"Charlie, Mommy's going to run just to the end of the hall to the laundry room, okay?" She plugged in the baby monitor's transmitter, and clipped the receiver to her belt. "Mommy can hear you, so don't you worry."

His eyes followed her to the door and she smiled reassuringly at him. She locked the door behind her, and jogged down to the laundry room. As she was plugging quarters into the machine, the monitor crackled and she heard him begin to whimper. By the time she reached her apartment door, he was in full wail. She heard it now coming from both the apartment and the receiver clipped to her. As she was reaching for her key, the door next to hers opened a few inches, and Renata felt herself examined by a neighbor.

"I'm sorry, did the noise bother you?" Renata fumbled to turn down the volume on the monitor; instead she turned it up by mistake. The door opened wider and the woman's eyes traveled to Renata's waist.

"What is that contraption?" She was old, but narrow and straight as a ramrod, with beautiful white hair pulled back in a knot.

"It's so I can hear the baby," Renata explained.

"I shouldn't think you'd have much trouble," the woman said, one corner of her mouth tugging up briefly in what Renata presumed was a smile.

"I'm sorry. He won't cry as soon as I go to him."

"Don't apologize," the woman said. "I'm Eleanor MacGregor." She held out her hand. It was dry and cool.

"Renata Rivera. That's Charlie you hear. We're moving in." Renata opened her apartment door so Charlie could see her. He stopped crying and grinned, trying to stretch his arms across the distance. "He's just inside, if you'd like to meet him."

The woman stepped into the hall to look through Renata's doorway. Her face remained impassive, but she said, "He certainly is a fine boy."

"Would you like to come in? I was just about to call for a pizza. Won't you join us?"

"Oh, no, dear, thank you. I'll leave you to your unpacking." Charlie had been quiet while he stared back at Eleanor MacGregor; now he began to fuss. "I'd say that young man is impatient for your return," she said, nodding before she disappeared behind her door, its lock clicking into place after her.

RENATA ATE HER PIZZA in front of the rented television, and after the eleven o'clock news, she woke Charlie up for nursing. She loved to pick him up when he was half-asleep and he draped himself against her neck, making mewing sounds. Without turning on his bedroom light, she nursed him in the rocker, changed him, then lay him down in his crib. He went back to sleep immediately. When Renata got into her own bed, she stretched out luxuriously, then, still awake after ten minutes, rolled to her left side, then her right. She checked the baby monitor and found that its green light was glowing. She got up and tiptoed into his room to make sure he hadn't kicked off his blankets. He was breathing heavily in his sleep, covered the way she had left him. He didn't notice that they were apart for the first night in his life.

Renata wanted to pick him up and take him to bed with her. But if she did, it would so clearly be for her comfort and not his. She took herself back to bed, promising herself the compromise of bringing him to her room when he woke up during the night for a feeding.

At two A.M., Charlie was still sleeping, and Renata was still awake, turning in her empty bed. At three, she moved her pillows and blankets into his room, lying on the floor and waiting for him. At five, his cries woke her, and she finally carried him back to bed with her to nurse, and to hold on to him.

RENATA'S NEXT FEW DAYS were spent stocking up her kitchen, buying cleaning supplies and prints for the walls, and shopping for new clothes for both of them. The city was still a maze to her. Even along her regular errand routes she found herself making the same wrong turns day after day, as if she needed to run through a set course of errors before she would let herself find home.

The dark and chill were daunting. Winter in L.A. used to mean breaking out a heavy cotton sweater. Now she found herself combing the stores for a goose-down coat. She finally came upon the one she wanted: bright red and mid-calf, made of weightless down and nylon. Even on sale, it was close to three hundred dollars. She didn't care. It warmed the dark like a chili pepper, and its brightness made her think of California.

This had been the first time in her life she could go out and buy anything she needed in one fell swoop, without having to pay it off a little at a time. It pleased her that everything they used was new, that the apartment was so modern. But Renata needed to get back to work after the New Year so she could leave the rest of their savings intact. She wanted to keep enough for a down payment on a house for them someday—where, she didn't know. She had started to drive around neighborhoods, not because she was ready to think about a house yet, but because she was curious about what that life looked like. She knew now that houses didn't have to look like the one she grew up in, with unmowed grass and drawn curtains. But she had nothing else to go on. Some afternoons she drove down streets where children were climbing off school buses, lunch boxes and drawings in hand, and saw them run to the front doors opening to greet them. She studied the way Christmas lights encircled bedroom windows, and how families had their names printed neatly on their mailboxes. She watched children roller-skate on their sidewalks, chased by their dogs, and saw parents pull into their driveways with grocery bags and briefcases. She liked to think that the shouts and barks and happy calls going back and forth on these streets were weaving their way into Charlie's sleep, and that as he napped in his car seat, these were recorded in his being as the sounds of his life.

ELEANOR

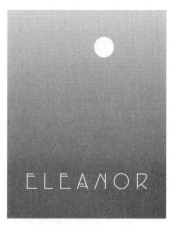

ELEANOR HAD GROWN UP in a house with servants. From birth through the age of twelve she had a nanny. The family also kept a cook, housekeeper, and gardener. Her father, Jackson Donleavy, was a button manufacturer who weathered the Depression by switching his emphasis from wholesale to retail in 1930, buying three small storefront businesses in Manhattan, Queens, and Brooklyn to sell sewing notions directly to the individual customer. Because more housewives were making their own clothes during those years, as well as keeping old clothes longer by mending or refurbishing them, he prospered in the notions business, opening more stores throughout the region, and actually increased button production when other manufacturers in the garment industry were closing their factories.

Although Eleanor had grown up somewhat luxuriously, she had, from the time of her marriage, lived a normal middle class life, at least until Robert's endless surgical residencies were finished and he began to earn enough not only to keep them very comfortably but to send Eleanor to law school. Only when she had begun her law studies did they hire household help—a nanny for the children, and a housekeeper. Having paid help was not an enormous adjustment for her; she was accustomed to the role that servants played in a house: they were to be treated fairly and kindly, and as long as they were competent and honest, they were entitled to every consideration an employer might extend to make the working conditions pleasant. This included inquiring in a general way after their welfare and that of their families, but, in Eleanor's mind, stopped short of forming a genuine friendship.

This was the very relationship Eleanor intended to create with her new helper, June. The girl certainly was eager to be useful to her, and had impressed Eleanor with her willingness to work. But the fact was that at this time in her life, Eleanor found it difficult to have a stranger coming and going in her house, although it did turn out to be a relief to have help—even light amounts of shopping and housework had been wearing her out lately. Eleanor would rather have avoided a lot of small talk with June, and simply wished to hand her lists of things to do, but June tended to chatter on. All the talking unnerved Eleanor in the beginning, accustomed as she was to the silence of living alone. But as June's visits passed, she began to grow used to it, letting it flow over her like music.

June's voice *was* musical; it had the lilt and optimism of youth as she told Eleanor about a new piece of choreography she was learning, the grade she had received on her statistics exam, or the bugs that she waged war against in her studio apartment. Little by little, and unasked by Eleanor, she began revealing things about her background: her parents' divorce and father's remarriage, how she wished she had not been an only child, and that she wished she had the courage to quit school and be a dancer in New York. Eleanor surprised herself by beginning to look forward to these visits, to be kept current in the life of June. She was not prepared, however, for June's curiosity about her own life, the questions about the boxes in the spare room, the need to know the names of all the characters whose photos were on her refrigerator, the wish to hear about what Eleanor had done over the weekend.

She was certainly not prepared when June asked for her assistance on a school project for some class fantastically called Dying and Grief.

"I just can't seem to begin the paper," June said. "It's about mourning. Do you think you could tell me some things about how you felt when your husband died? I mean, not really personal things, but did you go through some stages of grief? There are supposed to be four stages, you know—or maybe it's five—at least that's what the books say."

Eleanor was so taken aback by the question that she could only murmur something noncommittal and change the subject. She was sure June felt embarrassed, and she regretted that. But what in the devil did the girl expect her to tell her? June didn't bring it up again and Eleanor had no idea if she had begun writing her paper. Lately though, when Eleanor was sitting in her armchair having her morning coffee, watching the birds at her feeders, her thoughts kept turning to Robert, and their marriage, and his death. The feeder was now attracting several kinds of birds, and Eleanor kept meaning to get a book from the library to identify them. June had brought over a bag of mixed seed that her mother in Worcester concocted. "My mother makes the mix every year for Christmas presents," June announced. "She didn't mind me taking some early to give you when I told her you weren't having any luck with your feeders." Eleanor had been startled by the girl's observation, and even more by the fact that she had been right: it wasn't just a poor year for birds, as Eleanor had assumed; it was that the birds didn't want what she had been offering. They came now for June's seed.

Some sort of brown bird was now perched on the rim of the feeder; another, which might have been its mate, was grooming itself on the deck railing.

In many ways, she and Robert had been perfectly suited for each another. Both were disciplined, and more intellectual than emotional. They waited until they had both graduated from college to become engaged, and then, while Robert went to war, Eleanor worked for her father as a bookkeeper, saving money and living at home. They never made a misstep out of self-indulgence or recklessness. Robert's career proceeded just as they expected from someone so talented and ambitious; the children were never ill beyond the usual childhood maladies; and, after Peter was in kindergarten, Eleanor surprised neither of them by the way she sailed through her legal studies, graduating second in her class and rapidly achieving promotions at the Department of Public Welfare, where she became chief counsel.

Her life had not had too many disappointments. When she miscarried a baby between Helen and Janice, she remembered that she could not stop crying for a week. She and Robert both attributed the uncontrolled tears to hormonal shifts. When the week passed, she gave herself a list of spring-cleaning chores to do, and spent the next month cleaning closets, painting rooms, and digging up the soil in the garden. A few months later she was pregnant with Janice, and the miscarriage was forgotten. When Eleanor's father died she went through the customary mourning rituals, but really, his death was a relief. He had been so unhappy confined to bed for the last few years that Eleanor could not truly be sad at his passing.

Her mother's death fifteen years later was harder for Eleanor, who herself was beginning to feel the onset of arthritis and digestive problems, which were her family's hallmarks of aging. She had always identified with her cool, competent mother, and to see her shrink to ninety-seven pounds and then fall into a period of vague fretfulness before finally dying was frightening to Eleanor. In the last year or so that Charlotte rattled around the Forest Hills house, forgetting to eat, arguing with her housekeeper—who herself was seventy, but too loyal to retire—Eleanor worried constantly. Her mother would not hear of giving up the house, though the stairs were a clear danger to her and she had lost interest in its gardens and grounds. Eleanor and her sister, Isabel, were on the verge of hiring a twenty-four-hour nurse when Charlotte died in her sleep of a stroke.

By the time Eleanor came into her half of the Donleavy inheritance, she and Robert were well established in their fields. Their children were through with college and had their grandfather's trust funds to draw on for graduate school. Even after investing the bulk of her mother's estate, Eleanor and Robert had more money than they could easily spend. It was a period of second honeymoon for them: travels to Bombay one season, Kenya the next; fishing trips in Alaska and the Florida Keys; castle tours of Europe and a walking excursion in the Scottish Highlands. Eleanor felt them growing younger with each journey, as if the good luck of having extra money could buy time as well as exotic sights.

IN RETROSPECT, ELEANOR FOUND IT IRONIC that her doctor husband could never be bothered to get himself regular physicals. It wasn't arrogance, exactly, that made him assume that he could diagnose himself. Partly it was a kind of supreme confidence that someone who was so successful at treating other people's maladies could not fall prey to any himself. And, in fact, he was rarely sick. Eleanor thought that Robert saw sickness as somehow beneath him personally, though he was compassionate to his patients. Maybe it was because he saw so many weak and vulnerable people—powerful men brought low by a heart valve or a blood vessel, reduced to wearing those backless hospital smocks—that he, Robert, decided that will alone could keep him healthy.

Though she knew it was a fallacy to correlate what kind of failure the body experienced with personality, Eleanor could not help thinking that for her husband's body to repay him for all his self-discipline and intelligence with an inoperable brain tumor was a kind of gross cosmic insult. He claimed later that he had had very few symptoms in the beginning, and she was forced to believe it, because otherwise she would have been too angry with him for not seeing a doctor sooner. By the time his headaches and blurred vision made it impossible for him to perform surgery, it was too late. Less than a year later, he was an irascible stranger who would wander muttering down the street in his robe and slippers. The loss of control over his personality was the hardest part for Eleanor to watch, and she knew that in his moments of clarity it was what caused Robert himself the most humiliation and pain. Overnight he had become the kind of person to whom busy specialists spoke too loudly and talked about in the third person, as if he were not in the room.

Her children were with her when she buried her husband, and Peter, especially, stepped in to oversee the arrangements. It was a dignified Presbyterian service, though Robert hadn't been much of a churchgoer. His colleagues paid their respects in dark expensive suits, and spoke movingly of the Robert who ran the surgery department, omitting all reference to the eccentric and distraught character they had paid embarrassed visits to in the last three months. She supposed she had been, if not comforted by the burial rituals, at least occupied enough by them to propel her through the first period of shock. Her daughters provided a buffet back at the house after the funeral, and as Eleanor held the familiar party crystal in her hand, receiving condolences, she fought the surreal feeling that they were having a few people in for cocktails to celebrate someone's birthday or promotion, and that Robert would be back shortly from stepping out to get more ice.

It was not as if Eleanor hadn't been given time to rehearse his death. She had, and during the last months, when illness filled the house, hanging over her life with its sour smell and its released chaos of emotions, she had longed for the equilibrium of normalcy—which, given the scenario that lay ahead, meant she had longed for Robert's impending death. She had never wanted him to leave her, but when he already had left her, and the wasting stranger who was blind, bedridden, and did not know her transformed her life into a state of siege, she wanted Robert's body to die with the rest of him.

She shocked her children by taking a leave of absence and going on a cruise within a month of the funeral.

"Mother, don't you think it would be better for you if you

stayed home where all your friends are?" Helen asked on the phone from Houston. "Or, if you need a change of scene, why not come here?" Eleanor could hear her five- and seven-year-old grandsons fighting in the background. This was about the time Helen had first begun to speak to her in a tone that suggested that she, Helen, was the aggrieved parent and Eleanor the misguided child. Her daughter's tone was plaintive and demanding at the same time, as if somehow her mother were not being fair for making an independent decision that Helen could not see the logic of.

Eleanor spent a week poring over cruise-line brochures, and then booked three weeks on a mid-size ship departing from Florida. She took a few thick novels with her, but spent most of her time on a shaded deck chair just staring at the line where the sky and sea met. She was able to discern enormous complexity in that line after a few days of watching it—how sometimes it was invisible to her eye, yet certainly there; how at sunset it would sometimes reveal to her a quick flash of the most improbable green. She didn't remember much afterward about her fellow passengers, although she surely must have talked to them every night at dinner. She did receive the attentions of a seventy-ish widower who pressed her to accompany him on shore excursions and to dance with him in the Cabaret Room. She refused these invitations, as well as the inappropriately expensive bracelet he tried to give her as a farewell gift before they docked, but did take from him his business card, which she stared at absently when she unpacked back in Belmont, putting it on her dresser, where it remained for a year.

After the cruise, Eleanor seemed outwardly like her old self, just as, years before, after the brisk spring cleaning one could see no traces of mourning for the miscarried baby. She was efficient this way, giving herself some activity to purge the affliction of sadness, and then putting the cause of the sadness behind her. But a marriage of more than four decades was not to be so easily put aside. At first, everything Eleanor did was tinged with Robert's presence. Reading the newspaper in the morning reminded her of the way he would read interesting bits to her without looking up, and how he could not start his day until he had digested the contents of the *Times*, the *Globe*, and the *Journal*. She began reading the paper at night over her supper, something neither of them had done. When the car needed an oil change, she let the maintenance light stay on for six weeks before she finally drove to a service station—Robert had always made this his job. His favorite devil's food cookies remained on the cupboard shelves for months before she was able to throw them away, and she finally had Peter come down and take what clothes he wanted of his father's before bundling the rest up for the Salvation Army just short of the first anniversary of his death.

She tried to remember what daydreams she occasionally had had about things she would do if she lived alone. They turned out to be less satisfying in practice than in fantasy. She took a drawing class at the Cambridge Center for Adult Education, and went to only half the sessions, having filled a sketchbook with ten pages of lumpy, unpromising life studies. For several months she ate the kind of spicy takeout she enjoyed, and which had given Robert indigestion, until she tired of the flavors and went back to broiling plain chicken and fish at home. She bought herself a cat, an animal Robert had been violently allergic to, and found that for the most part the creature and she ignored each other, though it was nice to have it sleeping warm at the foot of her bed at night.

She had resented very little in marriage, and found herself missing much. Things that had irritated her about her husband—how he never put a single thing back that he had used, for instance, as if he thought a surgical scrub nurse was standing by to receive and dispose of anything he was finished with—now seemed insignificant next to the loss of his jokes, his conversation, and his faintly soapy smell.

These things occupied Eleanor's mind after June's earnest inquiry, and yet there was nothing to say in reply to the girl. The question, after all, was absurd. Grief was an intangible companion that moved in quietly after a death and came and went according to its own schedule. One day it seemed to leave for good, without letting you know its plans. Then came moments when you couldn't clearly picture the face of your own husband, and you actually had to look at photographs to remind yourself of that other life you led. As she stared at the busy activity at her feeder in the mornings, Eleanor often felt a bewilderment. How had she gotten here? One day she was dipping Easter eggs with Isabel in a great sun-filled kitchen, her mother and nurse looking on. The next she was driving her three school-aged children to the pond, the car filled with black rubber inner tubes baking in the backseat. Now Eleanor had a silent white room to live in, as plain and empty as a box, and she drifted asleep in it, loose on some great tide she neither welcomed nor feared.

JUNE WAS WORKING ON TURNING HER AURA pink again, on the advice of Miriam Lightcap, psychic adviser. She thought her aura must have turned to its present dark purple—the color of a bruise, Miriam said—at the moment of her father's phone call. The jagged red and yellow borders probably emerged during their lunch together.

He had been enthused about his newest real estate venture and laughing over Melanie's extravagances at a spa in Florida. June stared at his necktie, trying to remember if it was one she had sent him. Ties were the only present she had given him since he had left them. At lunch he was wearing an expensive-looking jacquard weave of blue and green; she didn't recognize it.

"So, why do you waste time on these dance classes, Junie?" He had never stopped calling her by her childhood name. "I mean, I'm sure they're fun and all, but I don't see why you have to pay good tuition money to take them. Why not use your electives for some business or computer classes, and take the dance classes at the Y?"

"I could teach those classes at the Y, Dad. You know I've been taking dance for fifteen years now."

"Well, why don't you? Earn some extra money, get your exercise in, and use tuition credits for something useful."

"I don't dance for exercise."

"Well, what, then? Oh, never mind, Junie. I can see you getting mad at me. Take whatever you want at school. I'm just trying to be a father here, you know, help you think practically about things. But if you want the dance classes, for God's sake, take them. Just do me a favor and see that the degree is worth something by the time you finish, okay? Take some meat-and-potatoes courses, not just dessert. I'm happy to put you through school, but afterward you've got to be able to cut it yourself, you know, kiddo. Everybody does. Part of growing up."

June toyed with her salad.

"Christ, you're just like Melanie. Won't order anything but salad and mineral water, and then you barely eat three bites."

June forced herself to ask. "How is Melanie?"

Her father beamed at her. "Just great. You'd never know that woman was thirty-five. She could pass for your sister if you two were shopping together." He sawed at his steak. "Actually, June, we've got some news. Melanie wanted to be here to help tell it, but this was the only week she could get in at the spa. And when I tell you what's up, you'll understand why the spa is so important to her right now."

June waited.

"We're gonna have a kid, June. What do you think about that? I sure as hell never imagined myself starting over at this age, and Melanie always said she never cared about children—I mean having them," he corrected himself. "But here we are, going for it. I think that biological-clock thing started to get to her." Her father popped a French fry into his mouth. "You just going to sit there and stare at me?"

June wasn't just sitting there. She was extremely busy telling herself, *Don't change your face, don't cry, this doesn't affect you in the least. This does not concern you.*

"That's great, Dad."

"Yeah, it is, kind of." Her father cleared his throat. "June-bug,

I know I wasn't there for you much in the last eight years. I'm sorry about that, but I can't get those years back. This is a second chance for me to be a dad, so it means a lot that you feel happy for us. I appreciate that. More than you know." He reached over and squeezed her motionless hand. "And," he continued dramatically, "it's going to be a boy. I never thought about it one way or the other when the doctor handed us you," he said, winking at her. "I thought you were a pretty special package. But now that it's all going to happen again and we hear that it's a boy, I'm thinking, great! We'll do the father-son thing: Cubs tickets, dude ranches, whatever the hell else. I'll have to read up."

"Dad, you hate baseball and you hate dust."

"I do hate that shit, Junie. You know me pretty well. Do you think he'll be born with a fondness for single-malt whiskey and eighteen holes of golf?"

June shrugged. "If he knows what's good for him."

Her father didn't react to her tone. He signed the restaurant charge slip, snapping off his copy of the receipt. Then he got out his checkbook. "Here's a little something for Christmas, Junie. Get yourself something nice." He wrote the check in his illegible hand, and waved it to dry the ink. June accepted it without looking at the amount.

"Thanks, Dad."

"Don't mention it. I had a good year, so it's a little bigger than usual. But don't expect that much all the time," he said, lifting his index finger in a mock scold.

"When's the baby due?"

"Wha?"

"My brother. When's he due?"

"Jeez. He will sort of be your brother, won't he? The due date's June twelfth. That's a nice coincidence, isn't it? You want to be dropped, Junie?"

"No, I'll walk."

"Just like Melanie—an exercise nut."

"Mom's doing fine, by the way," June said.

"That's great, just great. Listen, I gotta get to that meeting. You're sure you don't want a ride somewhere?"

June waved him away. "Merry Christmas," she called to his back.

"Oh, hell yes," he said over his shoulder. "Merry Christmas."

JUNE WAS TEMPTED TO RIP THE CHECK IN HALF, but it was for five hundred dollars. She decided that part of it would go for another consultation with Miriam Lightcap. She took pleasure in picturing her father's reaction if he learned that his money was going to a psychic healer who was helping her to balance her energies. Her first visit to Miriam had been by chance; she had happened to see the sign in a Kenmore Square window and gone in on a lark. But now she was hooked on the calming mint tea she sipped in Miriam's waiting room, the New Age music of chimes and bird calls that floated in the background, and the gentle authority with which Miriam's fingertips rested on her temples to assess her spiritual health. Miriam said she had a lot of work to do with her energy channels.

Some of the rest of her father's money would go for Christmas shopping, although she really had hardly anyone to buy for. There was her mother's gift, of course, and her father's annual tie. June had no boyfriend. She had no real best friend, either; the people she knew from dance class were nice, but everyone she met seemed to already have all the friends they needed. June was shy about issuing invitations; she didn't want to appear friendless, though that's exactly what she was. Halfway into her second year, she still felt lost at the university, with its sprawl of buildings that melted into the pavement of the city.

June debated, then decided she would buy a Christmas gift for Mrs. MacGregor. Even though she knew Mrs. M. had family and friends in town, she didn't seem to see much of them. Whether she wanted to see June or not, she did twice a week, and June figured that was probably the most contact she had with anyone.

It was a hard present to choose. Clothing was too personal, and anyway, Mrs. M. didn't seem very interested in venturing beyond her uniform of stretch pants and sweaters. June knew she used to like clothes. She had dusted a silver-framed black-and-white photograph of a handsome young couple who looked as if they were straight out of the movies. The man was wearing wool trousers and a tweed jacket and his hair was lustrous and dark. His arm was flung loosely around the shoulders of a young woman in a closely fitted suit whose fair hair was twisted up and who was leaning her head back to smile. It was the unmistakable shape of the darkly lipsticked mouth that made June realize with a start that this was Mrs. MacGregor and her husband.

When she asked about the photo, Mrs. M. was briefly enthusiastic.

"We were on our first motoring trip," she said. "That suit was part of my trousseau—kind of a mossy green wool bouclé. I bought it in New York on my father's charge card at Saks. Very expensive at the time, but I knew I would be out of the house and married by the time he got the bill." Mrs. M. laughed, the first time June had heard her. It was a dry chuckle that stopped almost as soon as it had begun. "I still have that suit," she said. "When the styles changed I couldn't bear to throw it away. It's in one of those boxes, Lord knows where."

June knew. She had been fascinated with Mrs. M.'s labeling system when she discovered the boxes stacked up in the spare room, and each time she cleaned in there she furtively turned a few more cartons so that she could read the contents listed on the side. She was positive the suit was in CLOTHING: KEEPSAKES. She would have given anything to see what was in that carton and some of the others, but she had learned that the boxes were a line you didn't cross with Mrs. M. She was touchy about them. It was funny enough to write such detailed lists on the labels when you were moving only across town, but it was stranger still to get to your new place and decide not to unpack them at all. Having no knickknacks sitting around the apartment made the job of dusting a lot easier, but cleaning such a bare place always made June a little sad.

And it made it hard to know what Mrs. M. could possibly want for Christmas. She didn't need stuff for her apartment, clearly. She was vain in a funny kind of way, with her perfect makeup and chignon and *L'Air du Temps* perfume, but to buy her more of her favorite cologne would only be redundant, and if given some other kind, she would probably never wear it. The birdseed was a good gift, but she had given it too early for it to be a Christmas present.

THE SNOW BEGAN ON THE NINTH, a day when June was at Mrs. MacGregor's, and by the time she trudged back from the market, it was coming down in thick, feathery flakes that caused an early dusk. She took off her boots in the hallway before she let herself in.

"Mrs. MacGregor, I hope you don't mind, but I got more food than you had on the list. When I got to the store it was already starting to snow hard, and inside I heard people talking about the storm. It doesn't hurt to have a little extra on hand, does it? I didn't buy anything perishable, just soup and eggs and some bread that you can always freeze. I also noticed that you're low on tea bags, so I picked some up."

"June, I don't know what I'd do without your memory. I meant to put tea bags on the list," Mrs. MacGregor said. They unpacked the groceries together. June didn't have to ask anymore where things went.

Before leaving, June presented Mrs. M. with a string of tiny Christmas lights tied together with a red ribbon, and said she would be happy to put them up anywhere Mrs. M. wanted her to. June had bought them on impulse at Woolworth when she picked up some decorations for herself. She knew it was a risky gesture. Mrs. MacGregor liked to keep her surroundings so plain.

Mrs. M. seemed slightly taken aback, then simply nodded and said that June could put them around the glass door to the deck. June stood on a stepladder and used some tacks she found in the utility drawer.

"This is where I pictured them, too," June said. "That way, when you watch the birds you can see the lights at the same time." Glancing out at the feeders, she said, "Look how much they've eaten already! I'll have to tell my mother what a big hit her mix is with Brookline birds. She'll be pleased. I'll bring you some more seed at the beginning of the year."

"I'd like to buy it from your mother," Mrs. MacGregor said.

"Oh, she wouldn't hear of it. She makes a garageful of the stuff, believe me. I'll tell her you offered, but she'll say no way. I'll bring you a big sack next time."

When June finished, she insisted that they turn off all the lights before plugging in the strand. When they came on, twinkling in the dark, the apartment was transformed.

"They're lovely," Mrs. MacGregor said.

"Oh, good. I was afraid you might not like them. Some people don't. If you get tired of them blinking, you can just take this clear bulb off the end and they'll stay on." June headed for the bathroom, where she had hung her snowy coat and cap.

"I'll see you next Tuesday," she said. "If you need anything over the weekend, be sure and call." Every time she left on Fridays now, June worried that Mrs. M. wouldn't be able to cope without her. It was silly, really—after all, Mrs. MacGregor had a daughter of her own nearby. But June had noticed how Mrs. M. was beginning to let June decide what needed to be done around the apartment, and even to ask her personal favors, like once rubbing some arthritis cream into her neck and shoulders.

As June was waiting to take the elevator down, a dark-haired woman with a baby emerged from the door next to Mrs. M.'s. The baby was crying and the woman was jiggling it and trying to shush it. A folded stroller was hanging by its handle in the crook of one arm, and a large tote bag was slipping off her shoulder.

"Would it help if I held something for you?" June asked.

"Do you think you could just put this strap back on my shoulder?" the woman asked.

June lifted the tote bag back in place. "You must be Mrs. Mac-

Gregor's new neighbor. She mentioned a woman with a baby had moved in."

The woman smiled a greeting. "I'm Renata, and this is Charlie. Are you Eleanor's granddaughter?"

"Oh, no. I just work for Mrs. MacGregor a few hours a week—cleaning and shopping. I'm June."

The elevator bell rang and the baby stopped crying to stare at the light that went on above the door. Renata laughed. "Works every time. Sometimes we just go on elevator trips for the sheer thrill of it."

They got on and June reached for the stroller hanging from Renata's arm. "Let me take that for you until we get down."

"Thanks." Renata blew a stray bang out of her eyes and shifted the tote bag higher on her shoulder. Then she hoisted Charlie up so he could press the buttons. "I know I shouldn't do that," she said. "Now the elevator is going to stop on every floor going back up. But he loves to see the lights come on so much I just can't help it. Don't tell on us."

June was charmed. The woman was so slim and pretty. The baby was sweet, too. After he had made all the floor buttons light up, he looked at June with a proud smile, sucking on his fist.

"I see what you did," June told him. "That was very clever of you."

When they reached the lobby, June offered to carry the stroller out and open it.

"Thanks, June, but we're going down to the garage. It was nice to meet you."

June waved to Charlie as the elevator closed. He was in the process of reaching one wet hand toward her when Renata snatched it back out of the range of the doors. Mrs. M. had told her how cute the baby next door was, but June hadn't paid much attention. Babies were never her thing. But Renata and Charlie completed each other so perfectly that June couldn't help having the fleeting thought that it would be a nice thing to have a little warm baby keeping you company all the time.

As she passed by the front desk, the boy who worked there afternoons looked up and greeted her.

"You ready for a storm, June?"

"Sure, I guess. I don't mind snow."

Owen leaned forward, his bony wrists protruding from his white shirtsleeves. "Are you a skier?"

"Not really. I've tried it."

"I cross-country whenever I can. There's a good place out in Weston. Would you like to go with me sometime? You can rent skis there."

June's smile froze in place. She had had a feeling by the way Owen always made a point of talking to her when she passed by that it was only a matter of time before he asked her out. She had even toyed with the idea of accepting. A date was a date, even if he was too thin and had a faint line of acne creeping along his jaw. But now that the moment had come, she realized that she would rather be alone than make several hours of painful small talk with this glasses-wearing physics major from Northeastern who grinned all the time.

"You know, I really shouldn't risk pulling a muscle. I might be going to New York soon to audition for a dance company." As soon as she said it, June was appalled by her lie. She directed herself to laugh and say something like, "*I wish*," so the whole thing would be a joke. But instead she just said, "Take care, Owen," over her shoulder, and propelled herself—dateless, a liar—into the cold of a Friday night.

ELEANOR

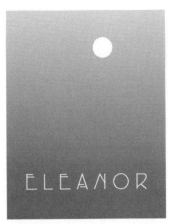

ELEANOR KEPT THE CHRISTMAS LIGHTS ON during the snowstorm and stayed up late watching her window on Friday. When she finally went to bed, the snow had thinned to lint-sized particles, and the drifts were up to the railing on her deck. The next morning, sun glittered blindingly on the snow's surface. Eleanor took a walk up and down the length of the building's hallways, then went down to the lobby to check her mail. More Christmas cards, though she hadn't sent any herself this year, and an invitation to an open house, an annual event given by a former colleague of hers on the bench. Eleanor had never skipped a year of the Bryces' Christmas parties, but she felt no interest in going this December. She put the card on her kitchen table to respond to later.

Janice called her around noon.

"Mother, I hope you're not thinking of canceling our Christmas shopping trip because of the weather. I'm just calling to tell you the streets are plowed. They've sanded everywhere. I'll pick you up under your awning, and we'll park right in the mall garage. You won't even need boots."

"Christmas shopping? We didn't have a date to go shopping." Eleanor glanced at the calendar square for today, which was blank.

"We sure did. I can't believe you forgot. We talked about it last Monday night when I stopped by."

Eleanor fought back her anger. She had been wondering lately just when Janice was going to stop by and see her; it certainly hadn't been as recently as last week.

"Hmm," Eleanor said.

"Mother, I'm going to start writing these things on the calendar for you. Then you can't deny them."

Eleanor remained silent.

"Well, whether you believe we had a date or not, let's go Christmas shopping today. The stores won't be as crowded because of the snow—not that the snow is anything to worry about," Janice said. "As I said, the streets are perfectly fine. We can have dinner afterward."

Eleanor looked out at the drifts on her deck. "The snow is four feet high, Janice. We can't go out in this."

"Where did you hear that? It snowed eight inches last night, but there's no problem driving."

Eleanor often found that the best way to get around her children's dogged arguments was to change points. She had learned long ago as a lawyer that it was fruitless to explore the nuances of a line of reasoning that would not be helpful to you.

"It's nice of you to want to take me, dear, but I don't need to do any shopping. I'm sending Helen's boys checks, and I can use catalogs for anything else."

"I just thought it would be nice for you to get out, Mother."

"When the snow melts. It's almost as if you're hoping I'll break my other hip," Eleanor gave a little laugh.

"You would see it that way, wouldn't you?"

Eleanor ignored her tone. "Anyway, you shouldn't be spending money on Christmas presents while you're still in school. Speaking of school, don't you have final exams to study for?"

"Mother, you know I don't have exams. I'm writing a thesis. It's a graduate degree."

"I know it's a graduate degree. How could I forget? How many is that now? You'll have more letters after your name than there are in a can of alphabet soup," Eleanor said, laughing.

"It's what I want." Her daughter's voice was sullen now, the way she had sounded when she was in high school.

"Dear, I would never want to interfere. All I'm saying is, don't waste your money shopping. Please don't get anything for me at any rate. I can't think of a thing I need."

"All right, Mother. If you change your mind about going out, call me. Don't try to walk anywhere alone. Do you have everything you need?"

"Oh, yes. June stocks me up every Friday. When will I see you?"

"You could have seen me today."

"Janice, why must you be so argumentative? I mean, after this dreadful storm."

"Sometime next week. I'll call."

"Fine. Good-bye, dear."

ELEANOR AND HER CHILDREN ALWAYS seemed to end up sniping at each other lately. When she did see them, they usually wanted to come by to sweep her away into some activity that she had altogether no interest in—always on their schedule, always at their pace. And they were so defensive about their lives. Their lives were their business; Eleanor had no wish to dictate to anyone. But all she had to do was make a simple observation about them and they either flew off the handle or started sulking. Eleanor could not recall feeling similarly insecure about herself when she talked to her own parents. But, then, she hadn't lived her life like a child, either: having secrets like Peter, or trying to remain in a perpetual never-never land of college like Janice. Helen was neurotic because she never had enough gumption to make herself the financial equal of her husband. Now she was a middle-aged housewife, her children almost through high school, and if Eleanor knew that slick son-in-law of hers, he was probably cheating on his wife. When the youngest boy started kindergarten, Eleanor had suggested that Helen go back to college and finish her B.A.

"The boys still need me at home, Mother," Helen had said.

"You're fooling yourself, Helen. When children are in school, they don't need their mothers sitting at home waiting for them. It's bad for the mothers, bad for the children. They need to see their mother doing something with her life."

"What would you know about it?" Helen had flashed at her. "Not every mother is itching to leave her children behind as soon as they can climb on a school bus. Some mothers like to go to PTA meetings and bake cookies."

"So, you're saying I was a bad mother because I worked."

"I am *not* saying you were a bad mother. I am saying I am a different person than you are. Roger earns enough to support us all. We both like it that I stay at home. Why is that so hard for you to accept?"

"Far be it from me to accept or not accept anything. I'm simply hoping for the best for you, and I never thought that finishing one's education harmed anybody. There may be a day when you'll wish you have it."

"What is that supposed to mean? That you think Roger and I won't stay married?"

Eleanor threw up her hands. They never spoke of it again, though through the years, Eleanor could see typical housewife quirks developing in Helen. The way she shopped, for instance. Helen was addicted—and addicted was not too strong a word—to clothes shopping. She expended much too much energy on frivolous things like hair and makeup, and, as far as Eleanor could see, hovered too closely over those boys. Eleanor didn't think they had turned out any better than if they had had a mother who practiced a profession; in fact, they probably turned out much worse for having one who would pick up every dirty sock they ever tossed on the floor. They were loud, noisy boys who took their mother's servitude utterly for granted.

Though Eleanor tried not to be critical, she truly did not

understand her children's choices, and it almost felt like an affront to her that they would grow themselves into lives that seemed so purposefully alien. Helen had turned out a lot like her aunt Isabel; she loved being useless and decorative, all the while talking about the sacrifices she had made for her family. Janice's life at first glance looked like the complete opposite of Helen's—but came to the same result of having accomplished nothing. And Peter was doing well professionally, but years ago had built a wall between himself and Eleanor that was seemingly impassable.

The rest of that day Eleanor sat reading, dozing, and watching the birds at her feeder. For dinner she heated herself some soup and toasted an English muffin. She ate a bowl of peppermint ice cream while watching a show on television about China, then filled a kettle of water to boil for tea. Around nine o'clock she started thinking about June's gifts to her, the birdseed and the lights, and wondered if she should give the girl something for Christmas. She had of course planned to write her a check as a seasonal gratuity, something on the order of thirty dollars, but that alone seemed too impersonal for June, who had been so thoughtful. She had no idea what a nineteen-year-old girl could use. In her day, monogrammed handkerchiefs would have been an appropriate gift for a young person at college, or perhaps a volume of poetry—Shakespeare or Millay.

Eleanor wondered if she might order her tickets to some dance troupe that was coming to town, but that seemed complicated to get right. The more she racked her brain, the more she leaned toward giving money. Money never disappointed. The thing was, Eleanor would have liked to do more than merely not disappoint; she hoped to please. What pleased June? She wore outlandish clothes sometimes, and told Eleanor that she combed thrift shops for vintage items. She loved that forties suit of Eleanor's that she saw in the photo, which amused Eleanor because Eleanor had loved it, too. She remembered buying it with her mother on a shopping trip to Manhattan to outfit her trousseau. The suit was French, and handsewn in an atelier. When the saleswoman brought it out for them to examine, Eleanor and her mother stroked the silk lining and admired the tiny precise stitches and horn buttons. Eleanor went into the fitting room, and when she emerged, her mother and the saleswoman actually applauded.

Eleanor remembered her mother's pleasure in buying it for her, and the way they giggled at lunch over the price tag and her father's probable reaction. She remembered wearing it on the steamer she and Robert took across Lake George on their honeymoon, and then again when they motored to Montreal. The suit was of a slim fitted style that served her well into the fifties. She wore it to her law-school interview at Harvard in '56, and then again, with minor alterations, to her interview at the Department of Public Welfare in '59. Quite simply, the suit was the kind of garment that you know on sight was made for you, fits you perfectly when you try it on, and brings you luck every time you wear it. Picturing herself in it again, Eleanor could taste the dry martinis she had sipped wearing it at the Union Oyster House with Robert on nights when they splurged for a baby-sitter. It symbolized, in a way, the best moments of her life.

She wanted to see it again. Eleanor went to the spare room and flipped on the light. She smiled. June had been in here vacuuming, and had stacked the boxes neatly against the wall, with the labeled sides facing out, so that you could find at a glance what you were looking for. It was just the way Eleanor would have done it if she had had the energy after pushing and lugging the boxes to the room. Eleanor surveyed the listed contents and was amazed to discover all the things she owned, and the pictures of her former self that leaped to life at the mere mention of certain objects: a flour sifter; gardening shears; Christmas crèche; briefcase.

Luckily, the box she wanted was not at the very bottom of a stack. CLOTHING: KEEPSAKES. She went to get a pair of scissors and slit the tape on top. She pulled the first layer of tissue off, and revealed a cashmere cardigan with yellowed beaded embroidery, a present from her children one birthday. Then a satin peignoir with matching robe from Robert. There, underneath some baby clothes, was the suit. It was a richer fabric than she had remembered even, woven from the softest wool. The deep green had a subtle vibrancy, like moss after a rain. Eleanor pulled the suit out and, on impulse, peeled off her clothes to try it on. It still fit; Eleanor's weight had never fluctuated much. The waistband was snugger and the seat of the skirt hung a little, but the expertly tailored shoulders with small pads still made her look sleek and well proportioned. As she turned in front of the mirror, she had an idea; June should have the suit as a present. They were the same height—they had joked about this, since neither one, when putting away groceries, ever utilized the top shelf. She guessed the suit would fit June fine. She took her scissors and opened up another box: GIFT WRAPPING MATERIALS. After she had a neatly wrapped Christmas present complete with tag and ribbon, Eleanor turned off the lights and went to bed.

WHEN ELEANOR WOKE, she didn't know where she was. A piercing horn reverberated through the air, and the room smelled smoky. Perhaps it was an air raid drill. They had them at school. But why the smoke, unless it was a real air raid? Eleanor rose, grabbing her robe from the foot of the bed. Where were Betty and Julia, the two girls she shared a room with? If they had left, it must have been a real emergency; but why wouldn't they have waited for her? Eleanor opened the door to the hall, staring at the other dorm room numbers. Which room was the Mitchell twins'? Doors started opening, and faces she didn't know were peering out. The siren seemed to be coming mainly from her room. Men were on the floor, which wasn't allowed. Perhaps they had come to help.

Someone came and grabbed her arm. The new girl on the floor.

"Are you okay, Eleanor?"

"What's happening?" Eleanor asked.

"It sounds like your smoke alarm, and there's smoke coming from your apartment. I've already called the fire department. Were you cooking?"

"Of course not. There's no cooking allowed," Eleanor said

indignantly. "What are all these men doing here?"

A man in a robe shouted something to the new girl and, before Eleanor could protest, rushed by them into her room. A moment later, he came back out, coughing.

"The bottom of a teakettle started to burn," he said. "I turned off the stove and opened all your windows," he said to Eleanor. "Are you all right?"

Eleanor nodded, staring at him.

"Okay, then," he said, tightening the belt on his robe. "It's going to be cold in your apartment for a while, but you need to clear the air. I heard the fire engine coming. I'll go talk to them. I'd leave your door open for cross-ventilation if I were you."

Just then a firefighter in a heavy canvas suit came from the stairway, carrying an ax. The man in the robe hurried over to talk to him, pointing at Eleanor and the open door of her room. Tears started to well up in her eyes. She didn't understand why there was a man in her dorm at night. And she certainly hadn't been making tea. She obeyed the rules.

She heard the wail of an infant. The new girl looked at her and said, "There's Charlie. Why don't you come to my place next door and have a cup of tea while your place airs out? We'll watch the kettle real carefully," she said, smiling.

Eleanor allowed herself to be steered by the girl, who seated her at a kitchen table and disappeared. The crying stopped. When she came back, she was holding a fat, smiling baby.

"Could you take him for a minute while I start the tea? He might fuss a little, but I'll feed him as soon as I take him back from you."

Without waiting for Eleanor to reply, the girl handed the baby to her. He was solid and heavy and warm, and searched her face soberly for an instant before deciding to smile, putting his fist in his mouth and making gurgling sounds deep in the back of his throat. As she held and jiggled the baby, using gestures that were suddenly as familiar to her as her whole life, the dream cleared from her mind. She wasn't at Vassar at all. She was home in Brookline, and she was sitting next door in the kitchen of the young woman who had just moved in with her baby.

Eleanor had her bearings now. The baby was intent on fingering the pink plastic buttons of her robe, which were molded in the shape of roses. Eleanor was embarrassed. She wondered if she had acted lunatic in the hall. The dream was gone now, little shreds of imagery blowing away.

She cleared her throat. Best to act as normally as possible. "How do you like the building?" she asked Renata.

"It's nice. You're the first neighbor I've really talked to."

Eleanor was ashamed of herself for not having been more welcoming earlier. A young mother apparently all on her own.

The kettle whistled. "Here we go," Renata said cheerfully, pouring the water.

Eleanor now knew what had happened. She had put the tea water on to boil and then gone to the spare room to look for the suit. After wrapping the present for June, she had gone straight to bed without ever remembering that she had intended to have tea. The clock on Renata's kitchen wall said two-thirty.

"I shouldn't be keeping you up," Eleanor said.

Renata laughed. "Are you kidding? Charlie would be awake now anyway. He was sleeping through the night at first, but ever since we stopped driving, his habits have gotten topsy-turvy."

Eleanor waited for her to explain where they were driving. When Renata didn't continue, Eleanor said, "He might be teething. Look how he's gnawing on his fist."

Renata looked surprised. "So soon? He's not even five months."

"They can start at that age. See, look at him drool. Mine all started at different times. They don't necessarily get a tooth right away, but they can be teething for months. My boy was this early, I think. He started waking up at night after he had been sleeping through, too." Eleanor smiled, remembering how she would wake up and say how nice it was that the baby had slept all night, only to be corrected by Robert, who would tell her, "No, *you* slept all night—the baby and I were up twice." He always heard the children crying before she did and got up with them; he said it was either the war or his medical residency that had trained him for fatherhood, but in either case he didn't seem to miss the sleep.

Renata put the steaming teacups in front of them and took the baby back from Eleanor. She adjusted her robe so that he could nurse, and Charlie lunged at the nipple, making little, satisfied grunts. Renata laughed. "That's why he's such a big boy. We've never had a problem with your appetite, have we, Charlie?"

Eleanor watched. "My, that's convenient for you. We never nursed in my day, you know. We'd be up heating bottles in the middle of the night."

"Why didn't people nurse?" Renata stroked the baby's head.

"They recommended against it. Talked about nutritionally fortified formulas and how they were an improvement on nature. We were told by pediatricians to adhere to strict feeding schedules, and that if we fed in between times, we'd be starting bad habits."

"Did you want to nurse?"

"Not really. You get conditioned to a way of thinking."

"That's true," Renata said.

"Does he eat solid foods yet?"

"No, but he'll start them soon. I'll need to look for a job after the first of the year, and it will be easier to leave him with a baby-sitter if he's partially weaned."

"Does he mind staying with baby-sitters?"

"I don't know. He's never had one."

Eleanor took this in. "In almost five months you've never had a minute away from him?"

"Well, I've never quite thought of it exactly like that, but no; I haven't."

Eleanor wanted to ask where the father was, but, after all, it was none of her business. It wasn't as if she hadn't seen unwed mothers before in her line of work; this girl's story was probably like a thousand others. But most mothers, married or not, had some friend or family member around to lend a hand once in a while.

"I can't imagine how you manage to get things done without help," Eleanor said.

"Charlie goes everywhere with me, don't you, sweetheart?" Renata said, stroking his hair. "We drove cross-country to move here, so he's already been in, oh, I don't know, at least fifteen states."

"My goodness. We were always told to keep newborns inside and not take them anywhere for months. We were so afraid of germs."

"Charlie hasn't even had a cold. It's the breast milk that gives them all kinds of immunities."

"I can see how sturdy he is."

They sat in silence for a moment, studying Charlie's obvious durability as his cheeks sucked rhythmically and his plump fist beat a little accompaniment against his mother's chest.

"I will need to find a baby-sitter soon, though," Renata said. "He's got to start getting used to other people."

"And you must be ready for a break. It's good to get away for an hour or two every once in a while. I remember feeling like I'd been on a vacation, just going to the market without my three youngsters. It gives you some time alone with your thoughts."

"What thoughts?" Renata laughed. "I haven't had any of those in quite some time."

Eleanor sipped her tea. "I'd volunteer to sit with him one afternoon, but I'm afraid I wouldn't be any good in an emergency. Look how foolish I was with the stove tonight."

"That could happen to anyone," Renata said.

Eleanor considered. "You know, I have a college girl who comes to my house on Tuesdays and Fridays to do chores and errands for me. You could leave the baby with us for an hour or two next week. She's really very capable, and with the two of us, I don't think this little fellow could get into much mischief."

"Is that June? I met her going down in the elevator. She seems very nice."

"She's wonderful," Eleanor said. "It's always hard for me to come up with enough to keep June busy, and I know she would enjoy it. Do come by," she said, afraid Renata would say no.

"Well," Renata said slowly, "I could use a haircut. And that's one thing that's hard to do with a baby along. The last time I had it cut he slept in his stroller, but I never know at this age how long he'll nap."

"Fine. Tuesday or Friday next week will be your salon day. The one thing a woman with a baby must not deprive herself of is a trip to the salon."

Renata raised her teacup. "To Mommy's first adventure without you, Charlie. Do you mind?"

Charlie was asleep at the breast, snoring like a tiny combustion engine.

"You've been very kind, Renata. But I really must let you two get to bed. June comes on her days from one to three P.M., but she can stay longer if I have more for her to do. You make your appointment and let me know, and we'll be waiting for you." Eleanor hesitated a moment. "I hope I didn't sound too eccentric when you found me in the hall. I don't think I had woken up properly, and for some reason I had been dreaming I was back at college."

"You sounded just fine. You should have seen how disoriented I got when I woke up in some of those motel rooms traveling with Charlie. Half the time I didn't have a clue where I was."

When she returned to her apartment, it was as cold as the outdoors, but the smoky smell was almost gone. Eleanor locked her windows and door, and turned up the heat. She threw her charred kettle in the garbage, and tossed an extra blanket on the bed. Warm in her pajamas and robe under the covers, Eleanor enjoyed the cold air on her face, and feeling as if she were camping in the mountains, she fell into a dreamless sleep.

WHEN MRS. M. BUZZED HER IN, the older woman had a look of excitement about her, almost bordering on gaiety.

"I have a surprise for you today, June."

June had never seen her this way, almost girlish.

"We're having a visitor, and I promised that you would help me entertain him."

"Him? Are you expecting a gentleman caller, Mrs. MacGregor?"

"You'll have to wait. They're not expected for another half hour, so you must stay in suspense while you do the vacuuming."

As June tidied up the apartment, she noticed that the Christmas lights were on. They glowed against the puddles of melting snow on the deck.

At one-thirty there was a knock on the apartment door. Mrs. MacGregor opened it and admitted Renata and Charlie.

"June, I believe you've already met my new neighbors. Renata has an appointment to keep at two, so you and I will be in charge of entertaining young Charlie. Are we equal to it?"

"Sure. How are you?" June greeted Renata, then went up to the baby and shook his sock-encased toe.

Charlie stared at her balefully.

"He just woke up from a nap, so he's a little fuzzy still. I'm afraid that means he'll be awake the whole time for you."

"That's good news for us, isn't it, June?"

June had never seen Mrs. MacGregor so animated. Renata and Mrs. M. both seemed to be expecting June to make some move. "Will he let me hold him?" June asked skeptically.

Renata handed Charlie to her, and June was surprised at the baby's dense weight. He seemed content to examine her face. "How old is Charlie?" she asked.

"Almost five months."

June had never been around babies much, so she didn't know if this one was an advanced specimen or not. But she figured that mothers always liked to hear that their offspring were thriving. "He's big," she told Renata.

"Isn't he? We went to the pediatrician yesterday, and found out that he's already sixteen pounds."

"Oh, that is big. What was he at birth?" Mrs. MacGregor asked.

"Only seven-two."

Mrs. M. and Renata talked baby stats for the next five minutes. Surprisingly, Mrs. M. knew the weights and lengths of her three children not only at birth but at several points during their first two years. June had never understood the fascination with these figures, but then it occurred to her that some people might not care how many calories were in a slice of honeydew melon either, one of approximately seven or eight hundred nutritional values she held in storage in her brain.

"Will he be getting hungry?" Mrs. MacGregor asked.

"I don't think so. I fed him before bringing him over. But just in case, I have a little bit of milk that I expressed." Renata fished inside the diaper bag for a bottle. "I was thinking about what we talked about—how he's never been with a baby-sitter yet. And I realized Charlie's never had to drink from a bottle. Not once. Can you believe that never occurred to me before?"

Mrs. MacGregor nodded sympathetically. "Well, you wouldn't think of it if you didn't need him to take a bottle, now, would you?"

"I don't know what I was thinking. He'll need to have a babysitter when I go back to work. Anyway, I went out and got one of those pumps—I don't know if you've seen them—and expressed some breast milk to give him myself from a bottle."

"And?"

"He wasn't crazy about it. I had to kind of pace back and forth while I gave it to him, and he kept looking at me like I was nuts the whole time, didn't you, Charlie?"

Charlie was sitting on June's knee, staring at his mother's face.

"But he did take it. And I did the same thing yesterday, so if he does need a bottle today, he should know what to do with it. I'll be back soon enough that he probably won't even get hungry, though."

Renata showed them the disposable diapers and wipes in the bag, and Mrs. MacGregor marveled at how everything had gotten so much more practical since her day.

"You just run along to your appointment, and we'll be fine, won't we, June?"

"Of course we will. I think he likes me." Charlie had swiveled his head now from his mother to June. After studying her for a minute, he decided to smile.

"Okay. I know he'll be fine." Renata didn't seem to know what to do. She kissed the top of Charlie's head, and shifted uncertainly.

Mrs. MacGregor finally ushered her to the door. "You'll be late. And I wouldn't want you to be rushed. Salons are meant to be enjoyed."

"Thank you, Eleanor. I'll be back soon. Be good, Charlie."

Charlie stared at his mother's departing back and then at the door that closed behind her.

"Well, now," June said, shifting him around to look at her. "You were a good surprise," she told him.

"I thought you'd be pleased," said Mrs. MacGregor. "You've watched babies before, haven't you?"

"Never," June said.

"Oh."

They looked at each other and laughed.

"Well," said Mrs. MacGregor, "I have. Not in a while, of course. Though I don't expect babies have changed much since I had them. You can be the brawn in this operation and I'll be the brains."

"Well, thank you very much."

Just then Charlie decided to spit up part of his feeding. June dashed to the kitchen for a dishtowel while Mrs. MacGregor dug through the diaper bag for a burp cloth. June wiped the front of the baby and her arm, while Mrs. MacGregor saw to the couch. "I had forgotten about that," Mrs. M. said.

Charlie looked from June's face to Mrs. MacGregor's and his lower lip began to quiver. In a few seconds he tightened his eyes to slits and began to cry.

"What do we do now?" June said, jiggling him.

"Oh, dear. You were such a happy little boy when I saw you last," Mrs. MacGregor told him.

June paced. Mrs. MacGregor walked beside her, jingling keys and shaking the brightly colored dishcloth. Charlie howled. June shifted him to a new position over her shoulder, and in the process of being moved Charlie released a large burp.

"Well," they said together.

Charlie grinned.

Mrs. MacGregor held him on the couch while June spread a blanket on the floor and put out some toys Renata had brought over. Then she put him on his back and sat beside him, putting the toys in his hands one by one. He brought each one to his mouth and sucked vigorously for a few seconds before casting it aside. In a few moments he began to cry.

"Try sitting him up," Mrs. MacGregor suggested. "Maybe he doesn't like to be on his back." They experimented with various positions, and with each one Charlie cried louder, his face turning red and large tears squeezing out the corners of his eyes.

"Let me try," Mrs. MacGregor said. She put the baby over her shoulder and walked him back and forth across the room, murmuring in a low voice. The cries subsided to whimpers. "June, let's get that bottle. Could you warm it for me? Heat a pan of hot water on the burner and submerge the bottle in it for a few minutes. Then test the milk on the inside of your wrist. It should just be lukewarm on your skin."

June brought her the bottle and Mrs. MacGregor eased Charlie onto his back and put the nipple to his lips. He shook his head vigorously back and forth, pursing his mouth. She began to hum, walking him. Charlie quit crying and gazed up at her, his mouth slightly ajar. Mrs. MacGregor gently pushed the nipple between his lips, still humming. Without taking his eyes off her or blinking, Charlie began sucking. In five minutes he had finished the bottle. He let it fall from his mouth and smiled.

"I'm impressed," June said. "You certainly look experienced."

"It's funny how you don't forget some things. You take him now. My arms aren't as strong as they used to be."

Charlie welcomed June back with a smile, and began busily sucking and chewing on his fists. June played with him on the blanket for a while, and, at Mrs. MacGregor's suggestion, turned him over onto his stomach so he could practice crawling. He lay there squirming and lifting his head up, without going anywhere. When he got frustrated, June picked him up again, and was showing him the Christmas lights when Renata knocked. She had a sleek new haircut, which made her white neck look longer.

Charlie greeted her with enthusiastic razzing sounds when she picked him up. Back in his mother's arms he looked at June and Mrs. MacGregor, dividing beneficent smiles between them.

"How'd he do?"

"Just fine," Mrs. MacGregor said firmly. "You should leave him with a baby-sitter at least once a week. It's not healthy for you never to get away."

"You're right. I had completely forgotten what it was like to walk down the street without watching for ruts in the sidewalk that would catch on his stroller, or bending forward every two minutes to check on his hat. I actually just walked, looking in shop windows, crossing streets against the light, running up stairs. It was incredible. You get so you think the stroller is part of your body. Then, when you take a walk without it, you're suddenly just yourself again."

"Nice haircut," June said. She was thinking that maybe she should cut hers short like Renata's. It looked so clean and modern. June had kept her hair waist-length since she was fourteen.

"Thanks. That was heaven, too. You were so right, Eleanor. There's something about having someone else wash your hair that seems the height of luxury."

"When my children were small, I made sure I had my hair appointment and manicure once a week."

"Well, I really appreciate you two watching Charlie. I can tell he had a good time because he's so calm now." She turned to June. "Do you baby-sit a lot?"

"Not since high school. And not ever babies this young," June said.

"You seem very comfortable with him."

"She was excellent. Some people are naturally good with babies," Mrs. M. said.

"Well, I'm going to be looking for a regular sitter after the first of the year. Do you think you might be interested? I know Eleanor thinks the world of you. If we spent time together before I started the job, I think you'd be able to learn everything you need to know. One thing I found out when he was born is that nobody starts out an expert," Renata said, smiling.

"I go to school during the day," June said.

"I'm working nights at a downtown restaurant. I'll need a babysitter about thirty hours a week, but most of that will be after he goes to bed, so you could do homework while you're over. My shift is from five to midnight, Wednesday through Saturday."

June calculated fast. Her dance classes were first thing in the morning next semester, and the rest of her classes got out by two. Then she had Mrs. M. on Tuesdays and Fridays.

"I'm here until four-thirty on Fridays," June said. "What time do you have to leave for work?"

"Four-thirty, I'd say."

"That's perfect, June," Mrs. MacGregor said. "All you have to do is go right next door. You were telling me you were looking for another job. I'll be your baby consultant. But June has so much common sense, I doubt she'll ever need me," Mrs. MacGregor told Renata.

"Well—sure. I'd love to have the job," June said. It wasn't as if she needed to save her weekend nights for a boyfriend or anything.

"Great. Let's try it out, see how it goes," Renata said. "Do you think you could come over sometime next week and spend some more time with him? I'll show you all his routines." She turned to Mrs. MacGregor. "Why don't you join us when we're done, Eleanor, and I'll cook dinner."

June admired the way Renata could just say "Eleanor" instead of "Mrs. MacGregor." It made them seem woman-to-woman, as if age were an irrelevancy.

A WEEK LATER THE THREE OF THEM were having dinner together at Renata's. She had made spaghetti and salad and served little individual bakery tarts for dessert.

"You were right about June having a knack for babies," Renata was telling Mrs. M. "Today he went off into the other room to play with her without even so much as a backward glance at me. And then tonight he let her bathe him and put him down for bed with a bottle. I was amazed."

"You're lucky. I remember having a nanny once that the children simply loathed. One day I pretended to go out just so I could go down to the cellar and put my ear to the furnace duct, trying to hear if she beat them when I was gone."

"And did she?" Renata asked.

"I don't think so. My plan didn't work as well as I hoped. I could hear every word they said when they were in the kitchen, but as soon as they moved to the playroom I only heard murmurs.

But it didn't sound like she was being cruel. I think they just decided that she was repugnant for some reason—maybe she had foul breath, or a mole, who knows. Eventually I had to let her go because they made such a fuss about her. You'll see," Mrs. MacGregor said with a smile. "Your pleasant young man will find not-so-pleasant tactics for making his will known. They can be quite tyrannical, children."

June felt a little shy tonight. Mrs. M. and Renata found so much to talk about. Renata seemed to spark a liveliness in Mrs. MacGregor, this gossiping about feeding schedules and sleeping patterns, remedies for colic and cradle cap. June hadn't realized there was such a timelessness to the work of tending babies. She would have assumed that Mrs. M.'s experience would be somehow outdated next to Renata's. But it wasn't the case. As mothers, the two of them met across a divide of generations as casually as if it were a picket fence they shared between their yards. June knew they weren't trying to make her feel left out; but she did feel very much the spectator, the uninitiated. Yet it was cozy, listening to them.

Renata turned to her. "June, that nice guy at the desk, Owen, was telling me you're going to New York soon."

June was embarrassed. Renata's eyebrows were lifted in question. Mrs. MacGregor was looking at her closely. "Oh, no, not soon," she stammered. "I just mentioned that if I ever really wanted to be a dancer, New York would be the place to do it." Now she was lying about her lie.

"I didn't realize that you were a dancer," Renata said.

"Well, you know, I'd like to be. I've studied for years. And New York is where all the important dance companies are."

"You wouldn't quit school, would you, June?" Mrs. MacGregor asked.

"No, not if I didn't have anything definite lined up. But I could always go down this summer and check things out, and then come back to school in the fall." She was making it up as she went along, but it sounded good.

"That's probably what Owen was referring to. He made it sound like you were leaving next week," Renata said.

"I guess maybe I left him with that impression," June said. "He was trying to get me to go skiing with him, and I didn't really want to."

"He seems like a nice young man," Mrs. MacGregor observed.

"But you must admit, Eleanor," Renata said, "he's not exactly June's type. Too, too . . ."

"Nerdy," June said.

Renata laughed. "Exactly. We want someone a bit more fun for June."

"There's nothing wrong with a steady, reliable fellow. Fun wears out," Mrs. MacGregor warned.

"Tell us about your husband, Eleanor," Renata urged, pouring them more wine. "Was he steady and reliable, or was he fun?"

Mrs. MacGregor frowned slightly and sat back in her chair. June thought Renata had overstepped. You didn't barge into Mrs. M.'s personal life unless you were invited. To her surprise, Mrs. MacGregor took a sip of wine and reflected.

"He was steady and reliable, *and* fun," she pronounced. "He knew how to have a good time." She seemed on the verge of continuing, then took another sip of wine and stopped. She looked at June. "It *is* important that they know how to make you laugh," she said.

"But it's also important that there's more to them than that," Renata said, a sudden emphasis behind her words. "Listen to Eleanor, June, not me."

June and Mrs. MacGregor looked at her, waiting for her to elaborate. But Renata just stood and began clearing the table. June rose to help her.

"Well, ladies, should I open another bottle of wine?" Renata asked, holding up the empty bottle.

"Goodness, no," Mrs. MacGregor said. "I shouldn't be drinking at my age, and I don't think June shouldn't be drinking at *her* age."

"And I shouldn't be drinking at any age," Renata said.

June had begun to notice that Renata never fully explained herself. In fact, all three of them seemed to have little doors that they began to open to each other, but only partially. Just when you started to see around the door to what was inside, it closed. Even so, it was a wonderful evening. Sitting in Renata's kitchen with the two of them made June feel part of something. On the way back to her apartment, June found herself humming the song Renata had taught her as they did the dishes, something about three Irish maids, and their hard Irish luck.

ELEANOR

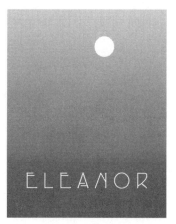

ELEANOR WAS FORCED TO OPEN ANOTHER BOX to get at something to wear to the Bryces' Christmas party on the twenty-third. She had forgotten to *RSVP*, and when Marjorie Bryce called her, Eleanor had an unguarded moment and said she would come. She would have liked to wear her usual clothes, but she knew everyone else would be in finery. Pride overcame her reluctance. She fished out a cherry red blazer piped with black velvet, and wide-legged black silk pants. She made up her face carefully, and rolled her hair in a French twist instead of her customary chignon. No one would say Eleanor MacGregor was going downhill.

At a quarter of eight she looked longingly at her armchair and newly begun novel, and called a cab. She hadn't driven in more than three months; she really should sell her car before it quit running.

Lionel greeted her at the door effusively, kissing her on both cheeks. She detested the affectation of a European kiss. A plain peck on the cheek was perfectly adequate. He led her through the crowded living room, taking her coat and saying, "Look who's here!" to anyone who would listen. Lionel always was a fool. He wasted time in his court making unnecessary conversation and telling jokes, so his docket was glutted with a huge backlog that never went away or seemed to trouble him. In family court, the nature of the cases often carried life-altering consequences for the children involved. Eleanor had considered it a duty and a kindness to deal with her cases briskly and without time-consuming pleasantries, so that her docket was kept current and her judgments delivered with dispatch.

The doorbell rang. Lionel deposited Eleanor with Marjorie, who effused over Eleanor's outfit. Marjorie was a tiny woman who wore fitted little suits that looked as though they were sized for dolls. She was vain about her hundred-pound frame, and always made a point of complimenting styles she never wore, saying, "I could never get away with that; I would simply swim in it. You'd never find me!"

"Lovely house, Marjorie," Eleanor said.

"Oh, you know, we have a tradition of doing it up. Every year I swear I'm going to leave half of the stuff down, but then we get the boxes from the attic and the decorations just sort of make their way to their usual places."

Eleanor agreed. It had been precisely that way in her Belmont home. Every wreath had had its appointed spot, every angel and candle its habitual place. This year she had no decorations whatsoever except June's strand of lights. The lights didn't feel Christmasy to her so much as they seemed magical, making her stark-white walls blink pastels.

"You're so smart to have scaled down, Eleanor. Lionel and I keep thinking we might sell and get a condo in town, but when it comes right down to it, I know I lack the courage. How did you ever fit everything into a little apartment?"

Somehow every time Marjorie offered praise it sounded backhanded. To converse with her was always to be slightly on the defensive, to say, "Oh but it's not *that* little, you know," so that Marjorie could come back with, "Of course it's not," as if she were generously sparing your feelings. Eleanor didn't want to play the game. She said, "I sold practically everything, and when I got to the new place I never unpacked my boxes."

Marjorie blinked, then brightened. "Wouldn't we all love to do that," she chirped, steering Eleanor over to the drinks table.

Eleanor asked for a hot buttered rum and sipped it from a chair near the fire. As always, the Bryces' house looked like a Talbots ad: wreaths in every window sporting giant tartan bows, a tall spruce Christmas tree with imported glass ornaments, and white votive candles flickering everywhere. Lionel was wearing a reindeer tie with a red lightbulb nose that actually lit up. Eleanor spent a minute speculating on how it worked, concluding that a tiny battery must be embedded directly in the fabric. The Bryces were very Cambridge. They voted Democrat but lived Republican, stabling horses in the country and putting all of their five children through the best private schools. Marjorie came from family money and made a career out of volunteer fund-raising for nonprofit arts organizations. Their names were listed under "Angels" in symphony and opera programs every year.

Did Lionel remember, Eleanor wondered, making a pass at her at one of these Christmas parties years ago? Robert had been talking deep-sea fishing with someone in the kitchen and Lionel had asked her to come see a new painting hanging on the second floor. As she looked at the painting she felt Lionel's arm encircle her waist, and the next thing she knew he had planted a sloppy, whiskey-soaked kiss on her lips. "You're the finest thing going, Eleanor," he whispered thickly in her ear. "I mean it; none of these women can hold a candle to you." This included, presumably, his wife, downstairs arranging more canapés on a platter. Eleanor felt no awkwardness in shoving him away, saying, "Lionel, don't be an ass," and going downstairs to rejoin her husband. She neither held it against him nor felt flattered by the episode. Eleanor had to respect a man before she could feel any attraction to him. Intellectually Lionel was a buffoon; had been appointed to his seat on the court through his political connections, and she suspected he had gotten into Harvard the same way. He was, for her, a pleasant enough host or guest once or twice a year, but as a man, or a real friend, she found him beneath notice. It never occurred to her that the rebuff had meant anything more to him than it had to her until one summer day at a barbecue in Belmont, Robert had teased her, saying, "You're hard, El," after she had said something sarcastic, and Lionel, who had been standing nearby, agreed, "Hard as nails." It was the way he had said it, with real feeling, that led Eleanor to believe he might be thinking of something specific, like the kiss in front of the painting.

Sitting there now, masking her boredom as she listened on the margins of a conversation about the condominium market, Eleanor couldn't imagine what she ever saw in these parties. She had loved dressing up for them, that was true. Robert and she had presented quite a stunning picture when they wanted to; he was magnificent in black tie, and she had a beautiful neck and shoulders that she often bared in an evening or cocktail dress. She passed most of those dresses on to her daughters—though, come to think of it, she had never seen either of them wear one. Helen would have to have them let out a size, and Janice didn't lead the kind of life that required off-the-shoulder gowns. She wondered if anyone did anymore. Even tonight at the Bryces' party, she and all the other women wore beaded sweaters or silk jackets with flowing pants rather than dresses. It was their age, she supposed. They were the last generation to dress formally for special occasions, which also meant they were of an age when it wasn't attractive to show too much flesh.

She began counting how many of the couples she knew were still with their original spouses, and how many had remarried. Of course even the long-standing marriages might be just for show; no one ever knew what was behind the façade of someone else's domestic life.

To this day she didn't know whether Robert had had the affair she had suspected, or not. He had worked with a female doctor, a surgical resident twenty years his junior named Deborah, who clearly had thought the world of him. When they had cocktail parties or holiday open houses, there was Deborah, hovering at

Robert's arm all night, laughing at his witticisms, smiling into his eyes as she tucked her hair behind one ear. Seeing this, Eleanor never worried. She was a confident woman, and felt her own value. The fact that Robert's protégé might have a crush on him seemed natural, something that they could laugh about together as they picked up glasses and napkins after a party. But this was during a cool period between them, when Eleanor had just been appointed to the bench and was spending long hours learning the job—a circumstance that had made Robert sulk—and somehow Eleanor never made the joke she intended to about Deborah's adoring looks. Then, when they threw a retirement cookout for a good friend of theirs, the chief attending surgeon Robert was later picked to replace, Deborah was there, but she kept a measured distance from Robert, and didn't seem to speak to him all night.

That was when it occurred to Eleanor that this woman might be having an affair with her husband. She watched them carefully, and although Robert and Deborah were not ever beside each other in the backyard where the Japanese lanterns bobbed around the patio, it seemed to Eleanor that they were somehow constantly in touch. She didn't see them looking at each other, but rather felt that they were ignoring each other with a hypersensitivity that could only mean they were absorbed with thoughts of the other person. Eleanor didn't know why she suddenly knew how Robert would act if he were having his lover over to the house under her nose, but she was sure that she did know, and that Robert was behaving exactly this way.

By the evening's end, when the suspicion had fully gripped her, Eleanor felt her mind become even more analytical and methodical than usual. A coolness imbued her thinking. First, she reminded herself that she might be entirely wrong. Deborah might have had other reasons to stay away from Robert; perhaps he had slighted her on an evaluation. Or she might have even flirted with him at work, felt herself to be rejected, and was now angry. These were possibilities. Eleanor owed it to everyone not to assume her intuition was infallible. But even with these counter-arguments running through her mind, Eleanor could not shake the feeling that something had happened, and nothing would be the same for her again.

She waited a week, maybe ten days, and, in a general conversation at the breakfast table about people at the hospital, Eleanor inquired as to how Deborah was doing. Robert kept his eyes on the knife buttering his toast as he told her that Deborah was doing great, and had gotten the best evaluation of any of his residents. Then he bit into his toast and discussed the chief attending job that was opening up, and whether he would accept it if offered. Eleanor counted this as changing the subject.

She never did find out if she was right. Perhaps she had fantasized the whole thing to remind herself that she still loved her husband, and what the stakes might be if they didn't get beyond this estrangement. Eleanor decided never to bring the matter up with Robert, nor to act as if she suspected anything. She began to come home at five-thirty on weekdays, and, if she absolutely had to work on weekends, bring the files home with her rather than drive in to her chambers. She began to invite her husband to do things with her—a golf game on Saturday, a museum benefit. Quietly, steadily, she waged her campaign. She was fifty-six years old; she was not about to make herself ridiculous, but she did buy herself some smart new clothes. Gradually Robert seemed to notice that Eleanor was around more, that she was interested in how his day went and in his company. At least that was the turn that Eleanor put on things, because one night they found themselves deciding to go to a movie, something they hadn't done in more than a year. Eleanor's birthday came around, and Robert bought her some large diamond earrings, the most extravagant jewelry he had ever given her. He took her out to dinner at the Ritz, and as the jewels sparkled in her ears and she looked at him across the table, she felt herself begin to relax inside again. She had her husband back; she was sure of it.

Two years later, an invitation arrived in the mail to attend Deborah's wedding in New York. Her residency was in its final year in Boston and she was moving in the spring to begin her practice in Manhattan.

"How long has this been going on?" Eleanor asked, waving the invitation.

"What?" Robert looked up from his newspaper. "Oh, Deborah and her fiancé? A year maybe, not sure. She's been commuting a lot." He resumed his reading.

So Eleanor never knew, and she surprised herself by not caring to know. Occasionally she examined her slim evidence, based on nothing, really—a feeling, a look—and decided that she must have simply been imagining things. But from the time of their reconciliation until Robert's death twelve years later, she could honestly say that she had a moment almost every day when she felt grateful to have her husband back. She would have hated being divorced. Being a widow was different. You lost the company of your husband, but you didn't lose all the years you had had with him. You didn't have to change the way you thought about the primary fact of your past.

The room was beginning to seem too close to Eleanor; she didn't feel as if she had quite enough air. She was grateful that she had taken a seat a few minutes ago, because suddenly she felt lightheaded. Surely two or three sips of rum weren't enough to do her in.

"Eleanor, what a pleasure to see you. It's been ages." Eleanor smiled and blinked at the woman, waiting for the name to come to her, or at least the face.

"So, how's the place in Brookline?"

"It's very convenient to everything," Eleanor said, completely at a loss as to whom she was talking. The woman was tall and olive-skinned, and somewhat younger than she was.

"Don't I know! You don't miss the gardening?"

"Frankly, no. Enough is enough of anything." Eleanor was having trouble focusing on the woman's words. They seemed to be bouncing around her ears, but not really penetrating.

"You're so right. Though you had such beautiful landscaping in Belmont. For years I coveted that flowering cherry of yours."

Eleanor began to panic. This face meant nothing to her, yet clearly they had known each other for years. She gamely tried to keep up her end of the conversation. "Finish your Christmas shopping yet?"

The woman looked at her strangely, then laughed. "Thank goodness I don't have to get involved in that scene. Hanukkah is so simple by comparison."

Eleanor laughed too, as if she had merely made a joke. But she was beginning to see that faking it was not simple.

"You're in the same place?" Eleanor asked.

"Well, yes. The same place I've been in for the last year. Didn't I send you my new address? I was sure I had." The woman fished in her bag for a pen and drew out a business card. "We're so close now, we really should get together for lunch. Give me a call when you get a chance," she said, scribbling a home address and phone number on the back.

When the woman moved on to speak with someone else, Eleanor stole a glance at the card. ELSA GREEN KATZ, M.D., PSYCHIATRY. Eleanor tried to survey the years, like looking backward down a telescope where her old friends and social life dwelled tiny in memory. Elsa, Elsa. A colleague of Robert's? Probably. She was fairly sure none of them had ever consulted a psychiatrist for anything. It wasn't like them. She shook her head to focus things.

She was suddenly exhausted. She could barely stand under the wave of tiredness that had swept over her. She made her way to Marjorie and Lionel, who were standing together telling some practiced story that they each took turns with. When Eleanor approached them, Lionel was waiting for his lines, an impatient smile playing on his lips. He winked at Eleanor, and returned his gaze to the couple who were their audience, trembling for his turn like a racehorse at the gate. Eleanor saw that they were only in the middle of their tale of lost luggage in Bermuda. Knowing how Lionel loved to draw out his anecdotes, she broke in just as he began to speak.

"I'm off, you two. Wonderful party."

Lionel looked annoyed at the interruption, but quickly put on his host manners, changing the irritation to concern. "So soon, Eleanor? You only just got here."

"Yes, don't go yet," said Marjorie. "We haven't even had a chance to talk."

"I really must. Early day tomorrow," Eleanor lied.

"Well, if you have to, let me get your coat for you," Lionel said, casting one last longing glance at his audience, who had now been distracted by a passing hors d'oeuvres plate.

IN THE TAXI, ELEANOR COLLAPSED WITH RELIEF. What had she been thinking of? Everyone talking about Florida and the stock market. Everyone so kissy and huggy. She gathered her coat around her and must have dozed, because the next thing she knew, the cabby was saying impatiently, "That's fifteen dollars, ma'am." She gave him twenty, because it was easier to let him keep the change than to try and put it away in the dark. He came around and opened her door and gave her a hand to grasp as she pulled herself out of the car. Goodness, she must give the appearance of being frail. Everyone was so solicitous of her these days.

That's what she liked about June. She was helpful without making her feel doddering. Eleanor always felt more awake after June's afternoons. Tuesday when she had been over, Eleanor presented her with the box containing the old suit.

"It was just a whim of mine," Eleanor said, half-embarrassed. Would June be insulted that as a Christmas present Eleanor was giving her old clothes? The gift now seemed like a stupid idea, but it was too late to change her mind. "You seemed interested in this, so I wanted you to have it."

Eleanor found the excitement in June's face almost unbearable. She had raised the girl's hopes for something nice in that big box, and now she was bound to be disappointed. Eleanor knew she'd be a good sport about it, and she resolved to write the check at the end of the day not only for what June was owed but for forty extra. Eleanor would laugh off the suit as a joke and they would both forget about it.

June slit each piece of Scotch tape with a fingernail. She didn't rip the paper, and it came off practically unrumpled. Before opening the box she carefully laid the Christmas wrap aside. She was prolonging the pleasure of opening her present as long as possible, Eleanor thought bitterly. Wrapping it was a mistake; it made too big a thing out of it.

Gingerly, June drew the tissue leaves apart and gasped. She stroked the fabric. "It's not the suit in the picture?" Her voice was filled with wonder.

Eleanor nodded, relief flooding her. "I wanted you to have it," she repeated.

"Oh," June said softly as she drew it out. The jacket's color was only slightly faded; it still was subtly rich and inviting. "Look at these buttons," June said, fingering them. "And the workmanship!" she said as she looked inside at the neatly stitched lining.

"It was handmade in Paris. I don't know if I told you that before."

"Paris!" June held the jacket up against her face. The color was made for her. "Would you mind if I tried it on right now?"

Eleanor flushed with pleasure. "Of course not. Go right ahead."

When June emerged from the bathroom, Eleanor remembered her mother's reaction the first time she had tried on the suit. She applauded for June. "I knew it would be just right for you. The coloring suits wonderfully, and you are the exact size I was then." It was a perfect fit. June twirled spontaneously, rising to her toes, and Eleanor saw the dancer in her.

"Oh, I love it, Mrs. M. It's the best present anyone ever gave me. I'll wear it for only special occasions." June threw her arms around her, and Eleanor's eyes watered for a moment.

"You're welcome, dear."

"I have a present for you, but I'm afraid it's not half as good as this one." June drew out a slim package from her backpack. She had curled a mass of red and green ribbon on top, and pasted gold stars all over white tissue paper. Eleanor opened it and held up the scarf.

"It's lovely, June. You've picked up on all the colors I like best. I can wear it with anything."

"I'm glad you like it. It's not much."

"It's beautiful," Eleanor said. "But you already gave me the presents of the birdseed and the lights."

"Oh, those were just things to bring over." June tidied up the wrappings and seemed reluctant to leave. "So, your daughter is coming to get you for dinner on Christmas?"

"That's right."

"Are you sure you don't have anything more for me to do before I go?"

"No, you run along. And have a wonderful holiday with your mother. Thank her again for the birdseed."

With June gone, Eleanor wandered around the apartment listlessly for a few moments. She turned on the kitchen radio. She had a sudden urge to see pictures of her children when they were young, from Christmases years ago. But the pictures were all packed away, in one of the boxes. She hated opening the boxes—loved how, sealed up, they kept the years contained in perfect order. She hesitated a moment, then got out her scissors and went to find the box marked PHOTOGRAPH ALBUMS AND SCRAPBOOKS.

JUNE ARRIVED HOME TO FIND HER MOTHER sitting on the living-room floor surrounded by bundles of dyed fibers. Her curly hair was too far between trims and stood out around her head in a great brown cloud. Little wisps of wool clung to her sweat suit, which was in need of washing and a half-size too tight. The couch and all the chairs were covered with weavings and sketches, and the loom occupied the space most people would leave open for walking. June looked around.

"No Christmas tree?"

"June, it is customary for a mother and a daughter who have not seen each other in a month to begin by saying hello. Some would even say a kiss would not be too extreme."

"Sorry. Hi, Mom," June said, giving her a peck on the cheek. "Don't we have a Christmas tree?"

Her mother sighed. "June, I just couldn't get around to it. If you want to go get a tree, take money from my purse."

"That's a lot of fun," June said under her breath.

"What, dear?" her mother asked, peering down her bifocals at two bundles she was comparing. "Which red do you like better with those colors over there, this cranberry or the burgundy?"

"They look the same to me." June stepped around the samples her mother had woven and spread out on the floor. "What's for dinner?" She didn't know why she was asking; she knew from long experience that dinner would be a do-it-yourself affair. But she wanted to imply that something *should* be for dinner when she came home for a visit.

"I thought you would have eaten before taking the bus. If you're hungry, there's sandwich stuff in the fridge."

"No, thanks."

"Why don't you sit down and talk to me while I weave this sample? How did the semester end?"

"Okay. I got A's and B's."

"That's wonderful, June." Her mother beamed at her. "You've always done so well. Have you thought about graduate school?"

"A little." She had been thinking about her fib to Owen about going to New York and joining a dance company. Maybe it *hadn't* been a lie; maybe she was trying to tell herself something.

"Would you stay with psychology?"

"I don't know. Probably." June played with a skein of yarn lying on the frayed arm of the overstuffed chair she was slumped in. "I saw Dad."

"Is that right?" Her mother stopped the clacking of the loom and frowned at the two inches she had woven. "How is he?"

"He and Melanie are going to have a kid."

Her mother stopped fussing with the weaving and put her hands in her lap. She gazed at June without speaking.

"How's that for a laugh," June went on, trying to sound light. Maybe if she played it up like a joke she could soften it for her mother. June supposed it was better that her mother heard it from her, anyway. And the sooner the better; give her a chance to get used to it. "Dad doing the family thing again. Wants to get it right this time, he said." She laughed, but it didn't sound right.

Her mother was still silent. June couldn't stop herself now.

"This is the best part, Mom. When I saw him, he said Melanie couldn't come to Boston because she was in Florida at a spa. She wanted to keep working on her figure, even during the pregnancy, he said."

"June—"

"Don't feel bad, Mom," June rushed in, afraid she had hurt her mother's feelings with the reference to Melanie's figure. "He's still a shit. He's exactly the same. You were so lucky to get out of that, you know." Her voice shook despite her best efforts.

"June." Her mother crossed the room and put her arms around her. June started bawling like a baby, nuzzling her face into her mother's sweatshirt until it was soaked.

"Oh, my poor little girl, my little June," her mother cooed, rocking her back and forth. "I'm so sorry."

THEY WENT OUT FOR HAMBURGERS and stopped at a lot on the way home to buy themselves a small Christmas tree. Her mother tied bows of colored yarn around the tips and June fished in the attic for the decorations. Every time she unwrapped a box, her childhood rose in images before her: holding her father's gloved hand while they waited in line for Santa; kissing her parents good night on New Year's Eve before they left her with the babysitter, her mother strange to her in perfume and lipstick, her father like someone on TV in his tuxedo. June put the boxes away. She came upon a Woolworth sack with a package of colored balls still sealed in their original plastic; her mother must have picked them up at an after-Christmas sale. She brought it down and hung the twelve glass balls, carefully spacing them.

"That's enough balls, don't you think?" she asked her mother. "I think I'll string some popcorn for it, too."

Her mother smiled and nodded, and kept the shuttle evenly moving back and forth on the loom. It was a soothing sound. Carols were playing on the stereo, and her mother had made cocoa. June went to the kitchen to microwave the popcorn, and surveyed the walls while she was waiting. Her mother still had practically every piece of artwork hanging that June had ever made her. Beside the window was a small dusty weaving made out of wool, grasses, and bark from summer camp. She took it down and brought it out to show her mother.

"I can't believe you still have this."

"Oh, I love that. Don't you remember? I thought it was so beautiful that I started collecting scraps of things to weave myself. That's what led me to take my first fiber class."

June remembered. She had been embarrassed by her mother's craft enthusiasms, but relieved that something finally interested her during that period after her father had first left them. For months after his departure, Alice had not cleaned, had not shifted things in the house to cover the bare spots where he had taken things from, and had bathed and changed clothes only sporadically. June had made excuses for her to her friends, saying that her mother had the flu, that they were getting rid of things and so the house was a mess, that they should go over to their houses instead of her own because her mother had gone back to school and had to have the house quiet to study. When Alice took up ceramics, and began spending hours at her potter's wheel, covering herself with little splashes of clay, June began to worry less. Her mother became like one possessed, staying up until three in the morning to get a pot thrown just right, silent for hours at a time while she painstakingly applied glazes.

Their Christmas Eve was quiet; only her father's relatives lived nearby, and June saw them even less than she saw her father. Alice cooked a pot roast and June made brownies from a mix. When they were finished baking, June cut them carefully into sixteen pieces so that she would know exactly how many calories were in each. After they ate, they sat by the Christmas tree and opened each other's presents. June handed her mother her gift. Alice unwrapped it eagerly.

"Oh, June, what a beautiful shade of blue. And I need a new robe." Her mother tried it on over her T-shirt and jeans and sat wearing it.

June's mother had filled a stocking for her: soaps, bubble bath, dance tights. Then she gave her a slim envelope and a large box.

"Which one first?" June asked.

Her mother shrugged. "The big one, I guess—it's riskier. I'm pretty sure you'll like the envelope."

June unwrapped the box and found a weaving of her mother's about a yard square, mounted for hanging on a rod. It was a mix of many colors, yet they were muted and soft, like a landscape in milky light. There were rough, nubby textures in it, shot through with silkier threads, and here and there a ribbon, a lace, a piece of cloth.

"I don't know if you like my weavings, June. You've never really said."

"You know I do, Mom. This one's great. Thanks."

"Well, this one was especially made for you. These silks are the color of your hair." Alice pointed to a coppery brown thread. "This lace is from a piece of a baby dress you wore. This is a hair ribbon from when you were a little girl. This string is from your first pair of dance shoes. Then there are some colors that make me think of you: pink June roses, a watery blue for the ocean we'd go to every summer around the time of your birthday." Her mother's eyes were bright. "I had such fun working on it. It felt like I was making something whole out of your childhood; I know we botched things up pretty horribly for you at the end."

"Don't say that. Dad was the one who ruined everything."

"It takes two, sweetheart. I guess I wasn't really paying attention to things he missed. Things got kind of old hat for him around here. I mean with me, the marriage—nothing to do with you."

"Mom, he's a shallow son of a bitch."

"June." Her mother tried to look stern. Then she laughed. "Well, you wouldn't really call him deep."

Her mother's other present to her was a pair of tickets for the Twyla Tharp company coming to Boston in February. Alice had always encouraged June's love of dance. From the time June was twirling around the house at the age of four, a make-believe ballerina, through the years when she was enrolled in first ballet, then tap and jazz, then finally modern dance, her serious love, her mother had gone faithfully to recitals, bought leotards, and run interference for her with her father over dance-class bills. Alice was the mother who could always be counted on to ferry carloads of little girls back and forth to the dance studio.

DURING THE REST OF THE VISIT, June ran every morning, wearing sweats layered over tights. Running wasn't her favorite kind of exercise; it made her leg muscles shorten and bulk up, and she had to stretch for an hour afterward to reverse the effects. But the exercise made up for all the junk food she ate when she visited her mother. The two of them watched television every night, and June couldn't help munching on everything she found in the cupboards. Every morning she was filled with such self-reproach that she added another mile to the run, until by the end of the week she was up to ten. Her knees ached with every step and she knew she should take a day off. But the next day she rose at six and slipped out of the house again. She couldn't stop after five miles anymore, or six, or seven; she needed to feel herself grow dizzy before she thought she had gone far enough. She loved her morning shower after the run, rubbing the concave space that was her stomach, knowing that she had eaten zero calories so far, and that she had burned off a thousand. It was the way she wished she could feel every minute of her life—her appetite as quenched as a saint's.

On the way to the bus station for her return to Boston, June stopped with her mother at the community art center where Alice had hung three weavings for sale on consignment. None had sold. June's mother took them off the walls and shook some dust out of them.

"I think I've come a long way since these, don't you, June?" Alice asked, unrolling her newest work to hang. "My textures are much more intricate now. I'm glad these didn't sell, because now I see how amateurish they were."

"Sure, Mom," June said, embarrassed for her. What her mother needed was a real job; her father reminded June every time he saw her that her mother's alimony would be running out when June finished college. But Alice seemed oblivious to this reality, and kept waiting for her "apprenticeship with the arts" to pay financial dividends. Even the rejection of having her pieces hung unsold for three months didn't faze her. She seemed happy, hummed even, as she rolled up the old weavings, while June burned with the shame of her mother's failure, which, inexplicably, felt like her own.

RENATA

RENATA STAYED IN ON CHRISTMAS and roasted a small turkey. Eleanor was visiting her daughter today, and June was at home with her mother. It would be just Renata and Charlie.

She helped Charlie unwrap his packages. She had bought him a toy plastic telephone he was not quite old enough to appreciate, a ball that he liked well enough until it rolled away from him twice in a row, and a soft stuffed dinosaur he didn't really notice. He had fun, though, crinkling the paper and chewing on the ribbon, until Renata noticed that the dye was coming off all over his chin and took it away. She opened a box that Marcia and the kids had sent her; it contained a cashmere scarf, with matching gloves and cap, in a shade of red just slightly too orangy to wear with her new red coat. There was also the present Jess had made Charlie: a Santa Claus doll made out of pipe cleaners. But she couldn't let him have because of the tiny sequins Jess had glued all over Santa's felt coat. Renata would call and thank them later, but she couldn't summon the energy yet.

There was nothing like Christmas to show you how many—or how few—people you had in your life. The baby had fallen asleep on a blanket in front of the Christmas tree. Renata wasn't ready to carry him to his crib yet. As soon as she put him down for the night, she would officially be alone. She stretched out on the sofa, lifting Charlie to a spot nestled inside the crook of her arm. They dozed together under a blanket as the room grew dark except for the tree lights glowing.

The phone rang, waking her. She groped for it, trying not to disturb the baby. Charlie continued to sleep beside her, nuzzling his face into her side as she shifted.

"Hey, Ren."

"Hi." Renata answered the familiar voice automatically, then went numb with shock.

"Surprised?"

"Yeah, kind of."

"Marcia didn't give me your number, don't worry. She's been real evasive."

"Well, I'm not listed."

"I asked Rick to get it from his friend. Rick said you're starting work next week for a guy he used to work for."

"That's right."

"Why so cold?"

"I'm not being cold, Bryan. I'm just surprised, that's all. Why'd you call?"

"Well, Merry Christmas, for one thing."

"You, too."

"Did Marcia tell you I wanted you to call me?"

"I guess she mentioned it."

"But you didn't feel like it."

"It's just that I didn't see the point. Nothing personal, but why?"

Bryan made a sound that was not quite a laugh. "No, you're not a bit cold."

"Bryan, what's this about?" Renata stroked Charlie's sleeping head. She was trying to leave her voice calm, so he wouldn't react and wake up. She needed to get off the phone quick.

"I just called you, that's all. Why are you so hostile?"

"It's not hostility." And it wasn't. It was panic. Renata twirled the phone cord. She would hang up, change her number.

"Then, what?"

"Listen, I've got to go, okay?"

"Is someone else there? You should have told me. I don't want to interrupt anything."

"You're not interrupting anything; I've just got to go. Merry Christmas." Renata put the receiver down quietly. Then she unplugged the phone. Charlie squeaked in his sleep. Renata wrapped her arms around him and breathed the warm baby smell coming off his scalp. If it weren't for her secret, she might have been glad to speak to Bryan, to sip a drink and curl up under the blanket and chat for an hour, finding out what he had been up to in the last year, and telling him all about her cross-country drive and Boston. Tears pricked her eyes. It frightened her that Bryan could be as suddenly nearby as his voice in her ear. But after hanging up, the apartment was emptier than before, the air more still. Even holding Charlie close enough to feel his soft breath on her arm didn't, surprisingly, ease the feeling that she was completely alone.

She dreamed of the baby's birth, except this time Bryan was in the delivery room coaching her. He was joking around like he always did, and Renata was laughing during the whole labor. In her dream, she didn't feel any pain at all, just a pleasant sense of exertion, but after a while she told him, "I don't think the baby can come out." Bryan told her, "Use your intuition," and she became angry with him, saying, "You have this baby if you think it's so easy." The next moment they handed her the baby, and she knew it was a boy because he had his father's face.

ON THE FIRST DAY OF HER NEW JOB, Renata was unexpectedly nervous. First she was afraid that June would forget or be late, although they had confirmed everything several times. But June rang the bell five minutes early, giving Renata time to dither through her final preparations, tying her black tie half a dozen times. It made it worse for her that Charlie was still napping when it was time to leave. He would wake up and find her gone, and there was no way to tell him why. She leaned over the crib and touched his cheek, causing a frown to wash over his brow like a brief disturbance in calm water.

Driving to the restaurant, she had time to worry about more things. Viva's was the fanciest place she had ever worked—waiters in starched black and white, eight-page wine list, the works. What if she spilled the wine, or knocked over some crystal, or dropped a whole tray of dinners? Thrust into the world without the baby, just Renata again, she felt jittery and awkward, as if she couldn't count on her arms and legs to know how to act.

THEO WAS TALKING with the phone tucked under his chin when she appeared in his office; he gave her a friendly wave and motioned for her to sit down. He was the owner, who had hired her on Rick's recommendation. The day of the interview she had brought Charlie; it was before meeting June and she hadn't known what else to do with him. Luckily, Theo was a father himself; he had ordered Renata a cappuccino while he held Charlie on his knee and made faces at him. Then he had shown her around the restaurant, which was decorated with milky-blue walls and pink shell-shaped sconces. A giant aquarium filled with electrically hued tropical fish separated the dining room from the bar. The fish seemed to swim silently among the tables, their fan-shaped bodies lit from an inner source.

Theo hung up the phone and greeted her, tossing her a freshly starched apron. All his movements were crisp, as if he were perpetually on the alert for a dinner rush.

"You can start with three tables to get your feet wet. It's going to be slow tonight—post-holiday slump. Gil's the shift manager; he'll tell you the specials and introduce you to the chef. Ask for tastes of anything you want so you can describe the food. Push the grilled tuna; it didn't sell at lunch and we don't want to get stuck with it. You can have that for your dinner, by the way. Eat early or late; you won't have a chance in the middle of your shift. Half hour for meals, plus a fifteen-minute break when Gil tells you you can go. Don't be afraid to ask questions."

Gil was a pudgy man with a slicked-back ponytail and a diamond earring. Renata could tell he was a lifer in the business; he handled trays and wine bottles completely unconsciously, as if they were extensions of his body.

"You've had a chance to read the menu at home?" he asked her.

Renata nodded.

"We like to recite the specials here from memory, but don't worry about it tonight. Here's a copy to read from. We do the tuna rare, but that freaks some people out. Tell them they can have it any way they like it, but the chef doesn't recommend going any better than medium. Don't worry, though, Ron's not a prima donna. He'll cook the fish to shoe leather if that's what the customer wants."

Gil gestured to the left and right as he talked, using his pen as a pointer. Renata met Ron, an unexpectedly muscular man wearing classic checked chef's trousers. She nodded hello to each of the prep cooks and to the rest of the wait staff. She remarked that she seemed to be the only woman.

"There's another woman, Susan, whose shift begins tomorrow, so you'll meet her. But you're right, Theo has a bias for male servers—a European quirk of his. Everyone's nice, though. Don't worry if Martin is rude to you; his New Year's resolution was to quit smoking, and it's making him a bitch. He's usually very sweet."

Renata went out to greet her first table, a couple of business types. They started with Coronas and lime, and she went to the bar to pick up the drinks. The bartender, Bill, winked at her.

"You're a nice change," he said, putting the drinks on her tray. She smiled and went to serve the bottles of beer. She poured a perfect inch of foam in the glasses and put a basket of bread between them. They stopped talking and leaned back to look at the menus.

"Let's see," Businessman One said expansively, looking up at

Renata with a smile she guessed was supposed to be charming. He had a small, even row of teeth and wore a splashy geometric tie. His short hair was perfectly groomed, as if he had just left a barber shop. "I'll have that tuna special. And a small Caesar."

"Sounds good for me, too," his companion said. They both wore dark, perfectly fitting suits and flawless white shirts. A little different scene, Renata thought, than the white linen gauze and Birkenstocks that walked into The Pelican, where she had worked in Venice.

Renata called in her order. This was a snap. As soon as she had felt the drink tray with its two beers perfectly balanced on her hand, it was as if she had never stopped working. The dress code was a little different here, and the prices a lot higher, but waiting tables was waiting tables. She went to greet her next table, a four-top with a family.

She recited the specials from memory, then took their drink orders. As she turned to go to the bar, she saw that the businessmen's glasses were empty. She poured the remaining beer out of each bottle, placing the empties on her tray. "Two more?" she asked. They nodded, engrossed in their conversation. Her third table sat down and she greeted them as she passed.

Bill's trade at the bar was picking up, but he smiled as he put the drinks in front of her. Gil caught her eye as she was on her way back to the dining room. "Good work," he said. "I can see why Theo hired you; you're a pro. You move really well."

Renata sold two more of the tuna specials at the family table, and one more at her third table, a couple dressed for a date, the woman in a short black dress, and the man in a silk weave jacket with a collarless linen shirt.

"Hey, you're moving my tuna," Ron said. "Great."

"The veal special would like her sauce on the side, if that's not a problem," Renata said. She knew how important it was to get along with cooks. They usually hated the dieters even more than they hated having their specials messed with.

"Not a problem."

She served the Beaujolais to the couple carefully and slowly, and, she thought, perfectly. When she was done she saw that both the businessmen's and the family's dinners were up. She hadn't removed the Caesar plates yet from table one, but made the swap gracefully. She walked as fast as she could without seeming to hurry back to the kitchen for the family's dinners.

Gil was at her side. "I'll back you up. Who's getting the tunas?"

"Mom and Dad. Mom gets the double vegetables, dad gets the garlic mashed," Renata said without consulting her pad.

"Right. Is that your calamari appetizer?"

"Yep. For three. I'll be right back for it."

On the way back from delivering the calamari to the couple, she picked up the empties from one and went to the bar for two more Coronas. Bill said, "They keeping you busy out there?"

"Not bad. I'm only starting with three tables, but they all sat down at once."

"Always the way."

Finally Renata's tables were all eating and she had checked back to see if everything was okay. Her busboy was doing a good job with their waters and bread baskets. She was just about to take a breather when she saw that a large order for one of Martin's tables had just come up. She came up behind him. "Follow you out?" she asked.

"My, aren't we the efficient one," he sneered. "Take the side dishes of vegetables," he said, turning and walking away.

Renata blinked, then picked up the three plates of vegetables. She guessed correctly who was getting them and then turned back to the kitchen without a word to Martin.

Ron looked at her and shook his head. "If he stays like that much longer, we're going to have to shoot him. And if we're going to shoot him anyway, then he might as well start smoking again."

Gil passed by. "Everything copacetic?"

"So far."

"You look good out there. Feel like picking up another table?"

"Sure."

By the end of the night, Renata had worked all six tables of her station, though the pace was leisurely. She was trained not to waste any motions. Anytime she was headed in a particular direction, she touched base with customers that way who were waiting for service, checked on how folks were enjoying their dinners, or picked up an empty plate. She loved finding the rhythm that made all her movements seem effortless and fluid. Her shifts always melted away then, and she was surprised when it was time to take a break or quit.

Stripping off her apron at closing time, Renata felt good. She already had a rapport with Gil and Ron, and she had plenty of time to settle in with the rest of the wait staff. She counted out tips for the busboy and maître d', then put some bread and left-over tuna Ron had wrapped for her into her tote. He had cooked the fish, chilled it, and wrapped it first in plastic so she could microwave it, then again in heavy foil for freezing. Renata had almost never cooked for herself during the time she worked at The Pelican. When chefs liked you, they fed you.

As they were filing out, Gil waiting until last with his ring of keys, Bill fell into step beside her. She almost didn't recognize him with his blue parka and ski hat. When she was picking up drinks from him, she had been too focused on getting the orders right to really look at him, even though he had been flirting with her all night. Now she saw him; he was cute in the way Bryan was cute—mussed and boyish.

"Want to go somewhere for coffee?" he asked her.

"I'd like to," she said, "but not tonight." Something stopped her from adding the rest of the sentence she had intended, that she had to get home to her baby. Instead she said, "Suddenly I'm exhausted."

"It's funny how that works," he agreed. "You go with this big energy wave that carries you over the shift, and then suddenly—boom—you're flattened."

"Especially the first night."

"Yeah. Hard to believe it was your first night, though. You looked like you've been out there forever."

"Well, in a way I have been." *Let that one out of the bag early*, Renata thought. Just in case he was tending bar as an interlude—a guy filling in a ski-bum winter, or someone in law school who would be doing this only for a semester or two. Renata was beginning to think that, like Gil, she would be a lifer. She might become a shift boss, or even a manager, but she didn't know anything except restaurants. In a month she would be twenty-seven, and somehow that seemed too old to go to school and learn something else. But she also liked the work. She liked the way she had an invisible window on people's lives as they sat at dinner talking business, or love, or divorce, or overdue bills, or work gossip. At first she had been amazed at how few people stopped their conversations, or censored them, when a waiter approached their table. Most continued talking as if she weren't even there, and as Renata silently removed a plate, or poured water, she was able to hear the most astonishing things. It made her feel protective toward her customers, this intimacy.

"You need a lift anywhere?" Bill asked.

"Nope. Thanks. My car's right here."

"Okay, then. I'll give you a rain check on that coffee." He smiled and turned the corner. He really did remind her of Bryan. The masculine confidence, so sure of his appeal and good looks, the insistent quality of the smile, as if to say, *You couldn't possibly have a reason for not smiling back, and if you do smile back, then I'll know you like me, and once we've got that straight, anything is negotiable.*

WHEN RENATA LET HERSELF INTO THE APARTMENT, she found June watching a movie on television, and Charlie sleeping in his crib, neatly tucked in.

"How'd it go?" she asked.

"He was great. A little fussy right before bedtime, but you said he probably would be. We had a good time playing with his gym on the floor, and then he drank the whole bottle you left, and I changed him into his sleeper, and by that time it was seven-thirty."

"He went right down?"

"Yep. By about ten of eight, he was out. How'd it go at Viva's?"

"Good," Renata said. "It's a nice place. The fanciest I've worked in, really. Want some French bread? I took home a whole loaf, and I know I can't eat it all."

June hesitated. "Just a small piece. For breakfast," she said.

Renata cut the bread and wrapped it, then looked in the refrigerator. "I need to come down from work," she said. "Do you want to have a glass of wine with me?"

"Okay," June said. "Was it busy at the restaurant?"

"Just enough. I like it when you have to keep moving; it's much better than standing around." She handed June a glass of wine, then kicked off her shoes and curled up on the end of the sofa opposite her. "So, tell me about Owen. Is he still after you to go out?"

June shook her head. "I think I hurt his feelings the other night. He still says hello, but he doesn't stop me to talk they way he used to."

"And that's how you want it?"

"Sure. It's better not to keep his hopes up, isn't it?"

"Don't look to me for any advice about men. Anyone else on the horizon?"

"No. I haven't really gone out with anyone since last year. And that guy was a jerk."

"How so?"

June made a face. "He was a musician in a local rock band. I met him at a party. All he liked to do was go to these really loud music clubs, and then when we'd get there he'd talk to his male friends and ignore me. It was like I wasn't even there. We went out for a couple of months and then I'd had enough."

"Good for you. You need someone who is going to appreciate you."

They drank their wine in silence for a moment.

"Were you ever married?" June asked.

"Nope." Renata took a drink of wine and let her gaze drift to the television. June had been watching a movie with Fred Astaire and Ginger Rogers. The volume was muted so that the black-and-white figures skipped and twirled across the screen without music, as if obeying some elfin impulse from within. Neither seemed able to stray too far from the other's orbit without gravity pulling them back, fusing them together again. It was beautiful, but Renata had always thought there was something wrong with the way Fred Astaire danced with women, no matter how graceful and perfect his steps. Somehow he didn't *see* his partners; though smiling at them and even mimicking a soulful gaze of love, the whole time you could see how little any single woman mattered to him. What mattered was that he had a partner, someone who would complete him beautifully.

"No, I was never married," Renata said again, as if she had not been clear before.

They ended up watching the rest of the movie, and microwaving popcorn. Renata noticed that when June ate popcorn, she extracted it piece by piece from the bowl; she never scooped up a handful. "You eat popcorn slower than anyone I've ever seen," Renata told her. "It's like you're counting it or something."

June blushed.

"Nothing wrong with that," Renata said. "You just make me feel like a pig, is all."

By the time the movie ended, Renata thought it was too late for June to go home, even in a cab.

"I'll be fine," June said.

"This city is dangerous at night," Renata told her. "Don't you watch the news? Just sleep here on the sofa bed and I'll run you home in the morning."

Renata lent June a nightgown and brought out some sheets and blankets. Then she looked in on Charlie again. When she entered her own bed, she fell asleep instantly, spreading out to fill the whole space.

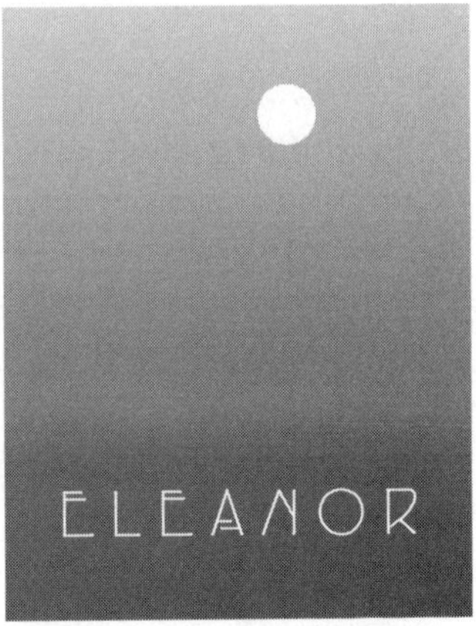

ELEANOR BEGAN EVERY YEAR with a complete physical. Her doctor for the last twenty years had once been a student of Robert's; he knew her very well. When Eleanor forgot her appointment this year, even though she had written it on the calendar, his office called to reschedule. On Monday the ninth, she took a cab to Dr. Brewster's office.

"Eleanor, you're looking as beautiful as ever. Feeling okay?"

"I can't complain, Ned."

"Still getting out, doing things?"

"Yes, except driving. I'm not comfortable with that anymore. I've asked Janice to sell my car for me."

"You won't even miss it, now that you live in town."

"That's what I thought."

"What about your state of mind? Any blues? Sleeplessness? Nervousness?"

"I'm probably more crotchety than ever, but no. My mood is fine. My memory seems to be going, though. I completely forgot that I had an appointment with you last week."

"Lots of people forget their appointments. My own memory's shot. Lucy has to remind me as I go out the door in the morning where we're going for dinner, and then, because she knows me, she calls in the afternoon to remind me again. I wouldn't worry about a little absentmindedness."

Ned prodded and thumped her, and dotted the cold disk of the stethoscope across her back. She had always been at home around medical people, because of Robert. Hospitals and clinics did not make her anxious. They were places where the world behaved in an orderly fashion. Though illness might strike unpredictably, the doctors and nurses themselves had procedures to follow, and a rational pattern to their actions.

"Your blood pressure is a little higher than I'd like, Eleanor." He consulted her chart. "Still taking the Aldactazide?"

She nodded.

"Any dizziness, headaches?"

"Some dizziness once in a while."

"Okay, let's get another reading next week. Just stop in some morning early in the day and the nurse will take it. If it's still high, we'll adjust the dose. I'm going to send you over to the lab now," Ned said. "We'll do the usual workup—blood count, electrolytes. Anything else in particular you're concerned about?"

She shook her head. Aside from a few chronic issues, mainly her blood pressure, arthritis, and hiatal hernia, Eleanor knew that at seventy-eight she was as healthy as a horse. Now that she had a new hip, she thought she was probably good for another twenty years. Her sister, Isabel, had finally succumbed to metastasized skin cancer two years earlier. It had been a slow and painful death, and her husband had been there until the end, with the bedpans, IV tubes, and a hospital bed he had bought for the living room of their Palm Beach condominium. Isabel had been so groundlessly worried about symptoms she exaggerated her whole adult life that everyone including herself was astonished that a painless mole on her back the size of a ladybug had finally killed her. It was odd burying a sister, even a sister you weren't close to. No one, not even a spouse, had shared the moments that formed the basic core of a person like one's sibling. With Isabel, Eleanor said good-bye to the only living companion of her childhood.

It was Isabel's death that set Eleanor thinking about her own. As she watched her birds come and go on the deck, Eleanor thought about preparations. Not that she thought her time was short. But Eleanor had always packed early for trips, had moved through life with organized closets and drawers, daily lists, and five-year plans. She hated to be taken unaware, and early on had formed the habit of being fully dressed at eight A.M. so that no one would catch her in her pajamas.

The other night she had had a marvelous dream in which Robert appeared in black tie and tails, asking her to dance. As they waltzed around and around in some magnificent chamber, Eleanor kept thinking, *But he doesn't dance; Robert has never been able to dance. Death must have taught him a few things.*

When she was first widowed, Eleanor negotiated nightly with the dark in their bedroom for any kind of sign from him while she slept. If it came, she never remembered it in the morning. But this invitation to dance, unasked for, unexpected, now teased her mind like a coded message, like a love letter in a language she could only half read.

WHEN JUNE CAME OVER THE NEXT DAY, she was practically bursting with excitement. She had just received a letter from one of her instructors inviting her to a special class with some famous choreographer. As June rattled on, Eleanor began looking around; speaking of mail, when had she last received any?

"Not everyone gets invited to these master classes, you know; it's an honor. But the best thing about it is that you get to know these really connected people. It can be almost like an audition if they have their own company—"

"June, would you run down and see if I have any mail?" Eleanor fished for the key to the box.

She noticed that June looked hurt.

"I'm sorry for interrupting you, dear. What were you saying? It's just that when you mentioned mail, I remembered that I hadn't received any for the longest time."

When June returned, her hands were full. "I'd say you had a few days' worth here, Mrs. MacGregor."

Eleanor stared at the pile. It did seem to be a lot. She flipped through the envelopes, becoming agitated. What were all these bank letters? As June started cleaning the bathroom, Eleanor sat at her desk with her stack of mail and opened each envelope with a neat slit. She threw the advertising circulars directly into the wastebasket and put the electric and phone bills to one side. Then she began opening the letters from the bank; there were four of them. She read the overdraft notices, uncomprehending. She had never overdrawn her bank account in her life. Every month she deposited her social security and annuity checks, which were more than enough to cover her monthly expenses. Someone had better take responsibility for this, she thought. There was no reason why she should be put to aggravating inconvenience because of some incompetent worker at the bank.

She checked her bank balance and saw that it should be around two thousand dollars, just as she thought. Then it occurred to her to look in her purse where she put her checks for deposit. There, neatly tucked in the zippered pocket with her deposit slip, was a bundle of checks totaling just over four thousand dollars: social security, two interest checks from annuities, and a pension check. Oh, how stupid of her; how very, very stupid. She had entered the deposit in her checkbook, but had never made the trip to the bank. She blamed the holidays, which, thank goodness, were behind her. All her routines had been upset by the unusual amount of visiting she had done in the last two weeks of December.

She examined the bank notices again. The checks presented for payment had been honored, since she had a companion savings account, but she was being charged twenty dollars per overdraft, a total of eighty dollars. Eleanor dropped her head in her hands. It seemed this kind of mix-up was happening to her more and more often, and she couldn't say why. She was not supposed to make mistakes like this; she was the one who sorted out other people's confusion. Hadn't it fallen to her to convince her fearful, aging mother that the meter reader was not a German spy? And wasn't it rational, patient Eleanor who had talked Robert back into the house when he stood shivering barefoot on the porch in January, waiting for his dead brother to arrive for a visit? Was it her turn now to be ill, to be old?

She shook her head briskly, to clear it of maudlin thoughts, though the sour taste of stomach acid lingered in her mouth, and a headache had started up. She entered the eighty-dollar charge in her checkbook, and thought she might ask Janice to go to the bank for her.

Her daughter emerged from the bathroom, sponge in hand.

"I think we need to put cleanser on the grocery list," she said. "Do you want me to go to the store now?"

"Yes, Jan, and would you take my bank deposit to my branch for me at the same time? I need to get these checks in right away."

"Sure."

"When you come home, dear, your father will probably be here, and we can eat."

"My father?"

Eleanor stared at her impatiently. "Janice, get going. We don't want the bank to close."

"Mrs. MacGregor, it's me, June. Not Janice."

"I don't think Peter will be eating with us tonight. Didn't he have chorale practice?"

"Mrs. MacGregor, your son is in New Hampshire, and your daughter is in Cambridge. I'm June. I work for you."

"I don't know what you're talking about. I want you to quit arguing with me, young lady, and do what I asked you to. You don't need to read those, they're all made out. Just skedaddle with them to the bank."

"Mrs. MacGregor, this deposit slip is dated almost a month ago. Do you want me to write in a new date?"

"If it makes you happy." Eleanor's voice was querulous.

"You know, you could get these checks to go directly to your bank account, and you would never have to worry about getting them in on time."

"Don't tell me how to run my affairs, miss."

"I'm sorry, Mrs. MacGregor. I'll be back in about a half an hour with your groceries and the bank receipt. Did you make a list?"

Eleanor stared at her blankly.

"Never mind, I know what you're out of. I'll need about thirty dollars, though."

Eleanor went to her purse and gave her the money. She was too irritated to speak. When the door closed, she rocked in her chair, fuming. She would be so glad when Janice was past this teenage stage of talking back and questioning her every move.

SHE MUST HAVE DOZED; June's key in the door woke her. She followed June into the kitchen and helped her unpack the grocery bags. She had a disturbing sense of having dreamed, but the images were obliterated by the present, like double-exposed film.

"Oh, you remembered cleanser; I meant to put that on the list," she said.

June looked at her. "Do you feel okay today, Mrs. MacGregor?"

"Well, I am tired," Eleanor admitted.

"You didn't seem well before I left. I think the bank upset you."

The feeling of powerlessness stole back. "The bank? Oh, those silly returned checks. I don't know what's wrong with my memory these days. I entered that deposit, but never walked it to the bank."

"The deposit's made now. I put the receipt on your desk as I came in. It's right beside your checkbook."

"Thank you, June."

"Have you ever thought of having your checks go directly to your account?"

"That's what Janice thinks I should do, but I just don't trust those computers. I feel much better going to a human being at the teller's window and getting a receipt."

June finished putting the fruit and cold cuts in the refrigerator, and neatly folded the bags, just the way Eleanor liked. Then she shrugged on her jacket, an old peacoat that Eleanor privately thought was a sorry sight. A young woman like June should not look so ragged all the time. All she wore were boys' clothes—jeans, sweatshirts that were much too large for her, and a coat that she had found in the army-navy store. If she were Eleanor's daughter, she would insist that June at least have a decent coat; something made for a girl.

June hesitated by the door. "Mrs. MacGregor, do you know that you thought I was Janice before I left for the grocery store?"

Eleanor blinked; again the sense of tilting, as if the room were not plumb. "Did I call you Jan? I'm sorry. You must admit that they are rather similar names: June, Jan. But I could never confuse the two of you; don't worry about that."

After June left, Eleanor stared absently toward the door. Then she looked down and saw that one gnarled old hand was patting the other at her waist, as if to reassure a friend.

JUNE WAS THE FIRST ONE IN DANCE CLASS on Friday. Her teacher, Mary Ann, was just setting up the tape.

"Excited about tomorrow?" she asked June.

"Very. Thanks for asking me. I love Richard's work."

June sat on the floor, her legs wide in a V, lowering her chest gradually to the ground in front of her. She lay there a few seconds, feeling the tension ease out of her hamstrings; this was no day to pull a muscle.

Other students started filtering into the studio wearing a motley assortment of leotards, T-shirts, and leggings. People tended to roll right out of bed for this seven-thirty class. They came in with unwashed faces and unbrushed hair hastily pulled back in an elastic. But it was a great way to start the day; afterward June felt warm and loose, every muscle humming awake as she showered and changed into jeans for class.

"Okay, people, let's start moving," Mary Ann said, clapping her hands.

The students stood in uneven rows, shaking out a foot or an arm muscle, facing Mary Ann, who had her back to the mirrors. She punched the button on the cassette and a recording of funk started playing.

"One, and two, and three, and four . . . " June closed her eyes during their usual warm-up, moving with the rhythms, feeling the energy from the music start to charge her up. They did some patterns together, then Mary Ann started them on movements traveling diagonally across the floor. One line of students waited in each corner, with new dancers moving into the middle space at eight-beat intervals, passing each other in improvised traffic patterns in the center, where they resembled a star in flux. Improvisation revealed who were the dancers and who were not. The real dancers used stillness as much as they used motion. Their movements took shape from within, and they never ran after the music, but let it travel through them.

During improv, June kept crossing against Max's turn, a tall black dancer who could get amazing height with his leaps and jumps. June was only five feet five; she wasn't about to jump with Max on the floor because her lack of elevation would only call attention to his strength. Instead she used her knack for making quick, complicated steps to counterpoint his streamlined running and leaping. Max caught on to her strategy, and the next time they met in the center of the floor, he made his movements even stronger, and June wove some tricky and almost comic turns around him. They had something going that resembled chase and pursuit, with June first baiting Max, then eluding him.

Mary Ann clapped her hands to end the freestyle moving. "Nice work, June, Max. You see how they worked the space together? They weren't just out there doing their own thing. Okay. Let's get in lines and start the cooldown. Wide legs, knees over toes, deep plié."

When class finished and the students gave themselves a ritual smattering of applause, June and Max high-fived each other.

"You going tomorrow?" he asked. There was no need to be more specific.

"Of course. You?"

"You bet," Max said. "I heard it's going to be small, just eight of us invited. I also heard something else," he teased.

"What did you hear?" June demanded.

"He's shopping."

"For dancers?" June squealed.

"No, for eggplants, you goose."

"How do you know this?"

"Judith mentioned it to Mary Ann, who mentioned it to me. She didn't know any details. But Richard is doing guest spots at about six schools in the next month, and Mary Ann said he usually invites a couple of new kids to apprentice in New York every summer." Max did a couple of quick steps around her, his muscles gleaming with sweat under the T-shirt he had cut down to a ragged tank top. "This is it, baby. Big Apple, here I come." He was the best dancer in the class; the students and instructors all tacitly acknowledged it. He also made no secret of his real ambitions, which were to leave school and dance with a company.

June picked up her towel in the women's locker room. This could be it for her, too; this was the opportunity Miriam had seen in her tarot cards last week. The most significant card in her array was the Judgment card. It was a picture of an angel with golden hair summoning souls as they rose from their coffins with arms outstretched. June was afraid of it, until Miriam told her it was most of all a card of outcomes and transitions—a card that heralded transforming change.

That afternoon at Mrs. MacGregor's, June waited until she determined Mrs. M.'s mood before chatting in her usual way. But Mrs. M. was her normal, quick-witted self; not a hint remained of the confusion she had shown the past Tuesday. She seemed cheerful, and was looking forward to her children's visit. Both Helen and Peter were coming into town on Saturday afternoon, and they planned to have a family dinner on Saturday night and a brunch on Sunday before Peter drove back to New Hampshire. June didn't mention the potential audition nature of tomorrow's class, but she did tell Mrs. M. again about Richard's visit. This time she heard her.

"It sounds like quite an honor, June, to be asked for the class. How long will it be?"

"Probably about two hours. They scheduled it early, for eight A.M., because his company performs in town in the evening."

"Well, make sure you get plenty of rest tonight. You'll be babysitting for Charlie?"

"Yes, but that's no problem. I'm usually home by one."

AT FOUR-THIRTY JUNE WENT NEXT DOOR. Renata was just finishing nursing Charlie, and in five minutes she fed herself haphazardly, grabbing some chips and soda, and taking a handful of cookies for the road.

"How do you eat that stuff and stay so skinny?" June asked her. Every time she saw her, Renata was casually munching down at least a thousand calories' worth of junk food.

"What stuff?" Renata said, blotting her lipstick in the mirror.

"Chips and cookies and Coke for dinner. If I ate like that, I'd be a blimp."

"I've always eaten like this. But since I've been nursing, I've also been starving all the time." She glanced at her watch. "Oh, shit, I've got to go. Have fun, you two. See you tonight." She kissed the top of Charlie's head and dashed out.

Charlie was delighted to see June and spent several minutes razzing energetically. They played together on the carpet, Charlie swaying dangerously as he grabbed at his toys, since he was just learning to sit unsupported. Whenever he saw something that he wanted to reach for, he began waving his arms and falling in slow motion to one side. June had put pillows all around him to soften his falls, and she caught him most of the time, but on the occasions when she wasn't quick enough, he toppled over with a puzzled, distant expression. June learned that if she didn't look concerned herself, he wouldn't cry after falling over. Instead, she swooped him up with a big smile, saying gaily, "Charlie fell over." It was the most amazing thing that he would decide whether to feel pain based on the expression on her face. Maybe she should let him decide himself when something hurt.

At six o'clock she set him up in his new high chair and mixed together a tiny portion of rice cereal. Charlie had begun solid foods this week, and he was very pleased with this new development in his life. He would grab for the spoon and help guide it, sometimes to his chin or cheek, and when a morsel made it successfully to his mouth, he would jam his fingers in after, smacking and sucking. By the time June fed him, and cleaned him and the high chair, it was just about time to get him ready for bed. In the two weeks she had spent with Charlie, June had learned some tricks. She discovered that he liked to dance with her, and for the transition from play to sleep, she waltzed them around in the darkened apartment, until Charlie finally quit grabbing her hair and prodding her in the ribs with his feet and relaxed, leaning his heavy head against her shoulder. Then she would rock him while he drank his bottle, and by seven o'clock he was usually either asleep or ready to lie in his crib, sucking on his pacifier while he drifted off.

Tonight Charlie went right to sleep, leaving June free to think about tomorrow. She almost wished Max hadn't told her what he had heard, because now she was thinking of the class as an audition. What if Bruce Richard asked them to do an improv? What could she impress him with? As she paced around the quiet apartment, she felt more and more fluttery. She started thinking about all the sweet things in the cupboards. *No, June*, she warned herself. If you make yourself sick tonight, you won't be able to dance tomorrow. Your body will be bloated and you will feel miserable and depressed, and the audition will be over before it even begins.

Still, she went to the refrigerator and stared in at the half-open containers and wrappers. Renata was messy in the kitchen. She never put lids back or wrapped anything so that it would keep. There was a whole bag of Snickers bars ripped open in the fridge, the small kind you buy to give out on Halloween. Renata was the only person June had ever met who routinely bought several kinds of candy bars in bulk packages, just to have on hand. She had so many back-up bags in the cupboards that a person could eat through a whole open package in the refrigerator, and then replace it, with Renata probably never even noticing. People who were normal about food usually didn't count how many of a thing were left. If something ran out sooner than they expected, they might register a slight feeling of surprise, but their first thought would never be that someone had eaten a whole package of cookies or candy in one sitting. June had discovered this axiom a few years ago, while baby-sitting as a high school student. There were other ways of doing it, too: taking one slice of cake, one scoop of ice cream, two cookies, and so on, proceeding all the way through the kitchen, so that the levels of everything dipped proportionately, with nothing appearing to be really missing.

June grabbed a carrot from the crisper and had to spend five minutes pulling off all the little root hairs that were growing out of it. Then she spent another five minutes scraping it carefully, and cutting it into smooth, even sticks. She still paced, chewing on the carrot sticks without even noticing they were in her mouth. She would screw it up tomorrow; she knew she would. Her thoughts went back to food. What had she had for dinner, anyway? Just a turkey sandwich. She did a calorie count and found that she had about two hundred to spare for the day. One candy bar would be fine. She heated water in the kettle and envisioned herself sitting down to savor the chocolate with a hot cup of tea to calm her down. But the tea water took so long to heat that she had already eaten the candy bar before she even unwrapped the tea bag. That was okay. How many calories were in one little bar—eighty, at the most? She could have another, and even a third, which would put her just forty calories over the day's total. She might not even be over, because she had figured her breakfast and lunch calories rather loosely, rounding up for good measure. This time she unwrapped two bars and sliced them into three pieces each. She arrayed them on a little plate, and by the time she was through, the water was boiling. She still needed to let the bag steep for three minutes or so, though. She paced around the living room, making herself stay out of the kitchen until the tea was ready. Then she sat down and ate the pieces of chocolate, one by one. She drank tea in between each bite to fill up with liquid. The chocolate worked on her like a drug. It was wonderfully smooth and rich. At least she was noticing what it tasted like; that was a good sign.

June tiptoed in to look at Charlie. He was sleeping deeply, his hands relaxed on top of his Winnie the Pooh quilt. His mouth was ajar and the pacifier had slipped out but was stuck hanging from one side of his lower lip, giving him a slightly dissolute look. June set the pacifier to one side of the crib and brushed her fingers over the top of his forehead. Her touch was more definite than she intended. The baby stirred in his sleep. June made herself leave the room before he caught her jumpiness and woke up.

She stopped in the living room and turned out all the lights. She had an overwhelming desire to make herself hurt. She would feel the pressure inside her stomach as she ate without stopping, and then she would feel the pain of forcing it up her throat. Her head would begin to throb from the sugar spike she gave herself, and a dull depression would settle over her like the lead apron they covered you with at the dentist's office. She had the power to make it hurt right now. She could feed herself so much food that she could split herself right open.

RENATA

"YOU WOULDN'T THINK SO MANY PEOPLE would be out on Friday the thirteenth," Bill said as he efficiently opened six Mooseheads and lined them up on her tray along with six frosted pilsner glasses. "It's nuts back here," he said, directing his chin toward the packed bar.

"It's crazy in the dining room, too. I forgot it was the thirteenth; maybe people want to be in a crowd tonight to feel safe."

"Believe me, this crowd's not safe," he said, grinning. The singles were out in full force, glossy men and women laughing loudly to their friends, all the while eyeing strangers across the room.

Renata hardly had time to think as she worked her station; she didn't have an empty table all night. People weren't lingering, either. They seemed full of nervous energy and wanted to get to a movie, or migrate to another bar, or wherever they figured that the evening would culminate in the maximum amount of entertainment. She didn't like the feel of this crowd, mostly hyper-stylish types from downtown and the Back Bay, everyone gleaming with hair gel and taking phone calls from tiny phones ringing in their purses and jacket pockets.

Even though things were hopping, she was having a good enough time. Ron was pleasant every time she put in an order or picked up her plates, and Bill was turning up the charm behind the bar. She and the other wait staff looked out for each other's tables. Gil had long ago ceased to treat her specially or keep an eye on her. Renata felt at home. Even Martin was over the worst of his nicotine withdrawal and turned out to be friendly.

When she counted up her money at the end of the evening, Renata was amazed: three hundred twenty dollars. She had had a birthday table of eight that chalked up a four-hundred-dollar bill, and group of lawyers from a conference who ate and drank themselves up to three hundred. These big groups got charged fifteen percent for service automatically. Best of all, both groups wanted to get somewhere to hear music or go dancing after dinner, so they didn't tie up her station all night. Even after tipping her busboy and the maître d', she still walked away with two hundred fifty to herself.

She was just putting her coat on when Bill loomed in front of her in his blue parka.

"How about that drink tonight?" he said.

Renata was inwardly amused. The rain check was for coffee, but suddenly the ante had risen to a drink. Oh, well, why not?

"Okay. I've got to call my baby-sitter first." She had been ashamed of herself for not mentioning her baby right away last time. At home that night watching Charlie's sweet concentration as he nursed, she had sworn never again to tiptoe around the issue. If a guy wanted to go out with her, he had to know straight away about her son.

Bill looked surprised, then he smiled. "Sure."

Renata dialed home. After four rings the answering machine clicked on. "June, it's me. Are you there?" She waited for June to pick up, drumming her nails. She knew June often fell asleep watching television, but why wouldn't the phone wake her? Then she remembered that she had turned down the volume of the ringer and the voice this afternoon when Charlie was having trouble taking a nap. June might easily sleep through a call, especially if she had one of her late movies playing in the background. "Okay,

I guess you're asleep. That's fine. I just wanted to tell you that I'm having a drink with a friend. I'll be home around one-thirty. See you then."

Even though she had left the message, Renata had misgivings. "I can't reach her," she said, hanging up. "She's probably just asleep, but I'm not so sure it's a good idea that I go out tonight."

"She has your work number, right?"

Renata nodded.

"So, she would have called you if anything was wrong, which leaves the explanation that she's sleeping. And if she's asleep, then the baby must be asleep, right?"

"Oh, all right." Renata laughed. "A quick drink."

"I know a great spot on the waterfront," Bill said. "Let's leave your car here and take mine."

"I'd feel better if we stayed in the neighborhood."

"Let's look at it from your baby-sitter's—what's her name?"

"June."

"From June's point of view. She sleeps, she gets paid by the hour. So, what happens if you get back at two instead of one-thirty?"

"She gets paid extra."

"Voilá."

Renata wanted to add that she also needed to nurse Charlie once more, but that seemed too intimate a detail to disclose. And in truth, she really didn't need to wake him up and nurse him. Since he had started solid food, he could sleep through until at least five in the morning. The ritual of getting him out of his crib after coming home from her shift had mostly been for her sake.

"All right. But how far is this place?"

"Fifteen minutes from here. I get so burned out on this Back Bay scene, I like to get to where I can smell water."

"Okay."

"You want to call June and leave another message?"

"No, I guess not." June certainly would have called if she were planning on leaving the apartment with Charlie for any reason.

And she would never leave without him. So, she was just asleep.

Renata had to admit that she was looking forward to this drink. When was the last time she had gone out with anyone? Or even ridden in someone else's car, for that matter? She was an adult, after all, entitled to a little companionship of her own. She would relax and enjoy herself.

"Good girl." Bill slipped his arm around her shoulder. It felt big and heavy. All her touch recently had been purely maternal. As soon as she could without seeming rude, she freed herself, and kept a space between them as they walked. He didn't seem to notice.

Bill's car was an old Porsche, a buffed and waxed creamy yellow.

"I guess you try to get women to go for a drive as soon as possible after meeting them," Renata teased.

Bill laughed. "Boy, are you suspicious. But it is a nice car, isn't it? My dad had it before me. He saved up for it all his life, then kept it looking like the day he bought it. In ten years he never let this car get dirty. When he died, I decided that I would do what it took to keep it nice. I probably could have been a millionaire by now if it weren't for pouring money into this thing. There's an irony there somewhere, but I haven't figured it out. Maybe you can help me."

"Oh, I'm not good at irony."

"That's what I was hoping. A nice, straight-forward girl."

The gears shifted under them with a sexual throb as he maneuvered them through the emptying streets. Not familiar with Boston outside of her own routes, Renata lost track of where they were going. They wound up at a bar overlooking the harbor, with sailboats moored at a nearby dock. She smelled creosote and salt as they got out: California, except for the bitter cold. The sky was icy clear, with stars as sharp as little pins.

Inside, it was warm and subdued, a small restaurant on one side that was closed, and a bar with a nautical theme on the other, half-filled with people. A fire burned low in the hearth. Renata had taken off her tie, but she wished for a scarf or something so she wouldn't look so much like a waiter in her black and white. Bill had put on a fisherman's sweater over his white shirt and looked for all the world as if he had been sitting by the fire for hours, a book or a pipe in his hand.

Renata almost regretted now that she had quit smoking. No, not regretted, of course not, because she did it for the baby as soon as she knew she was pregnant. But a cigarette was so useful for moments like this. He would help her light it, and she could draw slowly on the smoke and squint slightly at him as she exhaled, all the time looking guarded and cool. Smoking gave you something to do with your face, so you wouldn't have to let it betray you, your eagerness or your fear.

"So, am I reading things wrong, or does this make you a little nervous?" he asked her as soon as they had their brandies.

Renata was disarmed by the question. He wasn't as full of bullshit as she thought. "Does it really show? This is the first time, I guess, I've been alone with a guy since I had my son."

"How old?"

"Almost twenty-seven."

"I meant the son." Bill smiled.

Renata blushed. "Five and a half months."

"Thirty," he said. "Just to make us even."

"I thought you were older."

"Well, thanks."

"I didn't mean that you looked *old* old. Just a little older. You have a weathered face. A *nice* weathered face," she said, twisting a lock of hair. "I'll just be quiet now."

"Please don't. I sail a lot, so, yes, I know what you mean. A lot of people have told me I have skin like a road map."

"Now you're just fishing for compliments."

"And you're not going to give me any, are you?" he smiled again. He had a terrific smile. Aside from his dark, curly hair, the resemblance to Bryan was striking. Renata responded to his smile almost automatically, then felt a little guilty for her reaction, as if it were somehow disloyal. And it wasn't exactly Bryan's smile. Bryan's, though also charming, had a kind of vulnerability to it. Which was actually what had attracted Renata to him most.

"So, you have a baby," he began again. "But not a husband, I hope, or should I start looking over my shoulder?"

"Not a husband."

"Good. Because babies I get along with fine. But if you had a husband, he would have reason to be cross with me."

"You haven't done anything."

"But I want to," he said, reaching across the table and lightly brushing the back of her hand with his fingertips. Her hand felt paralyzed like a small, startled animal. "I think you must have figured that much out," he said.

THE SNIFTER OF BRANDY had been generously poured; it warmed Renata and relaxed her tired shoulders. The bartender gave last call and Bill ordered two more without asking her. What the hell. If June was asleep, she was asleep. Charlie wouldn't wake up, and if he did, there was plenty of breast milk in the freezer. The only difficulty Renata would have would be feeling a little full of milk herself. But the brandy seemed to be taking care of everything. She felt fine.

Bill didn't ask her any more about Charlie, and she was relieved. Charlie was her private life, the real part. Later she might introduce them. For now, she was content to listen to him talk about building boats, and sailing them to warm, faraway places.

"Have you ever been to the Caribbean?" he asked her.

She shook her head.

"There's nothing like it. Sailing from island to island, the water a turquoise so clear you can see right through. I like to work eight or nine months a year, and sail the rest. When you live on a boat, you literally can't find anything to worry about. If your engine breaks down, or bad weather's posted, that's just a fact of life you deal with. But you can't worry in the sense that you feel stress.

Three months at sea can set me up for the rest of the year in Boston."

"Why wouldn't you want to do it all the time?" she asked him.

"I'm getting there. I'm saving to start a charter business on Saint Kitts. A friend of mine already has a hotel there, and I could rent dock space from him. I figure another year of this, and I'll be ready to make the big leap."

The big leap. The phrase startled her, made her think of Bryan again, and the way he used to refer to his mother's attempted suicide. She shook thoughts of him away. Bill only superficially reminded her of Bryan. He had goals, after all.

"Closing, folks," the bartender said from the bar.

WHEN RENATA STOOD, the second brandy rushed through her, making her fingers and toes tingle. She wanted to tell Bill that her teeth were numb, because she considered it a very interesting fact, but then he would assume that she was drunk. And she didn't think she was drunk. Happy, yes, warm, yes, but drunk—definitely not. Not after two brandies. In the old days with Bryan, she could drink a whole bottle of wine herself, or a six-pack, or four brandies, and not be drunk. Old days. Was she really old enough to have old days? The thought made her giggle.

"What's so funny?" Bill said, snuggling her to him as they walked to his car.

"Old days." She started laughing and couldn't stop.

"Hey." He kissed the side of her temple. "You okay?"

"I'm better than okay."

"That's true. You're terrific." They stopped, and he tilted her chin up to kiss her. It was a long, serious kiss, the first she had had in she couldn't remember how long, and the heat rising inside her was frightening. She pulled back.

"Whoa," she said, swaying.

"I get it. Okay." He unlocked her door and she eased inside, grateful for the secure base under her. Then the car started spinning.

"Fast car," she said.

"Even faster when I start the engine." He turned to kiss her again, insistently, his hands moving under her coat.

"You're not trying to steal my tips are you?" She started giggling again.

"Why, did you make more than I did tonight? Probably. I'd tip you more than I would me."

"In L.A. we would call that low self-esteem."

"In Boston, we call that a compliment. You're beautiful." He kissed her some more, and she kissed him back. Decidedly, she was kissing back.

THEN THEY WERE BACK AT HIS HOUSE, in bed, and Renata was just drunk enough to be ravenous, starved. She couldn't get enough of him. But even through the brandy she felt how different sex was now. Her body was different. She had a moment's pain when he entered her, and then the size and weight and roughness of him half scared her after all the hours and days of cradling the unearthly softness of her baby. Scared her and excited her. He had condoms, which relieved her, since even though she didn't think she had started ovulating again yet, she wasn't prepared to risk another pregnancy for this. Then, when he was holding her, all of a sudden her breasts went hard, the way they did when Charlie started nursing, and then the milk let down, all over her, and him, and the bed.

"Oh, God," she said. "I'm sorry. You see, I usually feed him when I—"

"Shh," he silenced her. His mouth was on hers, then on her neck, then he was sucking the milk, moving back and forth between breasts, his mouth larger and wetter than her baby's, but, it was funny, also much clumsier, compared to the baby's neat precision. Charlie's use of the breast was so clear, so ordained, as he placed his tiny hands around it and looked up at her with his serious expression. Renata was shocked that this man was drinking her milk. It unnerved her that he should presume to go there; at the same time, she was sort of fascinated, and also glad not to be spilling it all over his bed.

They drifted in each other's arms, Renata peaceful, sated, dozing. So what if she was back at three instead of two. As he said, it wouldn't make much difference to June at this point. Renata was secretly a little proud of herself; motherhood hadn't made her any less sexy. He had wanted her from the moment he saw her, and when he got her, he wanted her some more.

THEN LIGHT FILTERED IN THROUGH THE SHADES and she tensed, waiting for Charlie's morning cry.

"Oh, my God. Oh, shit. Oh, fuck." She jumped out of bed and began fumbling for her clothes. Her heart was beating wildly. Little beads of perspiration stuck out on her forehead.

"What's going on?" Bill sat up, rubbing his eyes.

"How could I, how could I . . ." Renata was mumbling, half crying.

"How could you what? Come on, relax." Bill grabbed a wrist, trying to sit her back down on the bed. "It was great. You're great. I hope you want to keep seeing me. I really like you."

She wrenched away, tears of frustration in her eyes. "I can't talk about it now, don't you see? He's going to be hungry! We've never been apart this long! And June doesn't know where I am, and Charlie's going to wake up and I won't be there. I've never, never not been there." She dropped her face in her hands. "Oh, Christ, I'm a shit, I'm just a shit." She was really crying now.

Bill was out of bed, pulling on a pair of jeans that were crumpled on the floor.

"Renata, it's okay. Calm down. I'm going to drive you home now. Do you want to call your baby-sitter?"

She continued to cry.

"Renata, just call. You'll find out that everything is okay and you can relax. I'll drive you straight home. We can go back and get your car later. Come on, Renata." He coaxed the phone into her hand.

Through the blear of tears and headache, Renata punched in her number. It rang four times and the machine picked up. She heard her own voice, instructing her to leave a message.

"She's not there! Where is she? Oh, please, let's go, let's go now." Renata suddenly couldn't think of his name. She had no idea what part of town they were in. The room around her, with its clothes on the floor and rumpled king-size bed, was completely foreign.

"We're going now. Calm down. You're going to see your baby in a few minutes."

The car, at least, she remembered. She blessed the deep revs of its engine; she blessed the speedometer as it climbed to forty, fifty, sixty. She blessed the stranger beside her as he drove as fast as the traffic would let him, back to her child.

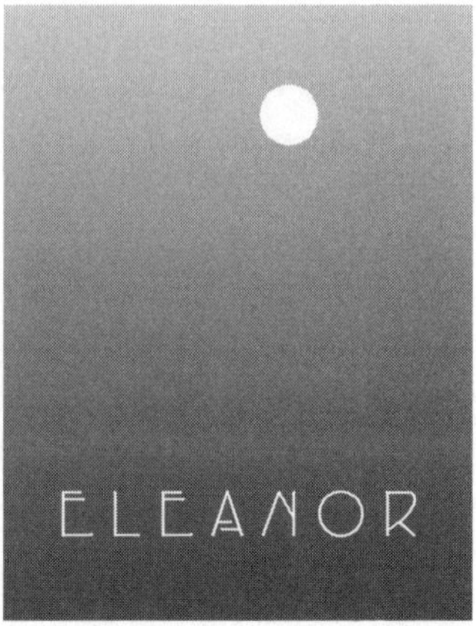

ELEANOR WAS DREAMING that the doorbell was ringing. As she rose to the top of sleep and her eyes opened to the pale light coming through her shade, she still heard it. What was she dreaming? The dream's substance vanished, but teasing strands of it tickled her conscious mind. Something about a journey, and her sister, something about the ocean. Where were they going, and who had interrupted them? The doorbell. It was ringing.

Eleanor wrapped her robe around her and crossed her living room, which was still dark with the draperies drawn. She opened the door to find June in the hall, Charlie in her arms. She stared uncomprehendingly for a moment. Was this June's day to come? Why was she bringing the baby over?

"Mrs. MacGregor, Renata isn't home yet. I fell asleep last night and there was a message on the machine from her saying she was going out after work—"

"Renata's going out?"

"Last night, after waitressing, she went out with a friend—"

The webs of sleep began to clear from Eleanor's mind.

"Come in, child. Don't stand there in the hall."

June came in with Charlie, who was whimpering in low tones, but was distracted from crying by studying Eleanor's face, and the change of scene.

"She left a message saying she was going out for a drink with a friend, and she hasn't come home yet. I don't know how to reach her and I've got to go to my dance class."

"Your dance class?" Eleanor was having a hard time keeping up.

"You remember, my master class. The special one I was invited to. It starts at eight o'clock, and its already six-thirty, and I have to get my dance clothes at home and get there early enough to do some stretching—"

Eleanor saw that June was near tears. Charlie was building up to tears. She was still a little foggy. Where was Renata?

"Let me hold the baby," she commanded, holding out her arms. Charlie let her take him, but fidgeted. "Has he eaten?"

"He woke up at five-thirty, and I warmed him a bottle then. He didn't want to take it, but he finally drank some. He's been fussing ever since. I'm sorry to wake you up, but I waited as long as I thought I could."

"Nonsense. You did exactly the right thing. When did Renata say she would be back?"

"That's just it. When I was sleeping she left a message saying she was going for a drink after work and that she would be home in a couple hours. I don't know where she is."

"Well, we can guess," Eleanor said. She had been wondering when a young girl like Renata was going to start needing to see men again. But she was disappointed in her for leaving June high and dry like this.

"Mrs. MacGregor, do you think you could—"

"Of course," Eleanor said firmly. "Go to your class. I know it's important to you. The baby and I will be fine until Renata gets home."

"I'll call right after my class to make sure she came."

"She'll be here," Eleanor said. "You go. You did the right thing."

June gave her a grateful hug, patted Charlie, and dashed out the door. Charlie stared at her retreating back, and looked at Eleanor. She had to laugh at the dubious expression.

"Well, yes. You're stuck with me for a little bit. But I'm sure we'll do just fine."

Charlie began to cry, the volume building until Eleanor's whole empty apartment seemed to reverberate. She rocked him for a little while, which did nothing. Neither she nor June had thought to get some of his supplies from next door. Eleanor didn't even have a pacifier for him. She tried offering him her arthritic knuckle, but he was too far gone in his crying to try sucking it. She got up and paced, thinking. June had been rattled; maybe she had left Renata's door open, or at least unlocked.

She left her own door ajar, and then, repositioning Charlie, who was beginning to weigh heavy in her arms, tried Renata's door. Locked. Inside she could hear a faint ringing from the telephone. If that was Renata, she had better be calling to say that she was on her way home.

Back in her own apartment, she had no idea what to do with Charlie. She gave him various things to suck on, a dishtowel, a wooden spoon, her sunglasses, and none of these interested him even briefly. He was upset. The double absence of his mother and June on an empty stomach was too much for him. She tried to remember what June had told her about Charlie and food. He had started eating some infant cereal, she thought. But of course Eleanor had none. Maybe she should walk with him to the corner store. Even if they didn't have the cereal, the fresh air on his face would probably quiet him.

Eleanor lay Charlie in the middle of her bed while she dressed. Then, finding a thick shawl to wrap him in, she put a ten dollar bill and her keys in her coat pocket and carried him to the elevator. His cries subsided to whimpers as he stared out from his shawl bunting at the elevator numbers glowing in red above him.

A young man sitting under the awning on the bench outside looked at her curiously, then rose to hold the front door open for her as she struggled with it.

"Thank you. Come on, Charlie, look at all the things there are to see outside."

By the time she was out on the sidewalk, her arms and shoulders were already beginning to ache from the baby's weight. She would need to find a couple of intermediate places to rest before they made it to the store. The cold on his face silenced Charlie, who stopped squirming a little to blink in the bright morning light.

"You like it outside, don't you, little fellow?" She jiggled the baby and tickled his cheek. "Don't you have a smile for me?"

A bench was up ahead. Eleanor sat on it gratefully, resting the baby on her lap. She was dizzy from the physical effort of carrying Charlie, coupled with the anxiety she was beginning to feel. Maybe taking him outside wasn't such a good idea. This predicament reminded her of the time she had gotten herself locked out of the house when Helen was just a newborn. Eleanor had taken the bus to the pediatrician for Helen's four-week checkup, and when they returned, the baby ready for her bottle and nap at home, Eleanor found that she had left her keys at the doctor's office, which was now closed. Neither of her neighbors were home, and Robert, although due within the hour, could not be depended on to be prompt. There was no public telephone nearby to call him. She walked with the crying baby for ten minutes back to the main street, where she found a phone booth, but there was no answer at his office. She took the baby to a coffee shop, where they warmed the bottle for her, and Helen ate and finally drifted off to sleep in her arms. In half an hour Eleanor rang Robert at home. He was there, and picked them up, ending what for Eleanor had been a frightening episode. She had felt so competent when they put the just-born baby in her arms; she had suffered from none of the new mother jitters that others had told her about. But that day, locked out with the baby, she had been struck by the enormous number of things that could go wrong. Helen's thin cry in the winter dusk had cut her like a knife. It was so easy to be a bad mother; a second's inattention could undo all the care and safeguarding you had lavished on a baby since its birth.

Charlie began to cry again. Eleanor bundled him up and trudged forward. She discovered that the corner store was closed until nine; if she walked another five minutes, she would be at the supermarket where June shopped for her. Surely it would open early. On the other hand, she felt her strength waning. Maybe she should just turn around and wait for Renata to come home. A baby could stand to be hungry for an hour or so. But what if she didn't come? What if she couldn't? The thought suddenly occurred to Eleanor that an accident might have befallen Renata. She would walk the five minutes to the supermarket and the ten minutes back home. Then, whatever happened, she would have some cereal to feed the baby. She might pick up some of those diapers, too.

There was another bench just before the supermarket parking lot. She sat down to rest once more before going in. Charlie was probably old enough to sit up in a shopping cart. Perhaps the store would let her wheel the carriage home, and she could get that nice young man at the front desk to push it back for her. This possibility cheered her, but she still needed to summon the energy to rise and walk the fifty yards or so to the store. Waves of lightheadedness were passing through her. She felt as if she were swaying. Hold on to the baby, she told herself. She could hear him crying at a distance. Why at a distance, she wondered, when he was right there on her lap? She mustn't let go of him, whatever happened.

Eleanor tried to shake herself out of the sudden stupor she felt. Why was she sitting here? Why wasn't she home? The baby was heavy. Peter shouldn't be out in this cold. Who was taking care of Helen and Janice?

She rose shakily. She looked around and didn't recognize the street she was on. This didn't look anything like her neighborhood. Perhaps she had gotten over one street too far. Eleanor tried to get her bearings. It looked like if she got off this busy street, she would be back into residential streets. Rosewood, the street her house was on, was surely in that direction.

Why was Peter crying so? She needed to get him home for a nap. "Hush, my darling," she whispered hoarsely. "We're almost there." But where was there? Eleanor walked for a block or two toward the residential streets and didn't recognize any of the names. How could she get so lost? Where was Robert? The girls must be with him, thank God. But Peter was turning beet-red with his cries. Her arms were breaking from the baby's weight. Panic rose in Eleanor as she turned this way and that, looking for home.

THE FEELING OF RELIEF JUNE HAD when Mrs. M. volunteered to take Charlie turned into nagging worry by the time the T deposited her in Kenmore Square. Mrs. MacGregor had gotten awfully confused the other day. But it was the problem with the bank that had made her so rattled. That day was the only time June had ever seen the older woman not completely sharp and lucid; Mrs. M.'s problems were physical, not mental. The only things that troubled her that June knew of were her arthritis and her stomach. After all, anyone who had the aisles of the supermarket memorized so completely that she wrote her lists in perfect order could not be senile. June had seen senile; her grandmother on her mother's side had died of Alzheimer's disease, and for years she had not recognized a single soul in her own family. But Mrs. M. was perfectly clear this morning. She had told June that she was right to go to her class; in fact, she had practically commanded her to go.

While changing into her leotard at her apartment, June had another thought: she hadn't brought over a bottle to leave with the baby. He had taken about two ounces at five-thirty; it was now seven. Renata would probably be home soon, if she wasn't already. He should be okay for another hour, June thought. He might get a little cranky on her, but Mrs. MacGregor could handle it. She had to focus on the task at hand, and that was getting to her class.

JUNE DRANK SOME JUICE FOR ENERGY, and walked the fifteen minutes to the studio to warm up her muscles. By a quarter of eight she was one of half a dozen students already there, stretching out. She went over to sit by Max.

"Have you seen him yet?" she asked.

"Nope. I think he's going to make an entrance."

They fell silent, concentrating on their stretching. Max wore a black thigh-length unitard with a T-back and low scooped armholes and neckline. His long, sinewy limbs were hairless and gleamed in the studio's overhead fluorescent light. Even his shaved head shone. June wore black as well; an ankle-length unitard cut with a tank top. Her skin was creamy next to the black leotard. Her long hair was coiled up at the back of her neck. Every dancer in the room looked scrubbed and awake, in contrast to the usual demeanor in early morning classes, and no one chatted. Each was absorbed in his or her own body, studying the flex of a foot, or the extension of a leg muscle.

Bruce Richard entered the studio flanked by Mary Ann and Judith, the two modern dancers on the faculty. The women seemed to disappear beside the aura of celebrity that he moved in. He looked older than the publicity photograph he used in newspaper advertisements for his company, but he still had the same flowing mane of curls and impishly curved lips. He was wearing a tie-dyed unitard with gray knit leg warmers, and sported a small hoop earring.

The class rose to their feet and waited, some students smiling nervously.

"Hi, I'm Bruce, and this is Marco," he said, pointing to a short, stocky man in a tank top and jeans who had followed the trio in, lugging a couple of cases. "Marco's going to drum for us, and we're going to dance, not talk.

"Okay,"—he clapped, without waiting for the drummer—

"let's stretch, two, three, four . . ." The students joined in as he led them in a series of lunging walks, hip circles, neck and shoulder rolls, and the other usual warm-up moves, which he somehow managed to make seem original with his emphatic and playful style. The drummer had finished setting up and now sat on a stool, closing his eyes and rocking his barrel-shaped chest back and forth as his hands traveled over the skins of the drums. Now the air was electric with rhythm. Bruce's warm-up started to be more complex, more dancelike. Without stopping, he shouted counts and directions as he milled among the eight students, correcting the position of a torso or the angle of a hip. He passed by June as she was holding an arabesque and said, "Good," as he swept by her.

Next they lined up and did some jumps across the room. With so few students, when you crossed the floor it was already your turn to reverse direction and go back; some students were panting after three or four trips. Max excelled here; June could see Richard's eyes following him with interest every time it was his turn. "Nice work," he said as Max crossed for the last time.

Marco slowed the pace of the drumming down to a meditative beat. Bruce led them in an improv across the floor. June was rapt watching him move catlike, then freeze, drawing his body up into a pose that suddenly exploded in a leap, then finish before she knew it in a series of small running steps.

They had several turns across the room, and June tried to change the mood of her improv at each crossing. Once he caught her eye afterward and nodded.

Max's improvisations, it seemed to June, always looked the same. He was the type of dancer who could interpret someone else's choreography with power, but wasn't too inventive himself. Even so, he was always impressive to watch, with his athletic sureness and the elevation he got on jumps, and June saw with a sinking feeling that Bruce Richard was visibly impressed with him.

Richard took the last improv turn and treated them to a three-minute sequence that June suspected wasn't so much improvisation as a set piece of signature moves that he used for classes like this. Still, the sheer professionalism of his execution took her breath away.

After the cooling down he led the class in a round of applause, which the class swelled and prolonged in appreciation of him. They broke out of lines. June watched with excitement as Richard walked over to Max and talked to him for a couple of minutes. Then Max followed him over to his bag, and Richard fished out a card and handed it to him. The students were filing out of class. Max looked like he was about to levitate from happiness. He kept staring at the card and looking up and grinning into thin air.

Richard was chatting with Mary Ann and Judith; he didn't seem to be talking to any other students. June knew she hadn't been singled out. Still, he was right here in this room. There was no law against asking him a question. June forced herself to walk over to him.

"Excuse me. I'm June. I really enjoyed the class. Thank you."

"You're welcome. You made some nice moves during improv." The compliment was made dismissively, and June could already feel him turning away. She rushed to hold his attention.

"Do you—does your company ever audition new people? As student dancers?"

"Yes, we do." He was looking at her now. Did he seem amused?

"Well, I was just wondering if, um, if I came to New York this summer, do you think I would have a chance? With your group?" He was just looking at her. "I really admire your work," she said inanely.

"Honey, let me save you some time. You've got nice moves and nice form—like a thousand other dancers who want to come to New York and audition. I've got twelve performing dancers, and five apprentice dancers, and that's as big as I get. The short answer to your question? Forget New York. Stay in school, get an education, and try out for local companies. There's lots of ways to be a dancer without going to New York and getting turned down every day."

Finished with this little speech—*Why not take dance classes at the Y Junie?*—Bruce Richard turned away, leaving June to arrange her face into a grateful smile as best she could.

RENATA

WHEN THEY DROVE UP TO HER BUILDING, Renata wanted Bill to drop her and leave, but he insisted on staying with her until they found out everything was okay. She really wanted him to go, because she didn't have time to think about him or what they had done last night. But she also didn't have time to argue with him, so she concentrated on getting to Charlie; Bill could do what he wanted. They didn't speak during the ride up the elevator. Renata watched the numbers crawling by, feeling as though she might explode. She had her key ready in her hand when they finally reached the seventh floor, and she dashed to her door, Bill trailing along behind.

A silent apartment greeted her. Everything was in order, down to the carefully washed baby bottles drying on the counter, but the objects mocked her without June and without Charlie. The domestic ordinariness of the scene seemed impossibly surreal. She didn't know where her baby was.

"Renata, June left you a note," Bill said. "It says, 'Charlie is next door with Mrs. M.; I had to leave at six-thirty' " he read from the refrigerator.

"Oh, God, that's right." Relief flooded her. "She had some special class to go to this morning. The baby's with the next-door neighbor; I'll be right back."

She left him in her apartment and went to knock on Eleanor's door. When there was no answer, she rang the bell. She pressed her ear to the wood to listen for a television or radio. Silence. In desperation she rang the bell again and again.

"She's not there," she said, reentering her apartment. "What should I do?" She was suddenly glad to have Bill with her. He was calm. He could think.

"Check your answering machine," he directed. The light was blinking with three messages.

The first message was her own from last night. She cursed the voice that blithely told June she was going out for a drink with a "friend." The second call was a hang-up; that, too, was Renata, from this morning. She must have called shortly after June left. Charlie hadn't been too long over at Eleanor's then. But where were they now?

The third message was a familiar voice. "Renata, it's me. I've been in town two days, trying to decide when and how to come see you. I've even been to Viva's, but you didn't see me. I was in the bar." Renata looked up at Bill, who was watching her curiously. "Here's the deal. I know about the baby. Rick told me, but I had already guessed it on my own, so don't be mad at anyone. It's Saturday morning, a little before seven, and I've decided to come over to talk to you. If you want me to turn around and go back to L.A., I will. But I want to see you, and I want to see the baby." There was a brief pause. "Actually, I've already seen the two of you. I've been in the coffee shop across the street and watched when you've taken him for walks. Anyway, I won't use up your message tape. We'll talk soon. I'm looking forward to seeing you. I'll wait for you downstairs if you're not home."

"You're white as a ghost," Bill said. "A voice from the old days?"

Renata nodded.

"The baby's father?"

She nodded again.

"Let me go three for three. You never told him about the baby?"

She stared at him mutely. She didn't need to nod.

"Wow." Bill whistled and shook his head. "You know, I think I can guess which one he was at the bar. A guy by himself was in the last two nights, and just sort of sat there, not talking to anyone. Blond?"

She nodded.

"Drinks Coors?"

"Sometimes," she said dully.

"Should I stay or go?"

"I don't know." She shook her head hopelessly. "Stay."

RENATA DIDN'T KNOW WHAT TO DO or whom to call. Bill convinced her that there was no reason to call the police, and of course he was right. If the police were to be called, she thought, it should probably be to report her for getting drunk and abandoning her child while she went off to have sex with someone she barely knew. She became conscious of her breasts, which were painfully hard and engorged; the front of her shirt was soaked with leaking milk.

"Excuse me," she said, and went to the bathroom with her breast pump. When she saw the milk spurting into the storage bottle, milk that Charlie should be drinking right now, she started to weep again, so that her shirt soon became soaked with tears and milk mixed together.

ELEANOR

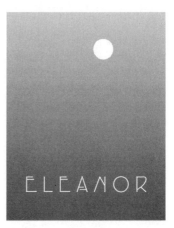

ARE YOU ALL RIGHT, MA'AM?"

Eleanor was sitting on the curb, her back straight, the bundled baby crying in her arms.

"Oh, Robert, thank God. Please, take the baby. It feels like I've been holding him for hours."

He took Peter from her and held him up.

"He's been crying like that for the longest time," Eleanor said.

"I think he's cold. Let's get you two in the car." He held the baby tightly in the shawl and murmured to him. "Hi, little guy. Hey there. Don't cry."

The baby stopped crying to stare at the new face. Then he began wailing again.

"I think he's hungry," Eleanor said. "Let's just go home, Robert, please."

"I think you're thinking of someone else, ma'am. I'm not Robert. But I'll be happy to take you home."

As Robert drove, Eleanor had a nauseated feeling in her stomach; she thought she might be sick. She couldn't imagine why she had started out for the grocery store like that. What had she been doing, anyway? Going for cereal. Rice cereal. For this baby, who—it suddenly occurred to her—wasn't Peter. Something cleared in her head. She felt her vision change, though she still had a pounding headache. Things became sharply outlined and familiar. She was on Washington Street, nowhere near Rosewood Avenue. This baby was Charlie, Renata's boy.

"I don't know you, do I?" said Eleanor suddenly, turning toward the man driving her.

"No, ma'am, we've never met. My name is Bryan Harmon. I saw you leave your apartment building, and I got a little worried about you because it seemed you had to rest a lot, carrying the baby. I got in my car and followed you," he said.

"Now, why would you do a thing like that?" Eleanor asked suspiciously.

"Because I was worried about the baby. And you," he added.

"Do you know this baby?"

Bryan laughed. "Yes, and no. This is Renata Rivera's baby, right?"

Eleanor hesitated. "Yes. I'm baby-sitting."

"Well, I know Renata Rivera. And I've heard about the baby. I was waiting for Renata when you came out. I heard you call him Charlie. I didn't think there would be too many babies that age named Charlie in your building. Of course, I could have been wrong."

"You weren't wrong." Eleanor was silent, trying to puzzle things out. "It's kind of you to give us a lift home," she said finally.

Charlie seemed to have given up on getting food for the moment. From his position in Eleanor's arms he stared up at the man driving, who also kept glancing down at him. For her part, Eleanor furtively studied Bryan Harmon's face, which seemed vaguely familiar. Then she looked down and examined Charlie, until things finally fit.

"Are you a relation, Mr. Harmon?" she asked.

"Yes, ma'am."

"Does Renata expect you?"

"She has a message waiting from me. But before that, no, she didn't expect to see me."

"Why are you here?"

"I don't know yet. To visit."

Eleanor reflected on that. Then she nodded. "You know, Renata's never talked about family. I never asked, although, of course, I haven't known her very long."

"I don't think anyone has known Renata very long," Bryan said.

"What a strange thing to say," Eleanor said. They sat in silence for a moment. "After all, Charlie has known her his whole life," she continued, cradling him. His eyes were now focused on her face, but the lids were fluttering closed, soothed by the warmth and the motion of the car.

Bryan laughed. "Well, yes. I see what you mean."

WHEN THEY GOT BACK TO THE BUILDING, Bryan offered to carry the baby.

"Have you ever held a baby, Mr. Harmon?"

"I've held this one—a few minutes ago, when I found you two. I think he likes me."

When I found you two. Where had she been? Eleanor knew she had better sit down, the sooner the better. The nausea was welling up again.

"Well, go ahead. My arms are aching. I'll follow along right behind you." Eleanor nodded to the young man at the front desk and Bryan accompanied her up to her floor, holding the baby. She rang Renata's doorbell and waited.

When the door opened, Renata stood there, with puffy eyes and a pale face. Her gaze flew down to Charlie, then went from Eleanor's face to Bryan's, who was standing there holding the sleeping Charlie.

"Renata, we'll talk later," Eleanor said. "I don't feel at all well right now and I'm going to my apartment to rest. Thank goodness for this young man; he appeared like my guardian angel when Charlie and I needed him."

AFTER LEAVING THE STUDIO, June talked to Max briefly in the hall, and tried to look as though she shared his excitement.

"He said I have to try out, like everyone else," Max said, his voice lilting with exhilaration. "And I have to pay my own expenses to New York for the audition. But if I make it, I get free room and board with the other apprentice dancers, and a small stipend. By the end of the summer, they'll tell me if I get to participate in the year-long program, which would put me on deck to be performing. There are a lot of odds to beat, but I've got a shot."

Max didn't seem to notice June's stretched, false smile as she nodded. Envy consumed her. She didn't begrudge Max his chance, but why didn't she deserve hers, too? She hated Richard for speaking to her so patronizingly—*Honey, let me save you some time*. She wasn't like a thousand other aspiring dancers. Maybe if you put her and Max side by side he looked flashier, more athletic, but he didn't have her intuitions, or her sensitivity. Why couldn't Bruce Richard see her for the dancer she was?

She fought off the invisible feeling that she used to get when her father arrived home after work and made a martini before dialing his first call of the evening. Every night her father returned from a day of business only to conduct still more business over the phone, sometimes even ignoring dinner on the table while June and her mother finally sat down. June remembered practicing her dancing in the living room in front of him as he talked interest rates and building permits and partnership shares. As a girl she would pirouette before him wearing her special pink tutu that was really supposed to be saved just for performances. She would keep her back straight and point her toes and hold an imaginary pear in each hand just as the teacher had instructed, and he never once saw her. If she spun all night in front of him, frozen in place like the plastic ballerina that rose smiling and perfect every time she lifted the lid of her jewelry box, her father would still see beyond her to the door, as if he were already planning his exit.

She couldn't decide whether she wanted to crawl off into a hole somewhere and be by herself, or talk to someone, although she didn't know to whom. She couldn't think of anyone who understood. Neither Mrs. M. nor Renata had a clue about dance, not really. She suddenly remembered the way she had rushed out and left Mrs. MacGregor with a hungry baby—and for what? So she could be insulted by some rude egomaniac.

She dialed Mrs. MacGregor's number and listened to it ring. Mrs. M. wouldn't be going anywhere yet, would she? It was only ten-thirty, and her children weren't due in until later. June had gotten her all the food she needed from the store yesterday. She tried Renata's number and got the machine. Worry began gnawing again; what if Renata had never come home? Charlie would be beside himself by now, and Mrs. M. would have no choice but to go to the store to buy him some baby formula or cereal. She could never manage to carry Charlie the whole way and shop as well.

Without bothering to change out of her leotard and Indian skirt, June threw on her peacoat and hopped on the T to Washington Street. For her two jobs she had a key to both Eleanor's apartment and Renata's. As the train stopped practically every block to let people off and on along the B.U. area, June grew more and more impatient. She really had been selfish to make Mrs. MacGregor take over her duties like that. Even if Mrs. M. had told her to go ahead and go to her class, what choice had June left her, standing there practically begging?

It was almost eleven o'clock when she let herself into the apartment building; she dashed through the lobby and took the elevator to the seventh floor. Mrs. MacGregor wasn't answering the doorbell. Before she used her key, she decided to check next door; maybe Renata was home and could tell her Mrs. M.'s whereabouts. No one answered there either. Alarmed, June let herself into Renata's apartment to see if she had been home. Someone had been, clearly. There were dishes in the sink, and half-filled coffee cups on the living-room table. June's note was on the kitchen table, instead of the refrigerator, where she had pinned it up with magnets. And when she went into the nursery, she saw that the sleeper Charlie had been wearing when June left had been balled up and tossed in the hamper. All was well. Renata had come home and taken Charlie from Mrs. MacGregor, and Mrs. MacGregor was now probably with one of her children. Maybe Janice drove over to get her early. At any rate, Renata was working again tonight, so June could see both of them and hear the details when she came to baby-sit.

Reassured, June locked Renata's door and took the elevator to the lobby. She had forgotten the humiliation of the morning for a moment. Now it came back to her full force.

ELEANOR WAS GONE BEFORE RENATA could even apologize or thank her. The sight of Charlie, rosy and sleeping, filled her eyes again with tears. She couldn't speak to Bryan yet. He handed the baby to her wordlessly.

"See you later," Bill said, touching her lightly on the shoulder and edging by Bryan with a nod. Then he was gone, too.

Cradling her baby in her arms, Renata turned and walked into her living room. Bryan followed, closing the door behind him. Charlie stirred, twisting this way and that to stretch.

"I'm sorry," she whispered in his ear, so only he could hear. "I love you, Charlie. I love you so much. I'm so sorry." She swallowed. "I have to feed him, Bryan," she said aloud, her back still facing him. "I'll be out in a few minutes." She headed for her bedroom door.

"Do you have to go in there to feed him?" Bryan said.

She stopped. She returned to the living room and sat on the couch. Charlie was waking, beginning a fussy little cry.

"All right." She sat down on the couch and pulled up her T-shirt. She had nursed in restaurants, and parks, and even once on the subway. Now, before Charlie's father, she was self-conscious.

Even though she had pumped, her breasts were still full and

hard. They began leaking as soon as she held Charlie, and as he fussed, the wetness spread into two circles on her shirt.

"Here you are, Charlie, back with Momma. There you go." Charlie began drinking deeply, little *mmm* and *nnn* sounds coming from his busy mouth. His eyes opened now, and fastened on her.

She was staring down at the baby, waiting for Bryan to speak, to ask her what the baby had been doing with Eleanor, to ask her what was the meaning of this baby, anyhow? When he didn't, she raised her eyes to look at him. He was watching Charlie nurse, a look of soft amazement on his face.

"Can I sit over there, closer to you two?" he asked. "I just want to look at him."

She nodded.

They sat there like that for some minutes, Charlie drinking, Renata and Bryan looking down at him. When Charlie had begun to get his fill, he broke off nursing and smiled at his mother.

"Hi, baby," she said back.

Then Charlie nursed again, stopping to smile, and to twist his head to look at Bryan. Finally he offered him a smile, too. When he was looking around more than he was nursing, Renata took him off the breast and pulled her shirt down. She held him up for Bryan to see. Charlie put his hands together at his mouth, looking solemnly at Bryan and suddenly belching hugely. They laughed.

"My God, he's beautiful, Renata."

"I know." She still waited for Bryan to begin asking her questions she couldn't answer, or to start berating her. Instead, he seemed content just to look at Charlie.

"Do you think I could hold him?"

Renata put the baby in Bryan's lap, and he adjusted Charlie so that he straddled his knee, facing him. He began gently bouncing the knee, saying, "Hey, Charlie, you riding a horse?"

Charlie laughed out loud. Bryan was encouraged, and started spouting nonsense in that singsongy register that adults automatically use with babies. The baby chortled and waved his hands in circles. Then Bryan played a game of offering his hair to the baby, which was as blond as Charlie's and just slightly longer than Renata's. Charlie grabbed fistfuls and tried to stuff it in his mouth. Renata watched them play, and began to relax. Bryan didn't seem to be coming on strong. She was surprised at how good he was with the baby, and how interested he was in him. Finally, curiosity got the better of her.

"Why did you come?" she asked.

"I figured out I probably had a kid with you, Renata. That's pretty big news to just ignore." He looked up at her from playing with the baby. "It's true, isn't it? I'm the father?"

"Of course."

They stared at each other for a moment. All her emotions were busy with the information that he might be here to interfere with her and Charlie. Her defenses were on high alert.

"When did you know?" she asked him.

"I'm not sure. It came in stages. When you wanted to break up, I thought you were just freaking out a little, a delayed reaction to your dad's death. I was sure you just needed time. Then you moved, and it blew me away."

"You didn't act too upset when we broke up."

"I wasn't going to beg you to stay with me. I couldn't see that working with you, anyway. I was going to give you time, see where you were at, and where I was at. But you didn't tell me you were leaving town—you just left, and I had to hear about it from the people you worked with."

She shrugged.

"After you had gone, all I could think about was why—what had I done to you? Things had been great—at least I thought so—and then you said you wanted to split up. I started going over everything. Like how your whole behavior seemed to change at the end—all the sleeping, the not eating. You quit smoking cold turkey, even though you had never talked about wanting to before. You made excuses for why you didn't want to have a drink. And I couldn't remember you having any periods at the end."

"So, you knew I was pregnant when I left?"

"No, after. And I didn't know for sure. It was a hunch. I kept thinking I'd drive up to Oregon and find your sister's place, but the next thing I knew, I ran into Rick and he told me you moved to Boston. I couldn't believe it. *Boston*. Totally the last place I would expect you to turn up."

"Why do you say that?"

"Renata Rivera? Who turns on the heat if it's fifty-five degrees outside? Who doesn't own a single coat, or any shoe that's not a sandal?"

"I own a coat now." She knew it was a stupid remark. "So, Rick told you about the baby," she said.

"Yeah. He called me up and said his friend Theo mentioned your cute baby boy, Charlie. Rick called *me* asking for details about the baby. Imagine how I felt telling him that's the first I'd heard about him." He looked at Charlie, who was hanging on to his finger, bending it back and forth with a furrowed brow of concentration. "Why, Renata? Why didn't you tell me? What were you afraid of?"

Renata was waiting for this question, the one she didn't know the answer to.

"I wasn't afraid of anything. I didn't think you'd be interested."

"That's such total bullshit. Did you think I wouldn't have wanted you to have it? *Him*," he corrected himself.

The answer was just the opposite. When she became pregnant, Renata had not only been sure she wanted to have the baby, but her intuition had warned her that Bryan would want the baby, too. And that frightened her. They hadn't ever said what they meant to each other, or if they wanted to stay together. She remembered almost telling Bryan, and then thinking about all the choices and decisions they would have to hash through, and how, from Renata's viewpoint at least, there were no satisfactory outcomes. She didn't want to get married because she had to, like her parents did; nor did she want Charlie to have a father she wasn't married to, and have her son always yearning for his father's presence. Telling Bryan was irrevocable. She needed the safety of her sister's house to think things through, but by the time she got to Oregon, the distance back to her life in Venice seemed impossible to bridge. The weeks turned into months, and the letter she had toyed with writing was forgotten.

"Renata?" he prompted.

"No, Bryan, I thought you'd probably want me to have him. But I didn't want to share him." There. She had said it.

She expected him to get angry, but instead he looked as though he had received a blow.

"Do you have a choice?" he said quietly.

The challenge of this took her breath away.

Bryan started to say something, but shook his head in a disgusted way and stopped. Charlie released Bryan's fingers and started to cry. Renata made a move to get him, but Bryan raised him upright against his shoulder, where Charlie promptly stopped crying and started looking around, grabbing a little bunch of Bryan's shirt fabric to suck on. She was starting to be annoyed at how much authority Bryan was assuming with the baby in her own living room. She wished Charlie would really scream so that Bryan would have to hand him back, but the baby looked content, his head resting on Bryan's shoulder.

He's a total stranger to you, Charlie, she told him telepathically, but Charlie just looked back at her and smiled.

"Renata, I'm not here to make your life miserable, or to harass you, or threaten you, or propose to you."

She snorted.

"What, you *want* me to propose to you?" he asked her.

"You just said you weren't here to do that."

"That's not what I asked."

"No," she said. "I don't."

"Fine. But Renata, for Christ's sake, I'm a father. You didn't decide to make me one, and maybe you wish I wasn't, but I am. You can't change that. Do you think Charlie wants you to change that? Have you for one second thought that he might like to know his father?"

"Of course I have," she said scornfully. "It's just that I wanted him to have someone he could depend on."

"What do you mean by that?" he demanded.

She was silent.

"Renata, you can't just drop these bombs and get away with them. Why don't you think he could depend on me? What gives you the right to judge?"

"I can judge. It fell to me to judge. I carried the baby, I had him, I've been nursing him and caring for him, and it's my job to judge."

"All right, Your Honor. Why don't you think I'm fit to be this baby's father? In practice, I mean. Not you or anyone can change the fact that I'm his natural father."

"For God's sakes, Bryan, you were dealing cocaine behind the bar when I left Venice. You think that makes you a fit candidate to be a father?"

"A couple of times I did a guy a favor and made a few hundred bucks. That's not exactly hard-core dealing, Renata. Besides, I don't use it anymore. Not that I ever was into it heavy. You know that."

"And you drink too much," she said.

"So do you," he countered.

"I don't. I haven't been drunk since—" *last night*, the sentence ended. Mercifully, he didn't press.

"What else? That's not it, and you know it, Renata."

"I just wanted it simple. I was pregnant, fine. I was actually happy about it. It didn't mean I wanted to be in a family."

"Renata, you don't get it. You and Charlie *are* a family. And even before I knew I had a son with you, he and I were family to each other. That's the way it is. It's what he deserves."

"You didn't know your father."

"And you think I liked it that way? You think I would have chosen that?" Bryan's expression was incredulous. "I don't care who my father may have been—not knowing is the worst thing. My mother didn't tell her relatives who my father was, and she didn't stick around long enough to tell me. If she had, I might at least have had one parent."

"Well, what about your mother?"

"What about her?" He suddenly had a little of the hurt, child-like expression that she knew.

"She tried to kill you," Renata said, her voice breaking. It didn't matter to her if what she said made sense. The image of his mother jumping off the roof represented a curse to Renata, and she was afraid that the seeds of its craziness or evil were tucked into Bryan's even row of stitch marks.

"My mother was sick, Renata. She was a manic-depressive." Bryan looked patient.

Renata watched the baby play with the sofa pillow over Bryan's shoulder.

"How do you know you're not like her," she said, her voice a near whisper.

Bryan stared at her blankly.

"How do you know you won't be bad for him, even if you don't want to be?"

Bryan looked at her helplessly for a long minute. "How does anyone know? How do *you* know?" he said.

Renata felt a chill, as if someone had suddenly opened all the windows in the apartment. She didn't have a scar, a place for the curse to raise pink welts that someone else could trace with a finger. But did she have the seeds of her parents' black disease? Frank and Mary Rivera had nurtured decay and chaos. They loved pain. They didn't grab hold of her and Marcia and jump out of a window, but in a sense they should have. Because it would have been quicker.

But all she said was, "Because I know. Because there's no way on earth I could ever harm him. Because I'm going to try to be good for him. " By the time she finished saying it, her voice was trailing away, her stomach turning with the memory of last night.

"Let me try, too," he said.

ELEANOR

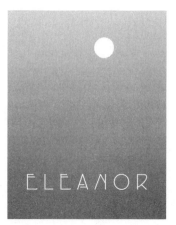

WHEN ELEANOR GOT BACK to her own apartment, it was as if years had passed. She looked with disbelief at the unmade bed from which June had roused her. How long ago had that been? An hour and a half? She shook her head. Incredible. She had been somewhere in that time, somewhere distant and inviting. She couldn't recollect it, as you can't get back to a dream, but she knew that she had traveled somehow.

She had had that baby with her, and then something had come over her, another life, and through it all she knew she must hold on tight to the child. But it had been a mistake to take charge of him in the first place. About herself she had no worries. She even welcomed the travel, the falling back through floors of time. But she mustn't put herself in that position again. She must be careful of forming ties that would hold her responsible to the young. Something was receding in her, like a tide backing away from shore, and she didn't want to be held back by any responsibilities. She had fulfilled her duties: a career and a marriage; three children launched into their lives.

She was tired, so tired. And her head was pounding. And then there was the nausea, which had come upon her so suddenly when she was in the car.

Eleanor removed her shoes and crawled into bed without undressing. She needed to rest. Gradually a tingling spread through her, a very pleasant sensation. Then the lightheadedness again, but she was in bed now. She could release herself to the spinning, whirling her through time. Scenes floated in her mind. Helen and Janice and Peter would be coming today. She hoped not to disappoint them, to be well enough to leave her bed, but there was this spinning, this irresistible spinning.

When she gave in to it, the paper dimensions of chronology disappeared as if eaten by flame. Faces and conversations buzzed in her head—her mother, Charlotte, teasing her for her narrow hips when she was thirteen as the cotton slip brushed down over her face and shoulders, falling straight. Her father, marching around the house with Eleanor at five on his shoulders, singing, "Hey Boom Bah! We are a parade! Hey Boom Bah! Let's drink some lemonade!" Her sister, whispering to her in their dark bedroom after she had received her first beau in the parlor, a grown-up visit, with Hetty bringing in cordials and leaving the door half-open behind her, as their mother had instructed. Isabel telling Eleanor every detail of how she had been kissed—furtively, as the young man took his leave, his mustache and wet mouth, his hands gripping Isabel's shoulders. How Eleanor had rubbed her hands over the flannel of her own nightgown sleeves, imagining it. Then Grandmother Donleavy's frightening face framed with a black crepe bonnet. Then Hetty rolling out circles of dough for Thanksgiving pies. Then the faces of her own children, turning toward her as they woke, blank as pools of water. Then Robert's face, saying something she couldn't make out because of the sudden humming in her ears. She strained to hear him, but she could only read his lips mouthing the familiar syllable, "El," his nickname for her, before it became darker and she could barely make him out—he was fading so—but he extended his hand. Could she go to him, could she really go?

WHEN JUNE WAS CROSSING THE LOBBY to leave the apartment building, she felt the pull of something unfinished. She swerved over to Owen's desk. His face lit up in a smile.

"Owen, did you see Mrs. MacGregor go out this morning? Maybe with her daughter?"

"She went out, early, with Ms. Rivera's baby. Came back with a man carrying the baby for her."

June wondered. Was Mrs. M.'s son in town already?

"I just knocked at her door and there was no answer. You didn't see her go out again?"

"I didn't see her. Of course I could have been busy talking to someone. Do you want me to ring her apartment for you?"

"Would you?"

He listened to the receiver for several seconds, then shook his head. "No answer. But I personally didn't see her go out. Maybe she's sleeping real hard or has the television turned up."

"What time did Renata and the baby leave?"

He squinted up at the clock. "Oh, I'd say about ten o'clock. They left with the same guy Mrs. MacGregor came in with. I'd never seen him before."

Now June was really confused. Who was the man? Maybe Renata's date from last night?

"I'm just going up to check on Mrs. MacGregor since you didn't see her leave. I have my own key to her apartment. Thanks a lot."

"Sure. Did you have your audition in New York?"

"I had one today in Boston, as a matter of fact. It went okay. I don't think I'll be going to New York for a while, actually." She fled before he could ask her anything more.

JUNE KNOCKED AGAIN on Mrs. MacGregor's door, rang for good measure, then let herself in with her key.

"Mrs. MacGregor? It's me, June," she called as she entered the living room.

The living room looked as it had this morning, neat and undisturbed from June's cleaning yesterday. The novel by the reading chair was just begun; Mrs. M.'s tasseled marker was inserted near the beginning.

The kitchen had no dirty dishes.

"Mrs. MacGregor?" June called softly as she approached the bedroom door. "Are you sleeping?"

June peered into the dark bedroom and saw that she was, her form silhouetted under the blankets. Her shoes were in the middle of the room. June's first thought was to back away and let herself out quietly. Then her eyes adjusted to the dark and she saw that Mrs. MacGregor had gone back to bed still wearing her turtleneck sweater.

"Mrs. M.? Are you feeling all right?" She didn't want to scare her. June crossed the room and bent over her. Mrs. M. was sleeping so still. Her mouth was slightly ajar. With a sudden foreboding, June reached out to touch her cheek. Cold.

"Mrs. MacGregor!" June pulled the covers back to expose the older woman's body curled into a semifetal position. June pressed her fingers to the cold neck to feel for a pulse. Nothing. Felt for a breath. Nothing.

"Oh, God, God, God, God." She needed to call a doctor, or

EMT, or something, but her mind was going blank. She punched in the number for the downstairs front desk; Mrs. MacGregor had it taped to the phone.

Owen answered pleasantly.

"Owen! Call 911. Mrs. MacGregor's sick or something. I can't make her wake up."

"Wait there. I'll call them and bring them up when they come."

June hung up and stood there in the quiet dark. When the shades were drawn, you couldn't tell whether it was night or day in this room. Mrs. MacGregor liked it that way.

She sat on the edge of the bed, frightened, but also strangely still inside, now that she knew help was coming. This wasn't happening; Mrs. MacGregor was surely sleeping, look at her—as whole and real as she had been this morning when they had had a conversation. She fixed a stray wisp of Mrs. M.'s white hair, which had unloosened a bit from the hairpins. Mrs. M. liked to be neat.

She should call Janice; the number was right there on the phone. She would, in a few seconds. She couldn't speak out loud again yet. Mrs. MacGregor looked beautiful and calm. She didn't have her makeup on today though, which made her look more fragile than usual. That was probably because June had woken her up early, and Charlie hadn't given her a chance to put it on.

The implications of this dawned a little at a time. She had pulled Mrs. MacGregor out of bed and thrust the baby in her arms, knowing full well that she was frail, knowing firsthand that Charlie was heavy, knowing that it was her own job to stay with the baby. She had killed her out of pure selfishness, to get to her class. In the distance she could hear the sirens coming, and her thoughts started crying *Run, run, run*, but June continued to sit immobile on the edge of the bed, as breathless and silent as Mrs. MacGregor.

RENATA

THEY HAD A LOT TO TALK ABOUT. They kept talking without even putting Charlie down for a nap because Renata forgot. He dozed in Bryan's arms and they were content to let him sleep like that, so they could look at him as they talked.

She was less afraid of Bryan's presence now that he was actually here. From the beginning she had imagined him as someone who would come between Charlie and herself, though now that she was with the two of them together, she didn't feel as possessive as she thought she would. A part of her even enjoyed the sudden perspective of seeing Charlie separate from herself, but held by someone who was—after all, it was true—his own flesh and blood.

Renata tried to explain her reasons for leaving. She needed to run away, she said, because it would have been bad luck to stay. Only by starting her life over as if it were the first page of a book could she give Charlie his own future. But Bryan didn't understand it, kept trying to argue with it, until finally they were exhausted and empty, and decided to go get some breakfast. Charlie woke from his nap and Renata changed him, and then they walked out past Owen, who always had a greeting for Charlie. Charlie seemed to enjoy the higher view that he had from Bryan's arms. He kept grinning at Renata from his position of being eye-level with her as if he were proud of himself and wanted her to see.

They went to the coffee shop across the street, where Bryan said he had sat and watched the two of them. He had seen them two days ago, he said, walking out. Charlie had been sitting up in the stroller, bundled in a white blanket and wearing a dark blue knitted cap. Bryan said it was all he could do to keep from running over to them then and there, but he didn't want to surprise Renata like that. So he had watched them turn a corner, until their profiles disappeared behind a hedge.

They got a table and Renata put Charlie in a high chair. The waitress who came to take their order probably assumed they were a family. They looked like a family.

"Where do we go from here?" Bryan asked her after the waitress left.

"I don't know; I need time to think."

"I want a chance to be in his life. Put yourself in my shoes, Renata. If you were me, and you knew you had a kid, how could you just go back to California and pick up where you left off?"

There was no answer to that. Maybe if she let Bryan play out some of his paternal urgings, they would go away. Maybe the less she resisted, the quicker he would see that he belonged back in California, not here with them. After all, he had no idea, really, what he was asking for.

"Okay, Bryan, you can see him, but we have to work this out a little at a time. This is about you and Charlie, not me and you. We're not a package deal."

Bryan accepted this with a nod as he fingered a pack of sugar. Charlie tried to reach the packet, and when Bryan put it on the high chair tray for him to play with, he immediately picked it up and stuck it in his mouth.

"Bryan, the paper's dissolving. Get it out of his mouth. He can't have sugar," Renata said crossly.

Bryan extricated the soggy packet, and Charlie screamed with disappointment. Renata felt a gleam of satisfaction. She gave Charlie a spoon and he stopped crying and stared at it, transfixed by the shiny metal. Then he banged it on the tray before jamming it into his mouth.

Watching Charlie turn off his cry as if a switch had been flipped, Renata felt ashamed of herself for wanting to show Bryan up. Of course she knew little gimmicks to keep the baby happy. Anyone who spent an hour around an infant learned them—look at June. By the end of the first week she had been completely comfortable with Charlie, and had come up with techniques of her own.

"You know what the hardest part of taking care of him is, Bryan?" she said. "Loving him so much you don't think you can stand it; you think you'll break from it. Then getting afraid that something will spoil it, and that it will be your fault. He came to me perfect, and sometimes I'm terrified that I'm going to have a moment when I won't watch him closely enough, and something horrible will happen."

"You never had to go it alone."

"That's not what I meant. I don't resent the responsibility."

They were silent when the waitress came with their plates of food, and they started to eat without speaking. Renata was starved. She had ordered eggs and pancakes and hash browns.

"You know, sometimes I think I remember my mother, although I probably just invent her from photographs," Bryan said.

"I'm sorry, Bryan. I don't know why I brought that up earlier. It was just crazy talk. I was upset."

He shook his head. "In my mind I see her face as closeup as if I'm on her lap. That can't be a real memory, can it?" Shrugging. "Anyway, when I was watching you feed Charlie, I had this good feeling. It jogged something familiar. Or like it should be familiar."

Renata nodded. She was thinking about how taking care of Charlie was a way of repairing her own childhood—as if she were offering the stuffed animals and night lights directly to the thin, speechless child she had been.

"You don't have to tell me this," he said. "But are you going with anybody now? That guy who was with you?"

"That's the kind of thing we're not going to talk about," Renata said firmly. She couldn't exactly tell him that she had no idea what her relationship with Bill was.

Bryan surprised her by reaching for the check as soon as the waitress put it down, waving Renata's money away. Then they took a little walk to get some fresh air, and their breath made frosty vapor clouds in front of them. The sky was a high, hard blue, and the sun gleaming on the houses and shops made the day look as if it should be warmer than it was.

"So, who was that lady, anyway, who had Charlie with her this morning?" he asked. "She said she was baby-sitting."

"She was doing me a favor," Renata said noncommittally.

"Kind of old to baby-sit, isn't she? She was confused when I found her. She was sitting on the curb. She called me Robert a few times, then she seemed to snap out of it. I had seen her leave the building with Charlie, and it didn't even look to me like she could carry him. I was worried, so I followed them, and I think it's a good thing I did. You don't use her to baby-sit very often, do you?"

"No, I don't," Renata said curtly. "I was in a bind."

"Where was she going with him?"

"Bryan, I said it was an unusual circumstance; did you arrive in Boston to interrogate me?"

Bryan said nothing, his mouth compressed into a line.

Renata was more frightened than annoyed; her heart started beating fast at the thought of Eleanor dropping Charlie. And she had no idea what they had been doing outside. Eleanor was confused the night her teakettle had burned, too. What had June been thinking? Bryan must never know the whole story of last night. He was being very humble and low-key now, but who could tell what he might be like once he got used to seeing Charlie?

They rounded the block back to the front of the apartment building, and Bryan handed Charlie to Renata. A siren approached. It got louder and louder, until Renata had to wrap her coat around Charlie's head to muffle the noise. The ambulance screeched to a halt under the awning of Renata's building, and the medics hurried to the door carrying a case of equipment and a folded stretcher. Owen buzzed them in and ushered them toward the elevators.

Bryan and Renata looked at each other.

"What's that about?" he asked.

She shrugged. The image of Eleanor flickered briefly. But after all, the building was full of people she didn't know, people who might have had a chest pain or cut a finger slicing tomatoes.

"You going to be okay?"

"Oh, sure," she said. They stood facing each other in a moment of uncomfortable silence.

"So, you're staying around," she said.

He nodded. "I'll call you tomorrow. Can I visit then? I'd like to take Charlie out in his stroller."

"Call in the morning. It's my day off. We can all do something together in the afternoon if you want." She was not about to let Bryan take Charlie off by himself.

"That's great." He kissed her cheek stiffly, and left her standing there, watching him. Bryan didn't seem the same away from Venice and out of his uniform of baggy shorts and T-shirts. Maybe it was the winter coat, but he looked more substantial than she remembered him, as if held by some stronger tie to earth.

AS SHE RODE UP THE ELEVATOR, Renata was trying to absorb the fact that she had apparently just agreed to let Bryan into their lives. Now that she was away from his engaging manner, that idea seemed absurd, crazy, dangerous. In an hour everything had changed; everything she had tried to do in the past few months to establish their independence had just collapsed.

When she stepped out on the seventh floor, she saw that Eleanor's door was open; she would stop by and thank her for watching Charlie, and apologize for the inconvenience she had put her to. But, as she approached the apartment she saw Owen standing in the living room, and beyond him the stooping white jackets of the medics. They were lifting something.

Eleanor.

Just then, June appeared in the tableau. Time stopped as Renata tried to make sense of what she saw. Then she cried, "June!" which startled Charlie, and unfroze the scene in front of her.

June walked over, and half-leaned against Renata, her face buried for a second against her chest next to the baby. One part of Renata's brain registered how pretty June was in her dancing clothes and skirt. Charlie reached out to grab June's hair, but she had it pinned up in a chignon. He tugged at a strand experimentally, testing its resistance.

"Where's Eleanor?" Renata said.

"They think it was a stroke, Renata. She's dead because of me. Because I had to go to a stupid dance class this morning when I should have known she wasn't up to carrying Charlie around. And then I forgot to leave him a bottle, so she probably tried to go out and get him something to eat, and it was all just too much for her."

Renata was staring in a daze at the narrow, white-sheeted form passing her by on the gurney. *Eleanor, in her apartment, telling her to get herself a baby-sitter so she could have some time to herself. Eleanor, confused, sitting on the sidewalk this morning holding Charlie.* Eleanor, dead. Because she, Renata, had gone out last night to get herself drunk and laid, leaving others with the responsibility of her child. "*Thank goodness for this young man. He appeared like my guardian angel. I don't feel at all well right now.*"

"Oh, June," she finally managed to say, reaching one hand up to stroke the head of the sobbing girl. "June, it's not your fault."

JUNE

BUT IT WAS HER FAULT, and even when Eleanor's daughter Janice explained that according to the medical examiner, the massive stroke that had taken her quickly and painlessly could have been triggered by anything, at any time, June still knew that it was her fault. The stroke could have come at any time, but it hadn't; it came the morning June woke Mrs. MacGregor out of a sound sleep and handed her a burden she couldn't possibly deal with.

June didn't know what to do with a grief and guilt so large. She told her mother about it. Her mother consoled her, and tried to reassure her that she had done nothing irresponsible. She suggested that if anyone had been irresponsible, the baby's mother had been. June knew Renata bore some fault, but she also knew that she had had charge of the baby, and the direct consequence of that was Mrs. MacGregor's death.

But even Mrs. MacGregor's children wanted to spare her. They were each very nice—Helen, with her faint Texas drawl and frosted hair and motherly tones; Peter, with his sober, quiet manner, like a minister, balding with a neatly trimmed gray beard; and Janice, who looked the most like her mother, and who was so nice to explain to June what had happened medically. Janice even tried to take some of the responsibility upon herself; she said she had noticed that her mother was getting mixed up at times, and kept meaning to call her doctor to discuss it, but hadn't managed to get around to it. It was possible that a series of small strokes had recently been causing her mother to have spells of confusion; brought about by episodes of reduced oxygen to the brain. But this only made June add to her own store of guilt, remembering the banking incident, and how she had thought then of calling Janice. At the time, she had decided against it, feeling somehow complicit with Mrs. MacGregor, who didn't want her children interfering. Now, of course, she saw it differently.

The funeral was Tuesday. June and Renata went together with Charlie, although there was an uncomfortable feeling growing between them, since neither could be around the other without thinking of the events that had led to Eleanor's death. June was astonished at the number of mourners who showed up. The Mrs. MacGregor she had known had been so solitary. Yet here were more than a hundred people; Janice told her a lot of them were judges and lawyers and doctors whom either Mrs. MacGregor or her husband had worked with. June had known that Mrs. M. had been a judge, but that had been an abstract, distant fact to her until she saw the number of important-looking people climbing out of limousines, coming to pay their respects.

A WEEK AFTER MRS. MACGREGOR DIED, June still couldn't go to any of her classes. She wasn't eating. She didn't waste time consulting Miriam, because she already knew that her aura was poisoned. Maybe she no longer even had an aura, or if she did, it was a halo of pure black. She and Renata didn't talk about Mrs. MacGregor at all. Renata came right home after her shift every night, and they talked about Charlie and how he had acted, and then June left.

One night when June was baby-sitting, she had been horrified to hear noises coming from Mrs. MacGregor's apartment next door. She pressed her ear to the wall and was positive she heard thumps and bumps, and the sound of something being moved. She felt suctioned to the wall like a limpet, until she heard a voice, which broke the spell of fear. Of course, someone needed to move Mrs. M.'s stuff out. June looked out the peephole in the door. Janice and Peter were hauling boxes into the hall. June didn't go out to say hello. She couldn't face them again. They were carting out Mrs. M.'s boxes, all labeled and sealed, that she had kept stored in the spare bedroom. It was funny how easy Mrs. M. had made the job for them by leaving her boxes closed like that.

Tuesday and Friday afternoons were the hardest. Instead of hurrying to catch the train after her classes to make it to Mrs. MacGregor's, June spent her time lying on her unmade futon with the shades in her apartment drawn. Sometimes she played music and sometimes she didn't. Mostly she stared at the ceiling. For the first time in years, she didn't think of food. She couldn't even feel her stomach anymore. As she floated through the afternoons, it was as if her body were not there.

At four, she had to drag herself out and go to Renata's. When she got a glimpse of herself in the mirror, she didn't even recognize herself: dark, hollow eyes; sharp cheekbones. A month ago, she really wanted to have cheekbones like that. Now she didn't care.

Owen greeted her these days in hospital tones, asking her with quiet concern how she was doing. She couldn't bear to talk to him. But no matter how clipped her response, he was always waiting to greet her the next time she passed, like one of those inflatable clowns that bounce back upright and smiling every time you punch them.

RENATA

JUNE WAS LATE AGAIN, and she was wearing the same dirty T-shirt and jeans she had on yesterday. Renata didn't care whether June could be cheerful for her sake, but she worried about the atmosphere that June was creating for Charlie. Of course they both felt horrible about Eleanor; of course they both felt guilty. But Renata would not allow herself to be depressed for Charlie's sake, and, damn it, she wouldn't hire depressed baby-sitters for him.

The whole question of keeping June on was up in the air, anyway. Bryan had found a job tending bar at a downtown hotel during the lunch shift, and he was pressing her to let him take care of Charlie when she worked at night. The idea was tempting, although she didn't know if she was ready to give Bryan so large a share of Charlie so soon. She had to admit that he was developing a knack for handling the baby. At first she had held her breath at the different style he had of picking him up, tickling him, jabbering in his face. Everything Bryan did seemed so loud and rough compared to the way Renata handled Charlie. But there was no denying that in Bryan's hands Charlie squealed, laughed, and generally acted totally delighted. Charlie might need a little of that kind of play.

She relaxed some then and quit scrutinizing Bryan's every move. She let him come by early a few mornings and take Charlie out in the stroller. The first time they had gone out without her, Renata realized she had never once been home by herself since Charlie was born. When they left, the apartment at first seemed unnaturally lifeless. Gradually, she remembered what it was like to have time on her hands. Sometimes she caught up on chores, and sometimes she just sat there, mesmerized by the calm. Yesterday, on impulse, she had painted her fingernails and toenails red. Charlie loved it, kept pouncing on her hands, trying to capture the shiny red ends.

June noticed right away, of course—she was always attuned to the nuances of Renata's dress, seemed to study her, almost. "What's the occasion?" she asked.

"No occasion. I had some time yesterday when Bryan came by and took Charlie out."

June didn't say any more. Renata was grateful that she was being tactful about Bryan's sudden appearance. After that horrible Saturday, Renata had told her that Charlie's father was now on the scene, but she hadn't gone into details, and June was too absorbed in herself to press for an explanation. She hated to disappoint June about the job, though. June seemed low enough without taking anything more away from her. But if she didn't have to pay a baby-sitter, Renata could save seven hundred dollars a month. It was substantial—enough to start a college fund for Charlie, or buy plane tickets to visit Marcia, or put toward a house someday. Renata did have to think of herself and Charlie first. If Bryan insisted on being in their lives, why not let him share the child care and help her reduce expenses? The idea had the advantage of keeping them on separate schedules, so Bryan could be with Charlie without being with Renata.

Not that it had been so bad seeing Bryan. Confusing, yes. When she let her guard down, as she sometimes did now that she was used to seeing him again, she caught herself almost reaching out to touch his arm when they were talking, or to brush the hair out of his eyes when they said good-bye. Watching Charlie grow attached to his father's face and voice and manner of handling him, Renata grew more and more tender toward Bryan, as if she were doomed to want him if Charlie did. But if they fell back into a relationship, then they were saying something about the future. She would be, anyway, because if Charlie grew up thinking of them as a pair, then any split between Renata and Bryan would be as devastating for him as a divorce. On the other hand, if Charlie grew up knowing that Renata was his mother, and Bryan was his father, two people who loved him but did not live together, he would never miss having them under the same roof.

It was a mess. But meanwhile, it didn't feel right to see Bill while she was trying to come to some understanding with Bryan. The Saturday everything had happened, she had called in sick to work. Bill left a couple of messages on her machine, which she didn't return. The following week, though, she couldn't avoid him. She explained about Eleanor's death.

Bill whistled. "Jesus, no wonder you called in sick. Was she a friend of yours?"

It seemed in a way presumptuous to say yes, since she hadn't known Eleanor long. But knowing that she could knock on the older woman's door for a visit had made Renata feel settled. When Eleanor gave her advice about Charlie, Renata took it. Eleanor had been a wise, comforting presence. She may have been the only real adult Renata had ever known. Then, on the last day of her life, she had done literally everything in her power for Renata's baby.

"Yes," she said. "We were friends."

Bill shook his head. "What was it that you said about Friday the thirteenth?" He reached across the table and covered her hand with his. "Except the part about being with you was lucky."

Renata withdrew her hand.

Bill took a sip of his coffee and smiled out the window into the dark. "Then there's the part about Charlie's father showing up," he said. "Ex-husband or ex-boyfriend?"

"Boyfriend."

"Ex-, though, right?"

"Right. But he wants to stick around and spend time with Charlie. I said okay."

"Long-term or short-term?"

"He said long. I say wait and see."

Bill nodded and fingered the napkin. "So, how are you feeling? You know, about us going out?"

"Everything is just too complicated for me right now to start something new."

"I'd say so," he said.

Renata felt a pang of disappointment over his response. She resisted the urge to say that they should still be friends, all the usual drivel. He didn't seem crushed, so to console him would be ridiculous. Maybe it was she who wanted consolation. Bill actually seemed quite offhand over the way things were turning out.

In the days that followed, they kept up the pretense of flirting. But it was a sham, and Renata began to understand something about Bill. He came and went with the seasons; he was aiming himself permanently in the direction of the Caribbean. She believed he had been sincere when he had said he was attracted to her and wanted to see more of her, but she also saw that his heart was in no way broken by not being able to. Well, why should it be, after one night together? She wasn't surprised. But she didn't know why, since she was the one who dropped him, that it was she who suddenly felt dropped. Sometimes things got twisted around in her mind like that; when she was on the road there had been moments—before she remembered the truth—when Renata actually felt gripped by a fierce anger toward Bryan for abandoning them.

And yet Bryan had followed her across the country.

But for Charlie's sake, not hers.

SHE WAS LATE AGAIN AND RENATA EXPLODED. June had been half waiting for something to happen, some reaction from someone that might break her trance. After it happened she made an effort to be on time for work; she also forced herself to go to some of her classes, although she still couldn't take notes during the lectures. Her professors' voices seemed to be talking in another language. June spent the class hours doodling stick figures in her notebooks. She didn't bother with dance class; what was the point?

The only thing that kept her from losing herself completely was seeing Charlie. It was impossible to stay silent, or sit slumped in a chair, or keep your face passive and expressionless, around him. During her baby-sitting hours she let Charlie show her what to do. He'd point to the toy he wanted and she'd bring it over to him. He'd reach up his hands to be held and she'd hold him. He'd clap his hands to the music on the radio and she would, too. Once, holding Charlie and turning the cardboard pages of an animal picture book, June felt her eyes fill with tears. It was a surprise; she had had no warning that she was about to cry. But the baby's weight on her lap got her thinking about Mrs. MacGregor's struggle to carry him that day, and the tears came. They were warm and, in a way, pleasant. Charlie didn't seem to mind if she cried. He hummed and gnawed the corner of his book, and June rocked with him, her face wet.

One day when she was on her way up to Renata's, she stopped at Owen's desk.

"I never really thanked you for all you did that day," she said.

He shook his head. "Please."

"No, really. I couldn't have talked to those paramedics without you. And I couldn't have handled the call to Mrs. MacGregor's daughter. You really saved me."

"It's okay. Whatever I could do."

He wasn't smiling his goofy, overeager smile now. June noticed for the first time that his gray eyes were really quite nice behind his glasses, and if he were a little more filled out, you could almost call him handsome.

"Owen, um, I don't really like skiing, but would you like to see a movie sometime?" She hadn't planned to ask him out; she wondered why she had.

He looked surprised. "Sure. I have weekend nights off."

"I have Sunday nights off."

"Sunday's great. Do you want to meet somewhere?"

She liked it that he didn't offer to come over to her apartment and pick her up. He was hanging back a little now, which made him more attractive. Maybe she had been too hasty about Owen. After all, who was she to put herself above him? Mrs. M. had thought he was nice. Renata liked him. And Owen liked her; that much was clear. What was wrong with liking someone who liked you? Always before, June had been drawn to guys who made a show of not being available. Even in high school, her crushes had been on the boys in torn black Levi's and leather jackets, the ones who smoked out in the parking lot between classes and turned the car radio up loud instead of making conversation. She had lost her virginity on a date with a guy who dumped her the next week because he wasn't interested in "being exclusive."

June was sitting on the floor in front of the television with Charlie when Owen buzzed her.

"Is it okay if Bryan Harmon comes up to get something he forgot?" he asked her.

June had never met Charlie's dad. Renata had talked about him a little, said that he had come from California, and that he was in town for a while. But June had never even seen a picture of him. She had time to run a brush through her hair and turn off the TV before he knocked. She answered with Charlie on her hip.

"You must be June," he said.

"Hi." She opened the door to let him in. He was gorgeous. Charlie smiled and stretched out his arms. "You want to go to your daddy? Okay, there you go," June said.

Bryan lifted Charlie high in front of him and made silly faces. Charlie chuckled and grabbed his nose, trying to twist it.

"Hey, that's Daddy's nose. I need that," Bryan said. He turned to June. "I'm sorry to barge in. I was over the other day and I left my camera here." He pointed to the kitchen counter where it sat.

"That's okay. Do you want a soda?"

"Sounds good. Me and Charlie'll just hang out on the floor over here." Bryan put Charlie down on all fours and assumed the same position, sniffing him and making friendly dog sounds. Charlie cracked up.

June put his soda on the coffee table.

"That's a nice camera. Are you a photographer?" she asked.

"I like fooling around with it. Renata tells me you're a dancer."

"Well, I've taken dance classes."

"She made it sound like a lot more than that."

"I flubbed this audition with a big-time choreographer. Well, actually, I didn't—that's even worse, because I danced about as well as I could, and he didn't think much of it. That was the same day that Mrs. MacGregor died. Since then, I haven't felt like going back to dance class." June didn't know why she was telling him all this.

"Well, my opinion is that you should do something if you enjoy it, and let the critics be damned."

June smiled.

"I mean it. If dancing is your thing, then dance."

"But the point is to do it for an audience," June said.

"I don't know this jerk who didn't like what you did, but I'll bet that he's not the only choreographer in the world."

June knew he was trying to cheer her up, but all she could do was shrug.

"I know, I know, easy to talk. You want me to go find this leotard guy and bust his nose?"

June laughed, and so did Charlie. Charlie loved jokes.

"You think that's funny? I'll show you funny." Bryan nuzzled Charlie over onto his back and growled into his tummy. Charlie was helpless with laughter, waving his arms and legs in the air like a bug.

"Okay, I'm headed home. Good to meet you. Renata has said great things about you. See you later, Charlie-O. We'll go out on Sunday, pal."

Charlie fussed when Bryan handed him back to June. To make up for the sudden quiet in the apartment after Bryan left, June hoisted Charlie up and razzed his stomach. He giggled. But not as much as when Bryan did it.

WHEN RENATA CAME HOME, June told her he had stopped by. Renata frowned slightly. Then she said, "What'd you think?"

"Of Bryan?"

Renata nodded, hanging up her coat.

"He's nice. Charlie was thrilled to see him."

"Yes," Renata said.

June decided to be bolder. "He really is good with the baby, isn't he?"

"Seems to be."

"And he's gorgeous. But he wasn't full of himself, the way good-looking guys usually are."

"I guess that's right," Renata said. She sat down on the couch. "So, you noticed how the baby responds to him."

"Oh, Charlie loves him, that's easy to see," June said. She stretched, and got up to get her backpack and jacket. "I don't mean to be nosy or anything, but why did you split up? Didn't he treat you okay?"

"He treated me all right," Renata said. "At the time I didn't think he was father material." She shrugged.

As June rode home in her cab, she compared Owen in her mind with Bryan. June wished now that she didn't have a date with Owen. She was bound to be disappointed.

RENATA

ELEANOR HAD BEEN DEAD exactly one month; Renata had not meant to equate that fact with Valentine's Day, but there it was. By imperceptible degrees the days were lengthening, so that when she set out for Viva's lately, it was still daylight. They had even had a couple of balmy springlike days that were offered tantalizingly, like soft fruits imported from a different latitude, then quickly withdrawn.

Valentine's Day fell on a Tuesday, her day off, so she was spared the irritation of waiting on couples ordering frothy drinks. She wasn't interested in watching that kind of advertisement for romance right now. Bill was openly flirting with a new woman on the wait staff who had replaced Martin, who had quit after learning that his lover's HIV had become full-blown AIDS. Martin took up smoking again. He and his lover moved to Florida, where they were living on the money they had been saving to open a restaurant together.

Bryan had not offered to see her today, and she wondered why. Even though he seemed to have taken her at her word that their new relationship would cover only their mutual commitment to Charlie, she had been operating under the assumption that he was just following the rules, and that he wished things could be different between them. She had half expected some kind of overture on Valentine's Day, but maybe she had been making things up, pretending she was more important to him than she was.

At least she didn't have to worry about finding a baby-sitter tonight. June would probably be unavailable, now that she and Owen had begun spending their time off together. Renata had first learned of this when June asked if it was okay if Owen stopped up one evening after Charlie was put to bed so that they could study together. Renata had been taken up short, not so much by the fact that June suddenly had a boyfriend, but that it had happened sometime recently and June hadn't mentioned it to her. She guessed she hadn't been asking June much about her life lately.

Last Saturday had been June's last regular night with Charlie, which made Renata feel bad. When she had told her about Bryan's offer to watch the baby, June said of course she understood. But she looked stricken. Renata wanted to give her a hug, but something told her that June needed to hold herself together just then, and that if Renata approached her she wouldn't be able to. They agreed that when Renata needed an occasional sitter, she would call June.

"I don't want to lose touch with him," June said of Charlie. "He's changing so fast now."

It was true. At six and a half months, Charlie was beginning to make creeping motions on the floor, and once Renata had come into his room to find him clinging to the rail of his crib and bleating for help; he was half standing but unable to move up or down, one foot bent awkwardly under him. Now that he was past the half-year mark, she would put him down somewhere, and five minutes later he would be in some tangle of his own limbs. In his lust for movement he smacked his head frequently on the furniture or the floor, which terrified Renata, but also gave her countless opportunities to soothe him, especially gratifying now that he had developed the habit of throwing his small arms around her when he was sobbing and burrowing his face into her neck.

Bryan had come by last week bearing a two-piece outfit for

Charlie wildly striped in neon colors—sweat pants and a little polo shirt complete with collar and ribbed cuffs. Wearing it, Charlie looked like a tiny Italian soccer player, and, suddenly, very much like a boy. In the one-piece stretch suits Renata had been dressing him in, he seemed so androgynously a baby, forever hers to cuddle and hold. Now Charlie was not exclusively hers, and not just because his father had shown up on their doorstep to claim a share of him. Charlie wanted more of the world, needed it, and was on the brink of crawling off to explore it.

So it was Valentine's Day, and tonight at least Renata and Charlie had each other, and no one else. At dinnertime she mixed his oatmeal with berry juice to make it pink for a Valentine's treat. She took pictures of him with his pink-oatmeal–smeared face and hands, and oatmeal-sculpted hair. Then she ran them a warm bath and stripped with him so they could sit in the water together, Renata nudging float toys within his reach as he sat in his swiveling bath chair. Now when he grabbed for something he twisted and lunged with his whole body. At times she had to blink to remind herself it was a baby's body, because he was so wiry and long, like a little boy. This is going to be over very soon, Renata told herself. Charlie will go to preschool, then kindergarten, and soon he will start getting invitations to other kids' houses and birthday parties, and when the phone rings it might even be for him. She should start picturing him that way, a year or two ahead of himself, so that time didn't sneak up on her and steal her baby right out of her arms without her at least expecting it.

And what about her? Should she really be a waitress forever? There was a time when some teacher had looked at her test scores and told her that she had what it took to go to college. Maybe it wasn't too late for her; she could use her father's money. But she didn't have the faintest idea what it was she should study. She had never been driven in a particular direction, like June to her dancing, and she had never had Eleanor's confident sense of the world. Renata reclined against the end of the tub, her breasts flattening out like water lilies. What she had really wanted to do, and had turned out to be good at doing, was taking care of Charlie. But that wasn't exactly a career move.

Bryan had taken some photography course in L.A. Since arriving in Boston he had been snapping away at them with his fancy new camera. Renata hadn't seen any of the prints yet, but she had been surprised that he seemed to take it so seriously. Something had happened to Bryan in her absence that had changed him into someone with more purpose. Or did she just see him differently now? In his new group house, where he lived not far from her apartment, he had already rigged himself a darkroom in the basement.

She had been impressed with how quickly he got himself organized. It had taken him precisely two days to find a room for a laughably low rent, and to get a good job bartending, thanks to a tip from Theo. He was also as good as his word when it came to showing up when he said he would to get Charlie, and returning him on time. There was really no evidence that she needed to protect herself from Bryan. He didn't seem to be the enemy at all; instead, she found herself looking forward to the times he would be coming by, and appreciating the extra hours he gave her when he spent time with the baby.

She rose from the tub and patted herself dry, then wrapped herself in a robe and lifted Charlie out of his bath seat. He rolled some r's on his tongue and drew his rubber duck out of the water with him, holding it and babbling *whoa-whoa whoa-whoa* as she carried him wrapped in a towel to his changing table and put him in a diaper and a sleeper for bed. She nursed him in the rocker until his eyes closed, and lay him already sleeping in his crib. Renata watched as he began his usual turning in his sleep until he was wedged into the corner of the crib, his foot protruding through the slats. It was as if even when sleeping he was restless, not content to be put down in a straight line where his mother lay him, but needing to find and test the outer reaches of his territory.

She let him stay the way he arranged himself, and tucked the blanket over him. The foot remained sticking out the side, a small, free-agent part of his body. Renata went to the kitchen and poured herself a glass of soda—she hadn't had a drink since the night with Bill—and carried it to the living room to watch television. *Gone With the Wind* was midway through. She stared idly at the screen, watching and brooding. She had always loved the outfit Scarlett made herself out of those green velvet curtains. But she couldn't bear to watch the riding accident with the little girl, so she spun through the channels, finding nothing else that interested her. She flicked the television off, and on impulse grabbed the phone and dialed Bryan's new number.

"Hello?" a female voice answered. Renata knew two women and two men besides Bryan lived at the house. Then, of course, there were all the friends of all of them who no doubt trooped through. Damn Bryan for being too cheap to get his own line, anyway.

"Is Bryan there?" She heard laughter in the background.

"Bryan? Sure, he's right here. Just a sec."

Renata heard him say something to the others, and heard them laugh. There seemed to be quite a crowd. Were they having a party?

"Hello?"

"Hi."

"Hey, Ren. What's up?"

Renata was feeling colossally stupid. What made her think he would just be sitting around watching *Gone With the Wind*, waiting to feel grateful that she called?

"Just checking in. We on for tomorrow?"

"Sure. Like we said. I'll be there at four-thirty, in plenty of time for you to leave for work. Okay? I'll come straight from my shift."

"Good. You know, you can shower and change at my place. And there will be food in the fridge. Whatever you want."

"Okay. We all set, then?" He sounded in a hurry.

"Yeah. See you. Happy Valentine's Day." Christ. Had she really said that? He probably had a girlfriend over there now. Maybe he was dating someone in his house, which would be like them living together already.

"Same to you." He did have a woman there. He couldn't even say the words to her; he had to code it. Fuck it, anyway. Why should she care? As long as he came on time to take care of Charlie tomorrow so she could go to work.

ON WEDNESDAY RENATA PACED the apartment, fuming. Charlie, playing with his toys on the floor, caught some of her tension and began to cry. That was how Bryan found them at 4:45 when he arrived.

"You're late," she said.

Bryan looked up at the wall clock in surprise. It had always driven her nuts that he refused to wear a watch. "Fifteen minutes," he said. "I had to circle a couple of times to find a place to park."

"Well, I needed time to tell you some things. You should have been early today. Now I'm going to be late."

"Relax, Renata." His voice was irritated. "I've been with him before, remember? I know where everything is."

"Oh, yeah? You're not interested in how long he slept today, and whether he ate much for lunch, and what new food I'm starting him on? That's totally irrelevant to you when you give him some dinner and try to put him down to bed?" She heard her voice rise in anger. Didn't he understand the first thing about taking care of babies? She and June always completely briefed each other when one of them was replacing the other.

Bryan put his hand on her arm. "What's wrong with you today, anyway?"

She jerked away. "I just want to know that you're taking this seriously, Bryan. I just want to be on time for work so I don't lose my goddamn job."

Charlie had been watching their conversation with wide eyes from his sitting position on the rug. Now he began to cry again, tilting back his head and closing his eyes.

"Now look what you did," Renata said, picking Charlie up and shushing him with kisses.

"What *I* did? Renata, go to work. When you come home everything's going to be fine. Call to check up on me during your break if it will make you feel better." Bryan reached out to take Charlie, which made him cry louder, stretching out his arms for his mother. Renata didn't want to release the baby until she had finished reassuring him, but she had no choice; if she didn't leave that instant, she really would be late.

She shut the door behind her as forcefully as she could without slamming it. What a mistake she had made in letting Bryan back into her life; now she was dependent on him to help with Charlie, and she hated being dependent. Why had she even told him the baby was his? Why didn't she say she had been seeing someone else on the side, and the baby was the other guy's? Now there was no going back.

Driving to work, Renata imagined midnight departures with their duffel bags, Charlie and Renata traveling light, the way it was in the beginning. She would leave on a Saturday night after work so that they could have three full days to get somewhere before Bryan even noticed. This time she would tell no one her address. She might even change their last name, so they couldn't be traced. Florida. That's where they should be, a warm seaside place with flowery winds where they would shed their winter clothes and feel the night air on their bare arms. But why should Renata sneak away like a criminal? What had she done that she needed to hide from, except want to bear and raise her son without interference? Why couldn't Bryan just go away and let her do that?

She remembered his initial words, that he would turn around and go right back to L.A. if she asked him to. Well, she might.

As Renata circled the block Viva's was on looking for a parking place, she saw the full moon hanging like a disk of ice against the dark. Every full moon had its own name, June had told her. She had been going to see some New Age psychic, and had been picking up lore like that. Renata was not interested in fortunetellers. There had been plenty of them on the boardwalk in Venice, but she had never bothered with a reading. For her, bad luck wore a plain enough appearance; you didn't need to go hunting it out in order to recognize it. When it came, it was simply what you had been dealt, and you lived past it. Even good luck, or a miraculous turn of events the likes of Charlie, she would rather not know about in advance. That way she wouldn't waste time waiting for it, and she couldn't be disappointed if it failed to show.

She finally found a spot three blocks away from the restaurant, and plugged the meter with four quarters to cover her until six o'clock. It was five o'clock exactly, and she would be at least ten minutes late by the time she got to the restaurant and put her apron on and punched her server code into the computerized wait station. It was a good thing that Gil and Theo liked her work well enough to cut her a little slack. She had been dragging in five and ten minutes late ever since Eleanor died, because June couldn't seem to get it together to arrive at her apartment on time. Now it looked like Bryan would have the same lackadaisical attitude.

The full moon hung directly in front of her the whole time she was hurrying toward Viva's; its cold light depressed her. What was February's moon called? The Hunger Moon. It did look starved up there, vapory and thin. Such a cold city. June said that the day Eleanor died, a full Wolf Moon was coming on. Renata pictured Eleanor's soul rising like a wild moan toward its light, solitary and mournful. Except Eleanor wasn't mournful; she was a very matter-of-fact person. She seemed to greet life head-on, and probably lifted herself up toward death the same way. Renata liked to think so. It wasn't so bad, was it, to die in your bed in a single instant after seventy-eight years of living?

AT WORK SHE STARTED TO CALM DOWN, soothed by the rhythms of waiting on tables. Her station filled up at a nice, steady rate—not fast enough to make her rush, but fast enough so that she didn't ever stop to watch the clock. At nine she turned over her tickets to Gil and sat down to eat the pasta and chicken Ron had cooked for the employees. Bill was just finishing his own meal, and motioned for her to sit down. She didn't feel like joining him, but she was taking pains not to seem disgruntled over his attentions to Sally, the new server.

"How are things?" he asked, pushing back his empty plate and taking a drink of his Coke.

"Oh, you know." Renata shrugged. "How about you?"

"Can't complain. I'm getting ready to take my annual leave, by the way. Actually, I'll be quitting, but for the last two years Theo has been rehiring me when I get back from sailing."

"Sounds fun," Renata said.

"I'd love to take you out on the boat sometime," he said. "I'll still be around for another two weeks."

"Oh, it's too cold for me. Besides, I'm not much for boats."

"You acted pretty interested when I was telling you about it before."

"Well, that's what brandy will do for you."

Bill looked at her, catching the chill in her tone. It surprised her, too.

"How's the boyfriend?"

"He's not; I told you that."

"Still in town?"

She nodded. "He spends a lot of time with Charlie."

Bill picked up his dishes and gave her a wink. "Well, you take care. See you around," he said.

"See you," she echoed. Whatever chemistry they had had between them was as flat as an old soda now. His smiles and winks came across as sleazy to her; she couldn't believe that a few weeks ago she was actually charmed by them.

WHEN SHE GOT OFF WORK, the moon was nowhere to be found. The city lights drowned the stars, if there were any. She hadn't called Bryan on her break, and wasn't sure exactly what she would find at home.

He was watching an old war movie, his feet up on her coffee table next to a pizza box and two empty Coke cans.

"Hey," he greeted her.

"Hi. How was he?"

"Fine. He ate cereal and carrots, played around a little, had a bottle and fell asleep watching TV with me. He didn't wake up when I put him to bed."

Renata flinched. She and June had always gotten Charlie to drop off to sleep in his crib. Now Bryan was going to undo all his good habits by hypnotizing him with the television. But she kept her criticism to herself and tiptoed into the nursery to see Charlie lying pressed up against the rails, curled on his stomach with his rump in the air. Bryan had him dressed only in a diaper and a T-shirt, even though the room was cool. She pulled the blanket up around his shoulders and kissed the back of his head. Charlie rolled over and began moving his lips. Renata picked up the pacifier and slipped it into his mouth just as he was beginning to sputter into a cry. As soon as he latched on to the rubber nipple, his body went limp again with sleep.

"Okay?" Bryan asked, looking at the screen instead of her. He had removed his feet from the coffee table.

"Sure. Thanks. You didn't have to order out, you know. I told you there was food."

"Yeah, I know. But I didn't feel like making anything. This was easier."

"How's the job going?" she asked him, sitting down in the armchair opposite. She wished he would turn the television off or at least down, but he kept staring at it.

"It's okay. Tending bar is tending bar."

Renata noticed his camera lying on the kitchen counter. "Did you take some pictures of the baby?"

"Yeah, practically a whole roll."

He didn't elaborate and Renata didn't press. She was a little hurt that for almost a month he had been taking pictures of Charlie and had given her none. She was too proud to mention it, but it seemed almost intentionally cruel.

"Were you late today?" he asked, finally looking at her.

"A few minutes."

"Sorry. I'll be earlier tomorrow."

"Well, I'm sorry I was such a bitch about it. I was tense today for some reason."

"New sitter," he said, grinning.

"You can't baby-sit your own child. I mean, you can't call it that."

"He is mine, isn't he? It's just beginning to sink in, that this isn't some sort of vacation. That he's really my son."

Renata didn't quite know what to make of this comment. Was he thinking of leaving them?

"You had nine months to think about it, and then you had the birth and all. You must have been able to ease into it."

That wasn't exactly how she would describe it, the sweaty July day she pushed Charlie into the world, feeling like it would tear her in two. It wasn't how she felt staring amazed at him in his bassinet afterward, either. The shock of him stayed with her for weeks. There was no easing into it.

She shrugged. "I guess. You getting cold feet?"

"No, of course not. It's just that it feels weird to wake up to, some days. It would be different if we had lived together first and then split up. It's just kind of tough never to have been under the same roof with him."

They let that one drift, hanging in the air between them. Bryan picked up his pizza box and cans and carried them to the kitchen.

THE NEXT FEW DAYS HE WAS ON TIME or even a little early, and they settled into a routine, as Renata had done with June. Charlie seemed content, except for his general angst over all the places he would like to go but couldn't quite manage to, his crawling still in neutral gear. Renata grew used to having Bryan around again. They traded stories about customers they waited on, trying to top each other with outrageous caricatures, just like before. She told him stories about the pregnancy, and the natural-labor classes she took with Marcia, even showing him a picture Marcia had snapped of her in the ninth month. In it, Renata was wearing a striped maternity bathing suit in the backyard, and Jess was spraying her with the garden hose. Some of the drops had gotten on the camera lens, so the effect was that of seeing Renata's swollen body through bleary eyesight. Bryan asked to keep it, and she was surprised but said yes, feeling a pang for him over the phases of Charlie he had missed.

One night after she arrived home, and Bryan had his usual feet and Coke cans on the coffee table as he watched TV, he asked her to tell him about Charlie's delivery, and she sat there for a moment, trying to get back to it.

She remembered labor to be like riding ocean waves with your body: at first the waves were spaced, so you could keep up with them if you concentrated. Then the contractions got rougher, but you could still pretty much hang in there and arrive at the other side with your wits about you, though you had less and less energy to fight with. Toward the end you were rolled over by waves so enormous you couldn't even see them coming; they slammed you to the bottom with a viciousness that almost shattered you there. At the dark bottom you had no idea which way the air was, or when you would be released. You knew that nothing you could do would slow this thing down or make it stop. It was just a matter of hoping you wouldn't die, or hoping you would, and feeling yourself at the mercy of the force that ground you to the bottom again and again. Finally, the thing spit you out of its jaws, and you lay sprawled there, abandoned by it. Except now there were two of you.

She tried her best to describe it, and after a silence Bryan said, "I wish I could have been there." The way he said it was not accusing but wistful, and Renata felt again that she had unwittingly stolen from him something she couldn't give back.

"I'm sorry, Bryan," she said, meaning it.

ON SATURDAY THE TWENTY-FIFTH, he arrived with a flat package wrapped in brown paper. He put it on the table and said, "Happy birthday."

She was astonished that he remembered. She scarcely had herself, running errands all day with Charlie. She was twenty-seven today. About a year ago she had left Bryan, and a year before that she had met him. Who could have said that the day she let him buy her a margarita at that restaurant in Malibu would be the day the cosmos started working to create Charlie? And the day that Renata and Bryan would be forever tied in some way no one could undo.

She opened the package before she left for work, and found an album of matted black-and-white prints of herself and Charlie. The first one in the collection was the snapshot she had given him of herself pregnant in Marcia's backyard, but Bryan had somehow copied it and enlarged it, printing it in black and white. The water-smeared lens gave the photo a dreamlike aspect, as if Renata were made of some element other than flesh and bone as she stood there with long white arms and legs, and huge pregnant belly, warding off the spray of the garden hose. The other eleven prints were taken during moments when Renata had not even realized she was being photographed. Bryan's camera had been so ubiquitous that she had soon learned to ignore it. Renata got to see for the first time just what the bond between herself and her son looked like: Charlie nursing at her breast, their eyes locked; Renata down on hands and knees trying to get him to crawl, the two of them grinning at each other; Renata leaning back to avoid being splashed as she kneeled beside the tub to bathe him. She was surprised at how professional the work was. The pictures glowed with suffused, complex light, and the printing was so crisp that she and Charlie seemed revealed in the photos as their essential selves.

"This is terrific, Bryan. You're really good at this." She was so happy to have the pictures that the photo she was staring at misted over. She had a million pictures of Charlie, but almost none of her holding him.

"They're not bad, are they," he agreed, pleased. "Of course I had to take a lot to get these good ones. I've got some other shots here in the envelope that didn't make the album, but that you might like to have."

She took them with her to work to look at on her break, and pulled them out over dinner. She was startled by some pictures of herself and Charlie taken at a distance, presumably when Bryan had been watching them before he announced his presence in town. He had used a telephoto lens to shoot a couple of pictures of Charlie as he sat in the stroller glaring into the winter sun. The photos had the look of being taken by a sly journalist, with Renata's blank expression unconscious of the photographer, and their blown-up faces slightly grainy, like newsprint. Then came a few pictures of Eleanor carrying Charlie, ones Bryan must have taken that Saturday as he followed her. She was stooped with the baby's weight, and the telephoto zeroed in mercilessly on her anxious, confused face. There was one of her sitting on the curb, just as Bryan had said he had found them, an image of a thin old woman wrapping her arms around a shawled infant. The background was obscure. The photo could have been taken anywhere, anytime, a picture of a forlorn refugee. As disturbing as it was, it was a stunning picture. Renata found she could barely look at it. She doubted Bryan was taunting her with the photo; he simply wanted her to see his work. She had been too absorbed in worrying about Charlie and in the tumultuous feelings accompanying Bryan's appearance to give much thought to Eleanor's fear on that day. Now she saw it before her, and it made her ashamed of her self-centeredness.

Driving home through the quiet streets, she felt restless, too keyed up to be alone; she realized she wanted Bryan to stay with her that night.

It was not just the fact of her birthday that made her want him to stay over. It was how everything had lately shifted, her balance becoming counterpoised against his presence. It was the queer way they were and were not a family; it was Charlie's new habit of raising his hands to be picked up and given a ride whenever Bryan entered the room; and now these photos—evidence of how closely he looked, how well he had seen the two of them. Right now she longed for someone to know her, someone whom she had a little history with. The fact that she had spent only a year with Bryan seemed insignificant next to the fact that together they had made Charlie. They had changed each other's life; what more can you know about a person than that?

WHEN SHE LET HERSELF INTO THE APARTMENT, Bryan was dozing on the couch. His expression was one of almost wounding sweetness, the way Charlie's was in sleep. Renata turned off the television, and the silence startled him awake. He rose to his elbows and looked at her, his eyes opaque and blank for an instant. Then he stretched and rubbed his face.

"Already?" he yawned.

Renata smiled. "It's twelve-thirty." She kicked off her shoes and sat down to put her feet up on the coffee table, nudging aside an empty beer bottle with her toe. Maybe she would have one, too.

Bryan swung himself up to a sitting position. The cushion had imprinted a line from his eye all the way down the side of his face, as if he had been scarred in a street fight. His flannel shirt was unbuttoned at the neck, and she could see how he still had some tan from California, slightly orange in this light. Her eyes kept straying back to that little triangle of skin; she used to know every part of him.

Renata had never had to seduce anyone. She had always been the one to say, *Maybe*; *we'll see; well, okay.* Now it seemed to her that Bryan should somehow fathom her willingness, should cross the room and need to ask no questions.

Instead he rose to get his coat.

"Um, Bryan?" She suddenly felt that if he left now, they would forever be watching each other from separate places. Like looking at someone in his car stopped next to you at a light.

"Yep. Do you know what did I with my hat? I thought it was right here."

Renata saw the hat on the floor beside the couch. She twirled a lock of hair.

"Would you like to stay and have a drink? For my birthday?" She felt cheap adding that, but she could see how he already had momentum toward the door, and thought she needed to throw out whatever ballast she could to slow him down.

He looked at her, and it seemed to her that his expression was the wrong one, his face softening in the wrong way.

"Oh, jeez, Renata . . ."

She felt herself close up, as surely as if she were one of those anemones in the glass tank at the restaurant, pulling their little spears of flame into a puckered fist meant to pass for a rock.

"Not tonight, okay? I mean, I know it's your birthday and all, but I didn't think—"

"That's okay."

"It's just that I promised to meet someone."

"Look, forget it. I'm wiped out, anyway. Your hat's over there," she added, pointing.

"We could do it another time."

"Sure, fine." *Just leave*, she thought.

The door closed behind him and she lay faceup on the sofa where he had been. It was still slightly warm from his body. Of course he had a girlfriend by now. Men didn't just wait around for months without finding someone. She felt a comforting anger begin to build. He probably had had two or three lovers in the year they had been apart. How dare he appear on her doorstep and pretend to be all wronged and outraged? As if her leaving him had been even a minor blip in his life. Well, fuck him. She had erased him once, and she could do it again.

JUNE

AT FIRST WHEN SHE STOPPED EATING, she kept it to herself. If she was planning to eat with Owen that night, she skipped breakfast and lunch. She couldn't keep that up for long, though, almost fainting one day in class after she rose from a psychology lecture. So she bought herself some high protein diet drinks to sip from cans three times a day. Owen discovered them in her cupboard and held one out in front of her, dangling it from its plastic six-pack holder as if it were a dead animal.

"What's this?" he asked. "Don't tell me you're dieting."

"Well, I am," June said.

"But June, you don't need to."

"I think that's my business, don't you?"

"This stuff isn't even food." Owen read her the list of chemical ingredients on the label, pronouncing them all correctly because he was a science major.

"Owen, excuse me, but whose body are we talking about here?"

He set his mouth in a superior, judging way, and put the can back in the cupboard. They returned to their homework without speaking.

It was worth it, though, to see her jeans gap around her waist, and to run her fingers over the shelf of bone her clavicle made. She loved how her bones were rising out of her like another June.

She couldn't tell Owen that the reason she had gained weight in the first place was because almost every time he left her, she paced her apartment nervously, her heart pounding, which set her off on an eating spell. The gauntness that had overtaken her following Mrs. MacGregor's death had puffed into extra pounds as soon as she began dating him. One day after vomiting a food binge, June was alarmed to see blood. She decided that she had to stop throwing up. Hence, she needed to diet, to balance the times when she lost control. So far, it was working. Since she had been dieting, she had binged once, but overall she had lost eleven pounds.

June didn't know why being with Owen would have this effect on her. There was nothing to fault him with. He was a completely nice guy. He told her how much he liked her; he bought her little surprise presents; he asked her about her day and listened when she told him. He worked hard and was putting himself through school. He earned good grades and was probably on his way to becoming a big success in life.

The problem was, he didn't excite her. She had enjoyed his company on their first date, and then the second, and by the third time they went out together, she knew she should be more receptive when he slipped his arm around her shoulders. When she did kiss him good night, she had to think of something else to distract herself from the loose, fleshy feel of his lips. She wished they could just be friends; June really wanted a friend. But Owen was clearly hoping they would get serious. Not that he was pushing her; he was too nice for that. She began sleeping with him, feeling that he somehow deserved it. This turn of events made him ecstatic. June pretended to enjoy it, too.

ON A SATURDAY MORNING IN EARLY MARCH when Owen was at work, June swept out the apartment, carried the garbage to the Dumpster, and scrubbed the bathroom. An apartment as small as hers took even less time to clean than Mrs. M's. June still missed Mrs. M., and Renata, too—for Renata seemed to have forgotten all about her, never once calling her to baby-sit. It had wounded her to lose her job, though she knew that things had changed now that Bryan was around. But she wished she could see Charlie and Renata. Maybe she would call Renata, ask if she could drop by for a visit.

After she finished cleaning, she took a shower and changed from sweats into jeans. She hated all her clothes; they hung like sacks on her, now that she was down to a hundred and seven pounds. She needed to buy new ones, but she had no money to go shopping with. The last of her savings from baby-sitting had dwindled to a hundred dollars, and she was going to need that for groceries. There was no cash coming in after that, none at all, and she hadn't had the energy to look for a new job. She hated to call her father for money, but it was time.

Of course she reached Melanie instead.

"June, what a surprise. Your father's just gone out to meet some clients. Do you want him to call you later?"

"Yeah, that would be good." June faltered. Was she supposed to try to have a conversation with Melanie out of politeness? Her father's wife—June had never been able to say *stepmother*—had never shown much interest in her.

"How are you doing?" June asked.

"Just fine, June, and you? How's school?"

"School's okay." Neither her father nor Melanie knew the first thing about her life. There was no point in going into any detail. "Are you feeling all right?" June asked. "You know, with the pregnancy and all?"

"Very well, thank you, June."

Was that all she was going to say? Didn't June count at all to be included? Couldn't Melanie just tell her something about it?

"Dad said you're having a boy."

"That's right, a little boy."

June was getting angry. She remembered the surprised look her father had when she had used the words *my brother*. She could picture it magnified a hundred times on Melanie's face in Chicago as she held the phone with manicured nails in their lakefront condominium.

"I hope I get to spend some time with him after he's born," June said. "You know, since he's my half-brother and all."

The silence on the line was stabbing. She had said it only to irritate Melanie, but as soon as the words were out they seemed true. She wanted to know that baby.

"Why June, what a lovely notion," Melanie said, smoothly recovering.

JUNE DIDN'T EXPECT OWEN until three. When he let himself in sometime before that, she was bent over the toilet bowl, vomiting up the last of the pound cake he had baked and left wrapped on the counter. He found her there, her hands gripping the freshly cleaned porcelain, her face an ugly twist of embarrassment.

His smile evaporated as he stared, then crouched by her in concern.

"June? You sick?"

She started to say yes, then began shaking her head no, faster and faster, until she stopped and sat back against the cold wall, her face buried in her sleeve.

"You're not pregnant?"

That made her laugh, a little smothered sound.

He tried to hug her but she stayed bent over, rejecting his touch. He was quiet for a moment. Then he said, "It's food, isn't it? You're getting rid of food?"

No, she wanted to say, *I mean yes,* but what she really meant was that the food wasn't the point at all.

"Okay," he said, patting her stiff shoulder. "Okay." Not *It's okay,* or *You're okay,* because those words would not be true, June thought, just *Okay.* It was what he had to offer, all she would let him give.

RENATA

RENATA WAS PERFECTLY POLITE TO BRYAN when he came by to pick up Charlie for a trip to the playground on Sunday, the day after her birthday. She declined the invitation to accompany them. She was also cordial on Wednesday when he came to baby-sit, and noticed that he had adopted her tone of distant civility. By the week's end, the civility was dissolving into simple distance. The tension grew more pronounced between them in the week that followed. Bryan showed up, stayed with Charlie while she worked, then went home. They talked only when necessary, and then in clipped, cool tones. On the weekend, Bryan didn't mention taking Charlie on Sunday, and the day came and went without his call.

The next Wednesday he was twenty minutes late, and she was sure he was doing it to spite her. She fumed in silence, trying not to upset Charlie as he sat in her lap, fingering her black tie. The phone rang. She answered it in cold anger.

"Is Bryan there?" It was a woman's voice—a girl's voice, really—high and perky.

"No, he's not," Renata said with emphasis.

"Would you ask him to call Cindy? He left his portfolio here, and I just wanted him to know so he wouldn't think he lost it."

"I'll tell him."

Renata was just finished scrawling "Call Cindy" on a note when Bryan showed up, breathless and apologetic.

"Forget it," she said icily, handing him Charlie and heading toward the door. "You had a call," she said, pointing to the note on the table.

FINALLY ON FRIDAY SHE BROKE THE SILENCE after work as he was getting ready to leave.

"Look, Bryan, I don't think we can keep going on like this."

"Like what?" he asked.

"You know exactly like what. This not-talking business."

"This is your silence, if you recall. You're calling the shots here, isn't that right?"

"What's that supposed to mean?"

"This whole arrangement. I revolve my life around yours, jump when you say 'Jump', say 'please' and 'ma'am.' Mr. Step 'n' Fetch It."

"Don't be ridiculous. I never asked you to do anything for me. It would probably make my life a whole lot easier if you wouldn't."

"Fine."

"What?"

"I said, fine. You tell me when I get to take Charlie for visits, and I'll come by and pick him up. If you want to do fifty-fifty custody, that's fine with me."

"What are you *talking* about?" Renata's heart was racing.

"I'm talking about what you're talking about. Ending our arrangement, starting tomorrow. I certainly have other things to do with my evenings than hang out in your apartment. But don't think I'm going to give up spending time with Charlie."

"Bryan, you are not sharing custody!"

"Then we'll work out some kind of visitation schedule. Something legal. I'll pay you child support, and we'll get a lawyer to write it all down. You'll have rights and I'll have rights."

Renata sat down, her pulse thudding in her ears. *Think, think*, she said to herself. *Say the right thing*.

"Get out," was what she finally thought of.

RENATA WAS UP UNTIL THREE, drinking beer and pacing. The word *custody* kept torturing her. Charlie was hers. She was the one who would say when and if Bryan could see him. This wasn't for lawyers to decide. It wasn't their business. She was his mother.

She began to see that it was impossible to stay in the same town as Bryan. And that he had lied to her—he had no intention of going back to Los Angeles if she asked him to. As unfair as it was, she was the one who had to leave. Renata walked from her kitchen to her bedroom, her bedroom to her living room. She didn't want to give up her apartment. It was her home. She had a good job. She didn't want to start all over somewhere else. Then the word, *custody*.

Renata woke at eight, with a hangover and the sour taste of beer on her breath. Charlie was screaming at the top of his lungs, and she was still in her work clothes from last night, stretched out on top of the bed. She let the baby scream a minute more while she lay there, looking at the blank ceiling.

By ten she was showered and dressed, Charlie was bathed and dressed, and she had two bags packed. Charlie was gay as he faced the full-length mirror at Renata's feet, patting his hands on the glass, saying *Hoo, hoo, hoo*, his mouth pursed in a small circle to kiss his reflection and then lean back to examine the mark he had made. Renata was trying to put on some makeup, but she couldn't get it right.

At ten-fifteen, the intercom buzzed. It was June. Renata had forgotten June's call, and the visit they had arranged for this morning. She looked at her watch. Oh, well, let her come up. It would be a chance to say good-bye.

When June appeared, Renata was shocked; her skin was white and papery, and she must have lost more than ten pounds since Renata saw her last.

"My God, June, are you starving yourself? You're a skeleton!"

"I've had the flu," June said, averting her eyes. She took in the two duffel bags, and the tote bag stuffed with diapers and baby food.

"You're going away?" she said.

"For a few days," Renata lied.

"You don't have to work tonight?"

"Nope, day off. June, you've really got to build yourself back up. Are you eating now?"

"Of course I'm eating," June said, bending down. "Come see me, Charlie. Look how big you are." Charlie still couldn't crawl, but he made creeping motions on the floor toward the toy June was holding in front of him. She picked him up and kissed his cheek. "I've missed you, buddy." Charlie stuck the cracker he was dragging around in her mouth, and June pretended to nibble it.

"See, even Charlie thinks you should eat."

"Now you sound like my mother."

"Well, listen to her."

"Where are you going?" June asked.

"Oh, maybe the Cape," Renata said. In fact, she was heading to Maine, flirting with the idea of Canada.

"The Cape's nice. We used to go there when I was a kid. It'll still be cold there, though."

"Where won't it be cold in this goddamn climate?" Renata asked. She smiled sourly. "Sorry. But I'm sick of this winter."

"Me, too," June said. "I can't keep warm, even with a coat on."

"It might have something to do with the fact that you don't have a gram of fat on your entire body," Renata said. "Seriously, are you trying to be this thin?"

"No," June said, her voice edgy. "I told you, I had a stomach virus. It's getting better."

"Well, take care of yourself."

"I will. Next week's spring break, and I plan to sleep for a whole week."

"Are you and Owen going to do something together?"

"No, I think that's ending."

"Oh, June. How come?"

"I know he's really nice and everything," June said.

"But not fun enough?"

"I don't want to say anything bad about him. He's been totally sweet to me. I'm just not in the mood to be with anyone, I guess."

"You still miss Eleanor, don't you?" Renata said. "I do, too. But you're taking it really hard."

June shrugged, her face contorting a little. Then she buried her face in Charlie's hair and Renata saw that she was crying.

Unexpectedly then, Renata was crying, too. She went over to where June was sitting on the couch and put her arm around her. Charlie reached up inquiringly, his hands touching both their cheeks, his mouth open. That made them laugh, and Renata reached for a box of Kleenex.

"Listen, how quick can you pack a bag?" Renata asked. As soon as she said it, she knew it was a mistake, a complication. But she couldn't take it back; June's face had lit up, and her arms were already squeezing Charlie with anticipation.

June was glad that they took the elevator straight down to the garage and bypassed Owen at his desk. It had been hard enough walking past him on the way in; he knew June had been making excuses lately for not seeing him, and she couldn't deal with his hurt feelings right now. When Renata had asked her to go on vacation with them, June felt as if she had been pulled miraculously out of a quagmire. If she weren't leaving town, she probably *would* have spent her spring break sleeping; it was the only thing she felt capable of. Now she was wide awake. But as they were driving toward her apartment, she was seized with a misgiving. Her father had sent her a check for five hundred dollars a couple of weeks ago, but he had told her to make it last until she found herself a new job.

"Renata? I don't have a lot of cash to spend on this trip, I just want to let you know. I want to pay my way, but I can't do anything really expensive."

"My treat," Renata said.

"Oh, no, that's not what I meant, I just didn't—"

"Forget it. I invited you. But listen, I wasn't quite straight with you about what I'm doing. For one thing, I'm thinking of going to Maine, not the Cape."

"Oh. That's okay." June was confused.

Renata was staring straight ahead as she drove. Charlie was dozing in his seat.

"The other thing is, I'm going to stay away. When your spring break is over, we'll put you on a bus back to Boston. But Charlie and I are moving on."

Now June was really bewildered. "You're not coming back?" she asked stupidly. Renata pulled up in front of her apartment.

"That's right. Do you still want to go?"

June nodded, her heart thumping. Something was wrong; she hadn't seen it before. But now she noticed how Renata's eyes were swollen and bloodshot, and she suddenly remembered the beer bottles on the counter in the apartment. "Yes, I do want to go," June said firmly. "Don't you leave without me. I'll be back here in five minutes." She left her knapsack on the front seat. Renata wouldn't drive away with June's wallet in the car; the knapsack would anchor her there in case she had second thoughts about taking her. June flew into her apartment and stuffed some clothes and underwear into an overnight bag. She went into her bathroom and scooped up makeup and her toothbrush. She ran back outside and was relieved to see Renata's car still there.

As she slid into the seat beside her, June felt more alert than she had in weeks. "Now tell me everything," she commanded as they pulled away from the curb.

It was like pulling teeth to get her started, but Renata finally told June about Bryan's threat, and how it went back to Renata leaving Bryan when she discovered she was pregnant, and his having to track them down. Renata made it sound as if Bryan were coming after her with an army of lawyers to take Charlie.

"He can't do that," June said. "Can he?"

"I don't know what he can do. The point is, I don't want to spend my savings hiring lawyers. It should be totally up to me whether Bryan gets to see Charlie. He won't accept that."

"But he is Charlie's father and he seems to love Charlie. Don't you want them to know each other?"

Renata glanced sharply at June. "June, put yourself in my place. Would you like a judge to tell you how much time you had to let your own son be apart from you? And Bryan probably has a girlfriend; he might even start living with someone. I'm just supposed to kiss Charlie on the cheek and wave bye-bye while he goes off with Bryan and some other woman? I can't do that." Renata shook her head, and June admired her fierceness. She knew how it felt to dread a stranger's presence.

"Does he really have a girlfriend? I thought he was in love with you."

Renata looked at her. "What makes you say that?"

June didn't know what had made her say that. Miriam would have said something like "emanations." She shrugged. "Just an impression. I only met him once. But he came all the way to Boston looking for you."

"Looking for Charlie," Renata corrected her. "And as far as having a girlfriend, who knows? He probably does. But it doesn't matter."

June looked at the set of her mouth and knew that it did matter; it mattered very much.

BY EVENING THEY WERE WELL UP THE COAST OF MAINE. Charlie was wild to get out of his car seat, in spite of the rest stops they had taken. Many of the motels they passed had not yet opened for the season. Finally they found one near a small fishing harbor that had a restaurant adjoining. Their room was paneled in pine and the beds were made up with burnt orange chenille spreads. A tin engraving of a schooner hung on the wall. The lamps had the kind of shades that looked like they had been stitched together by children at camp with large blunt needles and buckskin laces.

"Oh, lord," said Renata, unloading the car. "I forgot toys. The last time we traveled, he didn't need any."

"We'll find some," June said. But there was nothing inside to play with but a dusty black plastic ashtray. Charlie lay on the braided rug pushing it back and forth for a few seconds, then he began to cry.

Renata picked him up and nursed him. "You'll see, Charlie," she said. "We'll have fun."

AFTER FOUR DAYS IN MAINE, Renata had to admit that she no longer liked life on the road. It's true that they were in Maine out of season, the rain driving down on the windshield like penny nails, the dampness and loneliness thick in all the rooms they stayed in. But even if circumstances had been better, the fact was that Charlie needed stability. He could no longer wake and sleep according to the car's engine; he needed to be up at seven, down for a nap at ten, up at eleven-thirty, down at two, up at three-thirty, and down for the night at seven-thirty. He needed his plastic activity table and his baby-gym set. He needed a nice clean carpet to play on. He needed his regular high chair with its familiar view out to the deck.

What Renata needed was a plan. She had studied the small towns they passed through, trying to picture Charlie and herself living in one of them in warmer weather. In her fantasy, seagulls wheeled and called around their little cottage; Renata would serve lobster rolls to vacationing families in some homey café, the kind that tacked postcards to the wall by the cash register. The cost of living would be next to nothing, and she would find some high school girl to stop by afternoons to push Charlie around in his stroller while Renata waited tables during the dinner shift. It would be the kind of job where the high school girl could bring him in to visit on her break. The whole town would be friendly and casual that way, and Renata and Charlie would soon know everyone.

That was her mental picture, but the fact was, it was March twenty-first and there were no blue skies, let alone tourists, in sight. It would be June before anyone would want to hire her, and even then she would be as temporary as the season, out of work by Labor Day. Her thoughts turned to warmer places, Fort Lauderdale or New Orleans. She would put June on her bus to Boston at the end of the week and begin driving toward sun. Even though she could easily drop June in Boston on her way south, it was best to preserve the illusion in June's mind that Renata and Charlie were still somewhere north; that way June couldn't give them away once Bryan went searching for them, as he invariably would.

Renata was behaving like the fugitive she felt herself to be. She used no credit cards and signed a false name on every hotel register. She regretted the goodwill she had squandered by blowing off her job at Viva's: she had skipped work Saturday night without even a phone call. She regretted the apartment deposit she would be losing at the end of the month when she didn't show up at the manager's office to pay her rent. She also regretted the things she had bought for the apartment and left behind, simple things like tablecloths and picture frames, that had made her feel like she was putting down roots. Renata had toyed with the idea of asking June to pack up the apartment for her and send her some things. Then it seemed like a better idea to let the pieces fall where they would. Her life felt like a jackknifed truck, its freight scattered all over the road. She wouldn't try to minimize the consequences of the accident, or neaten the damage. She would simply walk away, and leave the wreckage complete.

Having June's company was allowing her to put off the inevitable. For whole moments of the day, Renata felt normal, as if this really were a vacation the three of them were taking, and she could go back. In spite of the bad weather, they found things to do: bowling, which Charlie loved; arcades, which he also loved; and gift shops, which made him cry because Renata kept him out of reach of all the pretty things he wanted to touch. Renata took a walk alone every day, because once June left, she didn't know how long it would be before she would have any time to herself. She took these walks without an umbrella, and taught herself not to flinch when the rain struck her.

On Friday, Renata proposed that they drive into town and get a bus schedule.

"I don't have class until Monday," June protested. She was panicked at the thought of going back to her studio apartment. There she would have to face the remnants of a semester in which she was behind in every class, and had received an official academic warning from the dean. She would also have to face Owen, who had left a faltering message on her machine while she was gone saying that he guessed she was busy, but would she please call him when she got the chance, because he'd like to know if he had done anything wrong. Once she was home, June knew she would go back to weighing herself four or five times a day, and sleeping until noon. She couldn't go back; staying with Renata and Charlie was her one hope of climbing out of the dark pit she was in.

Renata drove them to get the schedule anyway, to a little bus station that was nothing more than a bench under a rippled sheet-metal awning. The schedule was posted on a bulletin board: there was only one early-morning departure a day, and they had missed it.

"That gives us a whole day more," Renata said cheerfully. "Then, bright and early tomorrow, we'll have you on that bus."

June had been trying to frame arguments in her mind. But

when it came to making her request, all she could do was blurt it out. "Why can't I stay with you, Renata? I'll get a job, too, with hours different than yours, so that one of us can be with Charlie all the time. I'm really sick of school and was thinking of taking time off, anyway. I'm already failing everything this semester, so there's no point whatsoever in my going back."

Renata looked at her, her mouth open with surprise. "June," she said, "I wish you could stay with us, too. You're wonderful company, and Charlie and I will miss you. But you can't drop out of school; that's just plain crazy." Renata shook her head emphatically.

June stared at the dull green pine trees swishing by. They were headed back to a diner they had passed earlier called the Cuppa Coffee.

"Well, I'm dropping out anyway, whether I stay with you guys or not," June said stubbornly.

"And what will you do?"

"I'll get into a dance company somewhere," June said airily. "And I'll waitress."

Renata pulled over to the side of the road with a little screech of brakes and spray of gravel. When she turned to June, she looked angry. "Don't you dare throw away college because you had a couple of bad months," she said. "Do you know how lucky you are to have a mother at home, and a father who at least pays your tuition bills?" Her voice had risen and was shaking. "Do you think if I had had someone to send me off to college I would have *chosen* to be a waitress? *Do* you?"

June shrank back. Charlie began fussing from his car seat. Renata leaned her forehead onto the steering wheel. After a few seconds June reached out and patted her arm awkwardly.

"It's okay," she whispered. "I'll go back."

They sat there. A truck rumbled by. Charlie's crying had subsided into whimpers. He seemed to be getting used to the idea that he was a prisoner in the car seat.

"Renata," June said softly. "Why not go back, too? Your apartment's still there, and you can get another job. Why not just have a talk with Bryan? I'm sure he misses you."

"He doesn't miss me," Renata said, her voice muffled in her arm. "He misses Charlie."

They went to the Cuppa Coffee and pretended nothing had happened. June entertained Charlie with straws and spoons. Renata stared out the window and toyed with her eggs. June forced herself to eat some toast and part of an egg; every time she ate these days she suffered horrible stomach cramps. It was probably the shock of all the solid food she had been eating this week under Renata's scrutiny; tomorrow she would get back to the protein drinks to get rid of the pounds she was sure she had gained. A waitress who was at least fifty years old served them. June couldn't help but stare at her puffy ankles and the veins snaking up her calves. It had never occurred to her that Renata did not do exactly what she most wanted to in life. She seemed so free. She made waitressing look sophisticated and even glamorous, with her crisp black-and-white uniform and her fat roll of bills every night from her tips.

THE NEXT MORNING, RENATA HUGGED HER HARD when the bus pulled up. The sun had finally come out, making the wet trees shine. Mist rose from the road.

"I'm sorry I yelled at you," Renata said into her ear. Charlie was squished between them in the hug.

"How will I know where you are?" June asked, her voice squeaking with her effort to control it.

"You won't, for a while. But I'll be in touch. I have your mother's address and phone number."

June blinked hard. "I love you guys," she said, then grabbed her bag and hopped on the bus.

"Hey, don't you want me to put your bag underneath?" the driver called after her. June shook her head and kept walking until she reached a window seat facing Charlie and Renata. Renata was making Charlie wave, which he never did by himself until the person he was supposed to wave at totally disappeared from view. Then he began waving like crazy.

TEN MINUTES DOWN THE ROAD, June made her way up the aisle to the driver, her bag bumping the back of her leg.

"Excuse me, but could you pull over at that diner up there? I need to make a phone call."

"I can't wait for you, and there aren't any more buses coming today," the driver warned.

"That's okay. I changed my mind about going."

"Whatever you say." The driver pulled the bus over. June stepped off. The door wheezed shut behind her and the bus crunched across the gravel, back to the highway.

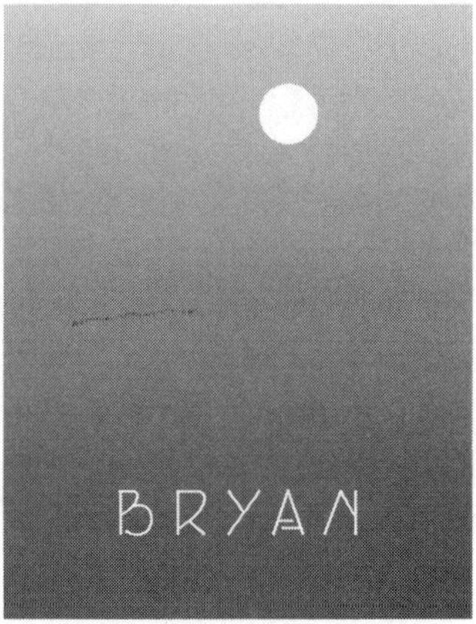

HIS ROOMMATE MELISSA WAS CALLING outside the bathroom door. "Bryan, phone!"

"I'm in the shower," Bryan shouted over the water. "Take a message."

A second later she returned to the door. "It's somebody named June. The message is that if you don't talk to her now you'll be sorry. You want me to hang up on her?"

But Bryan was already out of the shower, grabbing a towel to wrap around himself and running past Melissa for the phone, leaving wet puddles in the hall behind him.

Melissa said, "I hope you're going to clean that up!" and disappeared down the stairs.

Bryan stopped to catch his breath before he spoke.

"June?"

"Yes," June said.

"I've been leaving messages for you all week," he said. "Are you with Renata and Charlie? Where are you?"

"I got your messages. I've been traveling with them, but Renata sent me home because it's the end of my school vacation. I know where she is now, but by this afternoon she'll be gone, and I don't know where she's headed next. You don't have much time to catch up with her."

"Where is she? Just a minute; do I need to write this down?" Bryan clutched his towel with one hand and cradled the phone with his ear, looking frantically around for a pencil.

"I need to ask you some things first."

"You just said we needed to hurry."

"We do, but I'm not telling you where she is until you answer my questions."

He forced himself not to shout at her. "Go ahead."

"Do you love Renata, or just Charlie?"

"What?" His voice rose incredulously. "What kind of a game is this, June?"

"I need to know. Renata thinks you don't care about her."

"Of course I care about her," Bryan sputtered. "But she's made herself a little bit difficult to like these days."

"Do you have a girlfriend?"

"What is this?"

"Yes or no, and don't lie," June warned. "Miriam told me I have a psychic nature, so I'll be able to tell if you're lying."

"Who the hell is Miriam?"

"Yes or no."

"I've had some dates. There's nothing wrong with that. Those were the rules that Renata wanted—both of us free." Bryan was getting angry and feeling chilly. There was a slippery pool of water around his feet. Melissa came up the stairs pointedly offering him a sponge. He glared at her until she retreated.

"So, do you love Renata, or not? Tell the truth."

The truth. He had driven across the country to find out what Renata was hiding from him; he had found out, and fallen in love with his son; he had alternately been drawn to Renata and been made furious by her. At the moment he was furious. She had stolen his son from him, twice. This time he was aware of the loss; it felt like something ripped right out of his gut. Did he love Renata? He wanted to strangle her. She had treated him like dirt. He knew June wouldn't be satisfied unless he said yes. He said yes.

"*Why* do you love Renata?"

"June, this is crazy."

"It's not crazy, because I *do* love Renata. She's my friend. Do you think I want to ruin her life by letting you know where she is before I'm sure of your motives?"

"I'm Charlie's father," he said belligerently. "How about not ruining *my* life? And don't forget Charlie's."

"I'm hanging up now," June said. "I didn't call you to argue."

"Okay, okay, hang on. *Why* do I love Renata, that's the question?"

"Yes."

Bryan tried to remember how they were in California. The way she would stretch herself coming out of sleep and open her eyes smiling when she found him already awake, watching her. How, in the middle of the night, when he awoke with a jolt, his heart pounding, he could encircle her with his arms and go back to sleep almost immediately. He had been to bed with other women, lots of them, both before and after Renata, but she was the only one he had missed when she was gone. Hers was the only face he could recall in perfect detail. Hers and now their son's.

"June?" When he spoke again his voice was changed. "You're just going to have to trust me on this one. Please."

IT WAS SEVEN-THIRTY WHEN HE HUNG UP. June had told him he had four, maybe four and a half hours to get to them at the motel in Maine where they had spent last night. "I'm sure they won't check out until after Charlie's morning nap," she had said. "He wakes up at eleven-thirty. They'll be gone by twelve, at the latest."

As he threw on his jeans and sweatshirt, his mind raced. He could call ahead, speak to her. But he knew her stubbornness. Knew she'd bolt. He could call the motel manager, ask them to detain her in some way. But that would only make him seem suspicious; they'd probably warn her and she'd leave. He had no choice but to get there in four hours.

RENATA WATCHED JUNE'S BUS ROLL AWAY and felt like some part of her was leaving with it. Now she and Charlie were adrift, but without the same sense of adventure Renata had felt last fall; now she was running. She didn't let on, but when June was trying to persuade her to go back to Boston, she almost said yes. She would plead with Theo for her job back, and she would sit down and hash it out with Bryan. Then she remembered his voice, cold and punishing, talking about lawyers and custody. That gave her the strength she needed.

She hoped she did the right thing in sending June away. Surely she would go back to school and get over this slump. Renata had cautiously suggested that June find a counselor to talk to, maybe one at school. But June had said she was fine, in that brittle, irritated tone of hers that reminded Renata that the girl was still, after all, just a teenager, volatile and contrary. Maybe Renata should call her mother and tell her how thin June had gotten, and suggest that she be seen by a doctor. Or would her mother resent the interference?

Renata passed by the Cuppa Coffee and thought about swinging in for breakfast. But she had some muffins in her motel room; she would eat those. By the time they got to the room it was just seven-thirty, and Charlie wouldn't need a nap until ten. She dreaded making him sit confined in his car seat for long distances again. She decided to let him play in the room until his nap time, then load him into the car and drive while he slept. By the time he woke up they could stop somewhere for lunch and a stretch, and then she could drive again during his afternoon nap.

After packing up the car, Renata put Charlie in his stroller and wandered down to the harbor. It wasn't warm, but with the sun out everything was brightly colored. The waves had been the color of lead; now they were a deep sapphire. She picked Charlie up and pointed out the gulls and fishing boats and orange buoys. He took it in somberly. Then he rubbed his eyes. Renata read it as a signal that they should be off. She went into the motel office to drop off the key, and the grandmotherly woman behind the desk exclaimed, "Oh, thank heavens!" when she saw her. "That girl that was with you—"

"June? She left on the bus this morning from Rum Junction."

"She did? Well then, who was the girl who collapsed in the Cuppa Coffee ten minutes ago? They called and said she had one of our matchbooks in her pocket, and I was sure it was the girl who was with you because of the long hair."

"A girl collapsed? Collapsed how?"

"They just said she was unconscious. Found her in the bathroom. The paramedics took to her to the county hospital, about twelve miles north of here."

"Did they check her name? Didn't she have identification?"

"Well, now, we didn't get that far, because I thought I knew who it was. Let me call back and ask Irene at the Cuppa Coffee."

As she watched the woman talk, Renata rocked Charlie's stroller and tried to persuade herself that June was on the bus, safely headed back to Boston. Why on earth would she have gotten off? There of all places, where she would be completely stranded.

"So, it was her. Thanks a lot, Irene, and you take care now." The woman hung up, nodding. "It was your girl, all right. They got her name off her identification. And they didn't know how she got there, because there was no car in the lot, so she must have gotten off the bus you put her on."

WHEN RENATA SAW JUNE, she was surrounded by apparatus. Tubes entered her arms and were taped to her nose. She had just been wheeled out of emergency surgery and was still unconscious. Her skin was tinged with blue, and the hospital gown revealed her to be appallingly bony. In the week they had been together, June had changed clothes in the bathroom and worn a large flannel nightgown to bed. By day, under loose jeans and bulky sweaters, it was impossible to determine how underfed she actually was. Now, Renata saw.

Charlie had dozed in her arms while Renata sat through the surgery, and he was still sleeping when the doctor met her in the waiting area, dressed in his green surgical scrubs.

"Are you family?" he asked Renata.

"I'm a friend. We were traveling together. I've notified her mother and she's on her way. What happened to her?"

"She was hemorrhaging internally from the stomach. She was in real danger."

"But why? What caused it?"

"Repeated vomiting. Years of it, I'd say. This young woman has a serious eating disorder."

RENATA DIDN'T LEAVE JUNE'S ROOM. Charlie was delighted with the shiny hospital equipment. Whenever the nurse was out of the room, Renata let him play on the vacant bed next to June. With its rails up, it was as good as a playpen. Then the nurse happened to come in before Renata could pick him up, but all she said when she saw Charlie on the bed was, "That little guy needs some toys," and she came back a moment later with a small plastic pitcher and cup, and a rubber bulb syringe that Charlie immediately began gnawing on.

"Don't mention it," she said when Renata thanked her. "I've got a ten-month-old at home."

Sitting and waiting, Renata recalled the time by her father's bedside, and her detached, numb feeling then. Now she was locked to the sight of June's small white face. Renata felt as if she were breathing for her, and somehow using a portion of her energy and health to supplement June's own, to help lift her back to the surface.

Around noon, June opened her eyes. Renata's face was lowered to hers in an instant, talking in soothing tones, exactly the way she helped Charlie find his place back in the world after a deep sleep.

"You're okay now, June. Everything's okay now. Charlie and I are with you. Your mom will be here soon."

June's eyes widened. She moved her head in an agitated way. She made a dry sound with her throat.

"No, no, it's fine," Renata crooned. "Your mom is so worried about you. She just wants to be with you and make sure you're okay." She stroked June's hair and the girl drifted back asleep. When Renata heard footsteps hesitate in the doorway behind her, so unlike the busy, padded steps of the nurses, she assumed June's mother had arrived. With Charlie in her arms, she turned, presenting a reassuring smile.

Bryan smiled in a half-apologetic, half-pleading way and shrugged. Then he held out his arms, and she made him hold them there for several seconds before it occurred to her what she should do. She walked into them.

IT WAS MAY, ALMOST TOO HOT to wear Mrs. MacGregor's suit, but June felt that it would be lucky. She coiled her hair in a French twist, like Mrs. M. wore it in some of her pictures, and pinned the orchid Renata had given her to her lapel. She was the bridesmaid, but she was going to be holding Charlie instead of flowers. Renata's sister, who had flown in from Oregon, would also be standing up.

Since it was so warm, she didn't need a blouse under the jacket. Instead she fastened a thin gold chain with a single pearl around her neck. Her mother had given it to her the day June came home from her first visit with the counselor. The counselor, a woman with glasses and cropped gray hair, was nice. She didn't tell June what to do. Actually, she got June to do most of the talking. During their sessions she listened very hard; perhaps no one had ever listened to June quite so intently. When June faltered or struggled for words, she simply waited. Sometimes she had to wait a while. June was surprised at how much work it was to tell a secret.

At the courthouse they were milling around a little frantically, waiting for Renata and Bryan to be called before the judge. Renata's niece and nephew kept trying to make Charlie walk, which he was on the verge of learning to do himself, except that in their eagerness they kept making him lose his balance instead of letting him lean on their hands, the way he needed to. He didn't mind, though; he clearly worshiped them, crawling after whichever one of them was nearest. June had been surprised that Renata's sister looked so unlike her. Renata was tall and slender, Marcia petite and curvy. Renata had white skin and black hair, Marcia's skin was pinkish with freckles, her hair coppery. Renata said that Marcia got all the Irish and she got all the Spanish in their blood. But for some reason you could see a real resemblance between their children. Even though Charlie looked a lot like Bryan, his eyes crinkled up in a smile exactly the same way his cousins' did.

Renata and Bryan both seemed jumpy. Though they were nervously smiling a lot, they couldn't really look anyone in the eye. June supposed they had a lot of emotions to keep under control; anyone would, on a wedding day, even a couple who hadn't had as peculiar a romance as Renata and Bryan. They were so beautiful, though, that June found it hard to take her eyes off them—Bryan with his blond hair and black suit; Renata in a short white shift, white heels, gold locket, nothing in her short dark hair at all.

Their wedding day had turned out cloudless and sunny, with lilacs and azaleas blooming on every corner. June had decided to wear Mrs. M.'s suit the minute Renata invited her to be a bridesmaid. This suit had been picked out for Mrs. M.'s trousseau, and she had had a very happy marriage; you wanted to take advantage of karma like that. As June rode to the courthouse with Marcia's family, she saw another good omen: above them a creamy daylight moon, round as a saucer.

"Look, Jess, it's the Milk Moon," she said, pointing.

"A Milky Moon?" Jess giggled.

"May's full moon—it's called the Milk Moon," June said. She liked the sound of it, as if all you had to do was reach up and tip it toward you for a drink.

PRECISELY AT TWO, A BAILIFF OPENED the wooden door and motioned them into the judge's chambers. June picked up Charlie, and brushed some dust from his hands and knees. He twisted around to see where his cousins were, then relaxed when he saw that they were still with him, filing in beside their mother, who was walking in behind the bride.

RENATA

THEY WERE IN THE JUDGE'S ANTEROOM, where the chairs had all been pushed to the perimeter. Renata was relieved to see that they wouldn't be having the ceremony in the courtroom, where people were tried for crimes.

Bryan stood alone; he had no best man. Marcia and her kids were to the left of Renata, as were June and Charlie. From his perch in June's arms Charlie looked at her and clapped his palms over his eyes. Now she was supposed to say *Where's Charlie?* in her most worried tone, looking high and low. When he didn't hear her say it, he released his hands anyway, to see why she wasn't playing, and she mouthed *There he is!*, opening her eyes wide to convey her relief and astonishment. He snickered and clapped his hands over his eyes again, but she couldn't take her turn; the judge was beginning.

It was a woman judge; Renata wondered if Eleanor had ever performed marriages. Probably not. Eleanor was responsible for dealing with the destruction afterward, holding children aloft in the net of her judgment while she weighed the heaviness of one parent's failures against the balance of the other's until she could determine how to put the children down in the least harmful spot.

Renata looked down at her hands; remarkably, they were still.

Inside she had been trembling since daybreak. Bryan, too, had tossed and turned last night, although he didn't seem to have any nightmares. They were still with him, those dreams that he couldn't remember upon waking, but which visited him once or twice a week with some kind of torment that he could never turn into words. Since she had been sharing a bed with him again, Renata had realized that you could never be close enough to anyone to see inside his nightmares, just as you could never care for him enough to prevent them. What you could do, though, is be present outside them, waiting to welcome him back.

The judge concluded her greetings. She had a kind face, and wore a wedding ring herself, a plain gold band. That was good. Neither Bryan nor Renata knew one damn thing about marriage, having had absolutely no good examples of it in their combined lifetimes, so it was comforting to think that this stranger saying words over them might shed some of her own steadiness their way. For her part, Renata had observed all the superstitions she could, except for the groom not seeing the bride before the wedding, which was impossible because Bryan had already moved in with them. But she had her something old—her mother's heart-shaped locket, which had been empty until Renata carefully cut one tiny Charlie face and one tiny Bryan face from a contact sheet of prints and fitted them into the two halves of the heart. Her something new was her dress; her something borrowed was a Pocahontas sticker Jess had applied to the inside of her hem; and her something blue was her engagement ring. Bryan had sold four prints so far from his group photography show, and bought her the small sapphire ring from the proceeds.

They were supposed to say the words. The judge told them what they were, and then Bryan began repeating them to Renata, looking straight into her eyes with no trace of irony. He was promising her fantastic things, improbable things.

Maybe there were some futures that belonged to you once you had said yes to the initial premise. The first premise was Charlie. Or maybe it came earlier, the first night Bryan dreamed his motherless dream in her presence, and she held him afterward, not understanding a single thing about this man. Maybe it came even earlier than that: the day she bought herself a meal overlooking the ocean with her father's birthday money, and a breeze picked up Bryan's baseball hat and tossed it to Renata and she caught it without dropping it. But if you went back that far, there was no reason not to count the moment her father's vision cleared for a moment between glasses of Scotch, and he went to the drugstore to pick out a birthday card covered with flowers that said "For My Darling Daughter," and on the memo line of the enclosed check wrote "Gift."

Now they were turning to her. The judge was asking her a question. Charlie was humming in the background. Bryan was waiting. Renata took a breath.